BIG
TRUTH

ALSO BY DAVID PERLSTEIN

Fiction

The Odd Plight of Adonis Licht
Flight of the Spumonis
The Boy Walker
San Café
Slick!

* * *

Non-fiction

God's Others: Non-Israelites' Encounters With God in the Hebrew Bible
Solo Success: 100 Tips for Becoming a $100,000-a-Year Freelancer

BIG
TRUTH

New and Collected Stories

DAVID PERLSTEIN

BIG TRUTH
NEW AND COLLECTED STORIES

iUniverse books may be ordered through booksellers or by contacting:

iUniverse
1663 Liberty Drive
Bloomington, IN 47403
www.iuniverse.com
1-800-Authors (1-800-288-4677)

ISBN: 978-1-5320-7145-4 (sc)
ISBN: 978-1-5320-7146-1 (e)

Print information available on the last page.

iUniverse rev. date: 03/26/2019

For Howie Schnabolk, First Lieutenant, U.S. Army.
A medevac helicopter pilot serving in Vietnam,
Howie was killed on 3 August 1967.
His life represents a story of courage.

And for Larry Raphael,
a wonderful rabbi and wonderful friend
who loved stories and shared them with us.

"God made man because He loves stories."
Traditional Jewish saying

Contents

Beautiful!

"A MAN SHOT himself last night," Melinda said. "On Paradise Lane." The quaver in her voice told Hunter that she was serious. Although why, Hunter reflected, would she—or anyone—joke about something like that?

Melinda looked up from the newspaper. "Actually put a bullet through his..." Her cheeks paled despite the tan she'd developed playing golf upwards of four days a week. She peered at the framed crewelwork hanging above the kitchen table at which they sat. Against a deep blue background, brightly colored letters formed the word BEAUTIFUL! She'd done the crewel herself and chose to include the exclamation point. It bore witness to Hunter's emphatic response to what he saw up there.

Hunter gazed into his oatmeal as once he'd gazed down on Earth and across the Milky Way from two hundred miles up.

"Hunter, did you hear what I just said?"

Hunter nodded.

"You're not... how should I put it... dwelling on your birthday, are you? I mean, really, it's just another birthday today. Besides, they say eighty is the new sixty."

Hunter rested his hand—on a good day capable of meeting any man's grip—over his coffee mug. Deep-space blue, the mug displayed the insignia of his lone and unforgettable mission. It came from his congressman. He'd never gotten the hang of using the term representative. A member of the congressman's staff delivered it the day before along with a personal note. The mug honored both Hunter's eightieth birthday and his eight-day flight piloting the space shuttle all those years—those decades—earlier. Just refilled and covered by his palm, the mug provided his hand warmth and comfort. Excepting Air Force tours in Alaska and North Dakota, his birthday fell on warm spring days for which anyone would be—should be—grateful. Still, his arthritic knuckles pained him. "They say growing old isn't for sissies," he mumbled.

Melinda rested her hand on his. "You're hardly old. Didn't I just say that?"

He smiled. He had a wife for whom any man would be—should be—grateful.

"I'm really beginning to wonder though," she said. "About ordinary people being allowed to have guns."

"I have one."

"You're not ordinary. And you were a military man. Besides, you wouldn't hurt a fly."

"Why? Because I'm old?"

Melinda gave his hand a gentle pat. "Of course not. I mean, the way you came back. From up there."

The first flowers arrived just after ten o'clock. Hunter was in the back yard hosing off the patio. He'd insisted that this day be as ordinary as possible. Melinda was out running errands preparatory to an informal dinner with several friends. All local. Some of Hunter's peers had died. Others were scattered across the Sun Belt. None were particularly inclined to travel. He supposed that he and Melinda also had slowed down. Still, they'd driven north to Yosemite the month before. Then they'd gone on to San Francisco with a stop at Ames Research Center on the way south to see their son Morgan, who held on to his job despite all the cutbacks at NASA. Hunter considered that maybe eighty *was* the new sixty. He certainly felt inclined to fire up the grill. Turn on the gas, really. This despite Dr. Covington's advice—urging might be too strong a word—to watch his cholesterol. On the other hand, red meat was loaded with iron. And he still had his teeth. Chewing steak was not for sissies.

As Hunter finished brushing off the patio furniture, the doorbell rang again. More flowers, he suspected. They'd keep Melinda busy watering and fussing for the next few days. At least. A good thing. And while he neither requested nor expected them, he liked flowers. You had to marvel at them—the colors, the graceful lines and textures. And the delicacy. Beautiful things so fragile and short-lived. In their way, flowers were no less fascinating than the stars in their infinite clusters and galaxies. Stars. Flowers. Everything connected. One universe. One physics. One destiny.

Hunter went to the door.

A young Latino man in a crisp white shirt smiled. "Happy birthday, Colonel." He held out a large square box.

Hunter reached into his pocket.

"No thank you, sir," said the man. His smile widened. "Not today, sir."

Hunter took the box to the kitchen. Melinda said he should expect surprises, but this was very much anticipated. He loved chocolate cake, and the bakery in the village made the best. He'd received the same cake on each birthday over the past twenty years since they'd moved to the San Diego area and settled into the house. They intended the house to be their final stop. A final resting place, as it were.

He lifted the lid and grinned. Instead of *Happy Birthday, Hunter* scrawled in icing, the chocolate frosting bore the single word with which he had become associated: *BEAUTIFUL!* Not that Hunter had been unique in marveling at Earth from such a distance. He always made clear to the media that he wasn't the first to say what he'd said, even if he repeated it incessantly as the crew settled into orbit then while it carried out its mission and after they returned. It would have been unusual, he always emphasized, for any astronaut not to use that word. After all, the shuttle passed over Earth at such great speed and with such frequency that he witnessed sixteen sunsets in every twenty-four-hour period. During night traverses, he saw the lights of cities. People—during daylight, of course— were another matter. But if he *had* seen people, he said, he would not have been able to identify their race or nationality. That struck him as uplifting. Yet it often led him to feel that humans were insignificant. Distance and perspective prompted so many different thoughts. Conflicting thoughts. So yes, maybe he'd gotten a bit carried away, but he'd spoken from the heart.

Hunter closed the lid and noticed a small note taped to one corner. It exhibited the deliberate cursive he learned in grade school. *Do not refrigerate.*

Following lunch—tuna on whole wheat for him, salad with half a scoop of tuna for her—Hunter and Melinda drove to the supermarket that anchored one end of the strip mall near their house. The mall offered a variety of conveniences—Starbucks, an organic restaurant, a dry cleaner, a pizza place for Hunter's monthly indulgence and a shop selling a modest selection of office supplies and greeting cards. Their pharmacy—they required a minimum of medications—was located inside the supermarket.

They parked near the entrance. Not that Hunter couldn't walk. He loved to walk. He walked two to three miles each day. If it rained or grew too warm, he rode a stationary bike in the spare bedroom that served as his office. A desk stood in one corner, a TV in another. Hunter watched the news when he worked out—CNN during the day and the local news at its appointed times. The news generally was bad. War. Disease. Poverty. The local news gave traffic accidents lots of airtime. That man on Paradise Lane who shot himself—the early evening news would be all over it.

Hunter reached for a shopping cart but left his hand suspended in space. Not ten feet away stood one of those homeless people the news reported on now and then. *Probably* homeless, anyway. He looked the part. The man's brown hair was long and uncombed. He wore a gray overcoat riddled with holes—even in this weather. The coat hung limp from his narrow shoulders. A stained sweatshirt—even in this weather—rumpled khakis and shower clogs revealing dirty feet completed the picture of a man down on his luck. If he'd ever had any luck.

Melinda pulled on Hunter's arm.

Hunter grasped a cart and accompanied her inside.

Melinda produced a shopping list. It was mercifully short. She usually shopped alone, but she'd just had her nails done.

At Melinda's direction, Hunter plucked several cans and boxes from the shelves. He didn't mind the outing. There really wasn't all that much more to do to prepare for his birthday dinner. They'd also be home in plenty of time for that reporter from the local newspaper to come over. The paper wanted the interview to take place on Hunter's birthday, and

Hunter had been agreeable. Not that he craved publicity. He doubted he could add anything to whatever had been written about him. Still, he had a responsibility.

Hunter wheeled the cart into the produce section. Melinda wanted to serve something healthy for dessert along with the cake. She bent over and sniffed. Then she pointed to a cantaloupe. Hunter placed it in the cart. She pointed to another. He secured it. They repeated the process with honeydew melons and grapes.

"Well," said Melinda with a satisfied grin, "mission accomplished." She turned and walked towards the checkout counter. They went to the ones with human clerks, not the ones where you had to scan your items yourself. He didn't mind that particular technology. Technology fascinated him. That and the thrill of speed. And yes, the risk taking. Which is why he'd been who he'd been. But Melinda preferred what she called "the human touch." He could understand that.

He watched her walk away then pushed the cart forward several feet. He selected an organic apple. Then he went to the end of the counter and took a single ripe banana from a large bunch. Organic.

Melinda, sensing Hunter's absence, stopped and turned.

Hunter raised his index finger.

Melinda stepped towards him.

He wheeled the cart to the deli counter. A clerk—a young woman in a white apron and a clear plastic cap covering her piled-up blonde hair—offered a smile of recognition. He ordered a sandwich. Turkey and cheddar on whole wheat. Mustard, no mayo. Lettuce and tomato. "And sprouts, please."

Melinda tugged gently at his elbow. "Hunter, what on earth are you doing?"

Again, he raised his finger.

A moment later, the clerk handed the wrapped sandwich over the counter.

Skirting several young mothers with small children, Hunter went to the dairy section. He selected a pint container of one-percent milk. Organic.

"You've already had lunch," Melinda said. Her voice was matter-of-fact. It indicated puzzlement rather than annoyance. Hunter forgot things from time to time. In fairness, everyone had senior moments. But the stomach knew when it was full.

Hunter helped bag the groceries. They'd brought their own cloth bags to save trees. Still, he requested a paper bag. In it he placed the sandwich, the milk, the apple and the banana. Melinda's nails were still exposed to all sorts of ravages, so he used his credit card. Melinda liked the miles, but actually the miles were interchangeable.

Exiting the supermarket, Hunter looked to his left. The homeless man stood about twenty feet away. His head bobbed up and down. His feet shuffled as if he were dancing. He turned halfway round and shrugged a single shoulder as if he was engaged in conversation. If so, it was only with himself.

Hunter wheeled the cart towards the man and held out the paper bag. The Bible, he recalled, said that man does not live by bread alone. But without bread, Hunter knew, people starve to death. You just had to watch the news.

The reporter sat on the cream-colored sofa in the living room. A recent journalism graduate, she had long, honey-colored hair and pale skin. She struck Hunter as one of the few Southern Californians who avoided the sun. Or maybe she worked too much. He sat in an armchair upholstered in the same fabric. He and Melinda rarely used the living room. Hunter thought living rooms a waste of space.

Melinda busied herself in the kitchen, her nails now safe from harm. She'd offered the reporter a sandwich, but the young woman declined. She'd grabbed a couple of fish tacos before coming over.

The reporter crossed and uncrossed her legs. Her eyes checked the digital recorder she'd placed on the lamp table then darted up to an acrylic painting that hung over the fireplace. A local artist gave Hunter and Melissa the painting after they moved in. It reminded Hunter of the old 1970s LOVE postage stamp, itself based on a famous modern painting. Robert Indiana was the original artist, Hunter recalled. Their own painting featured a pile of red letters against a background of blue and green. Only the word was BEAUTIFUL! The reporter smiled. "After you came back, how were things different?"

Journalists loved asking Hunter "the question." They asked all astronauts "the question" in one form or another. It took patience to hear it over and over and provide "the answer." But Hunter had patience. It took years to hone his skills as a fighter pilot and years to train as an astronaut and years to adjust after his mission. He always began with the simple fact that he hadn't been the only astronaut to utter the word *beautiful!* But maybe, he would say, his constant use of "the word" had linked it to him more than to his peers. And yes, maybe *beautiful!* was a bit trite. But it was as fitting a word as he could summon to describe his feelings.

Hunter's feelings ran deep. He'd spoken with plenty of other astronauts. He'd even met separately with Neil Armstrong and Buzz Aldrin from Apollo 11 and absorbed every word as they spoke of being the first humans to walk on the Moon. But nothing adequately prepared him—could adequately prepare anyone—for the tidal wave of emotion that swept over him two hundred miles up. That statement, too, seemed trite. But he saw what he saw and felt what he felt.

His emotions might have remained under control if the planet hadn't revealed a terrible duality. On one hand, humans had escaped the confines of Earth's gravity because their curiosity stimulated their intellects to comprehend the enormity and complexity of the universe. They'd begun to unlock many of the secrets of the physical laws that bound everything in creation.

Then again, the human mind was confined in a body that failed even to approximate a small speck within the Milky Way, a galaxy that was, in the context of creation, itself a speck. So what then did the human race amount to? What purpose did he or any human being serve? What really mattered on Earth? And if humankind ever reached beyond the solar system to stare open-mouthed at the vastness confronting them all, what difference would that make?

There you had it. *Beautiful!* described what he saw and felt. The wonder of it all. What it failed to describe was his life after returning. True, he experienced an initial euphoria. But it quickly eroded. Listlessness followed. Then depression. He drank too much. He became sullen— withdrawn rather than abrasive. Went into therapy. Wriggled through the wormhole with a bit of a better grip but not much more. He did, however, became a gentler man. He could no longer imagine firing a missile at another plane or a ground target, although his flying days had ended. He retired from the Air Force and found a job with a bank in Houston. He and Melinda sought to raise the children in a stable environment. After the youngest completed college, they retired to the San Diego area with its milder weather.

"You've had your struggles," the reporter said.

Hunter smiled. She could never comprehend the sheer terror.

Hunter awakened from his late-afternoon nap.

Melinda stood over him. "I have to run out for a few minutes," she said. "No worries. We have time."

He smiled. He wondered if that meant he was happy. Did he care that in an hour and a half he would celebrate his eightieth birthday with two other couples and a pair of widows? Would he really be celebrating at all? When Melinda and their guests sang "Happy Birthday," would he be happy then? He'd long stopped caring about his birthdays—particularly the milestones every decade. He took a more prosaic view. Every sunrise on Earth brought another day. You lived that day as best you could, took what pleasures you could find. What it all meant in the scheme of things he didn't know. What was he really but a speck?

He heard the car back out of the driveway. He sat up and glanced at the clock on his nightstand. He had time to catch the opening of the early news before Melinda put him to work setting out the plates and silverware, straightening the seat cushions.

Seated at the desk in his office, he hefted the remote. It and the TV might well contain as much or more computing power as Apollo 11. He remembered the days of radio. Then television entered people's homes—vacuum tube sets in wooden boxes. Then the fuss over color. Now a single remote controlled the TV, the BluRay player and the Apple TV unit that let them stream all kinds of movies and shows off the Internet. Engineering displayed so much of the human intellect's capacity. Only, what was revealed by all those reality shows and the vampires and the zombies and actors butchering each other and practically having real sex? What did that say?

He clicked on the news. The anchors led with the man on Paradise Lane who shot himself the evening before. The story, they said, was evolving. *Evolving*, Hunter thought, was a code word. It meant, *You think you learned about this in the morning paper or on the radio or on the Web, but the investigation continues, and there's so much you haven't seen like multiple views of yellow police tape indicating a criminal investigation, which is standard procedure in a matter like this, and interviews with neighbors expressing their sadness and commentary from psychiatrists and psychologists who can offer no satisfactory explanation for such a tragedy.*

Still, he watched. Why had the man—a neighbor unknown to him—done it? On the other hand, how important was the man's life in the scheme of things? Somehow the latter thought failed to disturb him.

"Yet another startling death," the male anchor pronounced. "Stay tuned."

Hunter stayed tuned through the usual commercials for adult diapers, pain remedies, new prescription medicines for conditions of which most people were unaware, early-bird dining at a seafood restaurant in La Jolla overlooking the Pacific and sales at two car dealers.

"As we promised," the female anchor announced, "another startling death not far from the apparent suicide on Paradise Lane."

Hunter leaned forward. The second death, he learned, occurred only moments before he'd taken his nap. An SUV, apparently driven within the speed limit, struck a man near the supermarket where Hunter and Melinda had been shopping. Eyewitnesses reported a pedestrian attempted to cross in the middle of a trafficked boulevard without regard for oncoming vehicles. Identification had yet to be made, but the victim was a man and evidently homeless as suggested by his unkempt hair and tattered overcoat—a curious piece of clothing on such an otherwise delightful spring day.

Hunter turned away. The voices faded into near silence as if he'd turned the audio down. He didn't have to draw on his degree in aeronautics to recognize the victim as the man to whom he'd given the sandwich and the fruit and the milk. But why? Not why did he give a homeless man food but why was the man homeless? And why did he cross in the middle of a busy street? Did the news care about these people or was it all about the station's ratings? And what meaning could be teased out of this death and that of the man on Paradise Lane?

Of course, none of this could be seen from two hundred miles up. And what about that photo of Earth taken by the Cassini satellite from nine hundred million miles away? What was Earth but the tiniest of specks? And how insignificant a distance was nine hundred million miles in the scheme of the cosmos?

Hunter clenched his teeth. Despite the distances, humanity would never stop trying to connect with what lay beyond. Hadn't he tried to connect with that homeless man? And had the man's death sent him a message?

He sat motionless. Then he opened the top drawer of his desk and grasped a small key. With it he opened another drawer containing a metal box. He raised the lid and glanced at his Smith & Wesson .40 caliber. The muzzle's diameter spanned less than half an inch. The barrel ran only four inches. He brushed his finger along the trigger guard. The gun, too, represented nothing more than a speck. Yet how incredible—and frightening—that the human mind could conceive of such a device then identify and mine the metal, develop the polymer for the frame and grip, shape its parts and devise an explosive charge to propel a round. A small missile, actually. He contemplated that like the Shuttle that lifted him so high only to hurtle him earthward, the gun served as a vehicle for a journey of discovery.

He sighed. One way or another, every human undertook that same journey. Where it would lead him he could not imagine. What he knew was that each voyage to the unknown required departing the known. And one thing more he knew. Its certainty provided a considerable measure of comfort: he had the power to determine when and how he would embark.

Hunter slowly rotated the gun. Light glinted off the stainless steel slide. He saw again the white sunlight streaking Earth's horizon and gleaming across the planet's oceans. What he, a solitary human being—a speck—held in his hand connected him to the infinite.

"Beautiful!" he whispered. "Beautiful!"

"Beautiful!" appeared in Reed Magazine (2016).

Riser

JEFFREY HYER STARES into darkness he can almost touch. It suggests the plague that blinds sightless Egypt—the ninth divine admonition dismissed by Pharaoh.

"What time is it?" asks Danielle. Her soft whine reveals her unanticipated awakening.

Jeffrey slides out from beneath the comforter. "Five."

"Oh," she says. "It's today."

As Jeffrey navigates around the bed, he notes the familiar inhale and exhale of Danielle sinking back into sleep.

At the bathroom door, he reaches for the knob. His fingertips find only wood.

He rubs his eyes. Even for him the hour is early. The change of routine has affected him. Not good. Today he will launch his career to the next level. This is no time to lose focus.

His fingertips scuttle from side to side. The knob eludes them. This makes no sense. For three years, he and Danielle have lived here on a hillside in Marin County. When not sheltered from the world by blackout drapes, the master bedroom provides views of trees, rooftops and a sliver of Richardson Bay. It is a fine house. Not their dream house but a worthy way station. Their dream house will come soon. This morning will make it possible.

If he can find his way into the bathroom.

Jeffrey guides his fingertips upward. Nothing. His upper teeth meet his lower lip to form the beginning of an expletive. He separates them. He fears waking Danielle again. Well no, not fears. An attorney of his caliber does not yield to fear. His silence represents an act of consideration. In spite of the reputation he has achieved in some quarters, he thinks himself a considerate man. It just so happens that he reserves his consideration for his clients—giants in the complex world of social media. And start-ups with big ambitions. They share much in common with him. So yes, he is unfailingly considerate. And disciplined. It takes discipline to slip out from under the comforter at five-thirty before his alarm sounds.

Okay then, another strategy to get into the bathroom. He waggles his fingers then lowers his hand. Yes. He finds the doorknob. It's where it's supposed to be. But no. Not exactly. Or perhaps yes. Admittedly, he is sleep-deprived given the court case he's been working on. Still, Jeffrey brooks no excuses. He loathes weakness. Any kind. Always has.

Exercising discipline, he applies pressure to the knob and twists slowly. The door opens without a sound as if he were an astronaut on a spacewalk. Quality hardware. Expensive. Jeffrey and Danielle made many upgrades after purchasing the house. Details. He consumes details like a black hole sucks up matter.

Still swathed in darkness, he closes the door and reaches for the light switch. Again his fingertips find only smooth, enameled wood. Applying his recent lesson learned—a man in Jeffrey's position must be a quick study—he lowers his hand. His finger finds the switch. He presses it.

Let there be light.

Jeffrey blinks. He blinks again.

Everything in the master bathroom is lower than it should be as if the floors were raised in the middle of the night by some alien force unseen and unheard. Or everything *appears* to be lower. This defies rationality and flies in the face of all that Jeffrey believes he knows. He is as rational—most of the time—as he is considerate and disciplined. He knows damn well that what he sees is an illusion, although the line between illusion and reality hasn't always been clear. The white-and-gold marble vanity stands inexplicably lower. Also the toilet. And the showerheads in the glass-enclosed double shower along with the towel racks and the hooks holding matching terry robes.

Jeffrey calculates that everything seems lower by four inches.

He frowns. He is no longer prone to letting his senses deceive him. He has learned to control his emotions. Failure to do so risks misconstruing evidence and letting opposing counsel or a hostile witness slip something by him. This is why he's earned a reputation as one of the Bay Area's sharpest young litigators. The next few weeks will affirm his status. And yes, he has heard the occasional whisper that he is full of himself. He dismisses such criticism. He knows what he knows. He knows who he is.

But *where* is he?

He looks down. The soles of his feet hover four inches above the floor.

Jeffrey closes his eyes, takes a long, slow breath. He has crafted a reputation as a man who never panics, never stumbles, never pauses, never doubts. *Hard charging* serves as an apt description. Which is why he soon will become the youngest senior partner in the history of hard charging Hawke, Falco, Harrier & Kyte. Why someday, he will become managing partner. It's just a matter of time.

Granted, Jeffrey has made sacrifices to rise to the top. Everything worthwhile comes with a price.

He pinches his right cheek then his left. He is not dreaming. Not that he believes he's dreaming. Although in the past, he's had dreams no one could imagine. Nonetheless, Jeffrey Hyer not only is rational, considerate, disciplined and calculating, he's also practical. Add to that observant.

Exhaling, he opens his eyes and again looks down. In defiance of gravity and all related laws of physics, light appears under his feet.

I have risen, he whispers to himself, *above the ordinary*.

But this is no time for levity. And certainly not for levitation.

He raises his right foot and lowers it. He repeats this with his left. Although they hover above the floor, the soles of his feet feel the familiar texture of the tiles along with the pressure of the weight they bear. He steps toward the shower then back to the sink. Although he continues to float above the floor, his steps feel normal.

Under a time constraint and seeing no other option, Jeffrey showers and shaves with dispatch. True, he raises the showerhead and stoops lower over the vanity. He towels off then dresses. When he slips on a favorite pair of yellow socks—symbolic of his being unconventional, a maverick, someone daring to go against the grain—the cool silk caresses his skin. His shoes offer the comforting embrace of supple Italian leather.

His mint-green silk tie stylishly knotted, the jacket of his elegant gray suit slung over his left arm, he pauses at the top of the second-floor landing. He finds himself in a state of suspension. But he knows he can go only one way. Forward. Or as it happens, downstairs to the kitchen. Committed to his mission, he foregoes reaching down to grip the railing and models the sure-footed descent of a mountain goat.

Only as he backs out of the driveway does he realize that he has skipped his OJ.

The drive into the city proves uneventful. Light traffic flows unabated over the Golden Gate Bridge and through the tollbooths, which no longer employ people to collect revenue. All the while, his backside nestles into his seat, although he has to slide the seat back and adjust the mirrors. He thanks God—whom he considers a myth—that he feels pressure on the gas pedal and brake despite the gap under his right foot.

In the city, he parks beneath the building of which his firm is the major tenant. As he presses the elevator button for the lobby—for security reasons, the garage denies access to the upper floors—he bites his lip. Jeffrey is not one for leaving anything to chance. He must—he *will*—demonstrate this to the executive committee at this morning's briefing. Still, he registers disappointment with himself. He has not given thought to how he will respond to Melvin, the morning security man.

The door opens. He leans forward and peers around. This brings him to frown. Hesitance irks him. Jeffrey Hyer never does less than put pedal to metal. He steps out into the lobby.

"Morning, Mr. Hyer," says Melvin.

Jeffrey studies Melvin's yellow-brown face. The puffy cheeks. The grin that makes the round eyes seem eternally mirthful.

"Earlier than early, huh, Mr. Hyer?"

"Big day, Melvin."

Jeffrey steps into an office-access elevator, swipes his card and presses his floor. As the door closes, he experiences both relief and confusion.

Melvin seems not to have noticed anything amiss. Is he exercising professional discretion?

At six-fifteen, Jeffrey enters his office on the thirtieth floor. Among his peers and superiors, he's the first to arrive. As always. He sits at his desk. His backside rests on the seat of his ergonomic chair. As always. His feet, not as always, hover four inches above the carpeting. Perhaps five. He can no more close the gap than he can push the earth free from its orbit.

He powers up his laptop to review his presentation. He was scheduled to assist Thom Bertelsen, the senior partner leading this case against an upstart company's infringement on their client's intellectual property, but Thom suffered a massive coronary a month earlier. He's recovering in Hawaii. Incommunicado for the most part but not worried because Jeffrey has put together a case for the plaintiff that will do more than secure victory. It will cripple the defendant—and all the plaintiff's competitors. Put a crimp in the media's constant criticism of corporations that achieve great things. And if it halts a few careers in their tracks, so be it. Contending in the marketplace extracts its price. Losers pay.

Jeffrey takes a breath. He knows that winning also exacts a price.

At seven-thirty, knuckles tap on his door.

"Yes?" Jeffrey replies.

"Good morning, Mr. Hyer," calls Cheryl, the associate office manager. "Bagel and coffee?"

Jeffrey is hungry. A finely tuned engine requires fuel. "Please," he says. *Please* and *thank you* demonstrate his considerateness.

A moment later, Cheryl knocks.

Jeffrey remains seated. "Come in."

Halfway to his desk, she stumbles.

The bagel goes flying like a circus clown shot out of a cannon. Coffee soaks the carpet.

Cheryl falls to her knees.

Jeffrey leaps from his chair.

She looks up. "Oh God, I'm so sorry."

Jeffrey looks down at her from his new vantage point.

Her eyes betray no hint she sees anything unusual. "Really, Mr. Hyer. I *am*."

Jeffrey smiles. "Carpeting can be cleaned. But I'll take another coffee and bagel."

After Cheryl leaves, Jeffrey feels his hands shaking. What is happening? Why don't Cheryl and Melvin see what he sees?

He goes to the window and marvels at the insignificance of early birds like him—only not like him—coming to work. Has he always thought about people down there as trivial? At best, marginal? He wants to believe he hasn't. His unbidden four inches of elevation—perhaps five—seem to have altered his perspective. Or made it more clear. Regardless, he sees what he sees.

They are so small. We are all so small.

At nine forty-five, Jeffrey strides out of his office. His feet clear the floor by six inches, possibly seven. He cannot be sure. He loathes not being sure. His pulse races.

Several associates and staffers nod. He acknowledges them with grace. Ron Passmore waves. Another up-and-coming associate, Ron defers to Jeffrey in assessing their prospective places in the firm's hierarchy. An attractive paralegal whose name eludes Jeffrey offers a breathtaking smile. He knows that she—like everyone—has heard on the grapevine—planted and nurtured by him—that the firm stands on the cusp of a notable victory.

Like Melvin and Cheryl, no one responds to his curious elevation.

In the boardroom, Jeffrey stands—hovers—a foot above the Tigerwood Laminate flooring. A chill crawls along the back of his neck. He buttons his suit coat. Feeling awkwardly formal, he unbuttons it. Wary of wasting time, he sits at the north end of the table. Thankfully, his backside presses against the seat bottom. He slips his laptop out of its Spanish Bull leather case, connects it to the digital projector and boots up.

Everything—beyond his legs extended to avoid his knees grazing the underside of the table—appears normal.

At one minute before ten, six members of the executive committee file in.

Jeffrey leaps to his feet.

The committee members stand behind their chairs.

As per tradition, Joe Falco Jr., the managing partner, arrives last. Jeffrey glances around the room. Or more accurately, down at it. Joe Falco sits.

The committee members follow suit and lean slightly forward. Their faces reveal anticipation. Jeffrey will tell them what they want to hear. That despite Thom Bertelsen's absence, Falco, Harrier will eviscerate—he has chosen this word carefully—will eviscerate the other side. He will present an argument every member of the committee and every senior partner will agree is compelling. Airtight. Terrifying—yes, he has chosen that word, too—terrifying in its ability to produce the outcome they all desire.

Goliath will stamp David into the dust.

Joe Falco motions to Jeffrey. "Show us what you've got, Jeff. Show us—" He smiles. "Annihilation."

Jeffrey's heart pounds like a bellows. His breaths come long and deep, but it's not oxygen filling his lings. He feels like a balloon taking in helium. Lots of helium. And the balloon is rising. His head seems almost to abut the ceiling leaving his skull clearance of no more than two or three inches. Although he is not sure. From where he stands—or floats—he's no longer sure of anything.

Except that he's rising again. Without meeting resistance, his head pushes through the ceiling. He ascends the remaining eight floors, penetrates the roof then soars above the building. The city grows distant beneath his feet. His view takes in the Bay and the Pacific. The Napa Valley to the north. To the south Silicon Valley emerges, San Jose, the Santa Cruz Mountains. In the east, are those the foothills of the Sierra? He knows that the executive committee waits for him to begin, but his view no longer encompasses them. People are too small. Even these legal giants have become miniscule.

His vista of Northern California—unaided by wings and engines—stuns him. He has long desired to touch the clouds. Now his feet trample them from the home of the gods. It is glorious.

But as a god, can he abide to live among people?

A choice confronts him.

His heart palpitates. His cheeks flush.

Jeffrey descends.

The seven faces of the executive committee stare. Is Jeffrey engaging them in a bit of theater? Is he playing the role of a speaker who, on approaching the podium, holds aloft a sheaf of papers then tears it in two and tells the audience that he will not deliver his planned speech? That he has something more important to say? Something they—and he—have failed to anticipate?

Jeffrey's feet touch the floor. He glances down. No hint of daylight appears beneath them. His heartbeat slows. His cheeks cool. He glances out the window.

Then he turns and walks out the door.

At the elevator, he rises on his toes to press the down button. When the door opens, a man and a woman exit. They tower above him.

In the lobby, Jeffrey gazes nearly at eye level at polished marble glistening in the morning sunlight. He slithers across the lobby to the elevator going down to the garage.

No matter. He will rise again.

The Satan and God
Go Double or Nothing

In the Beginning

ONE DAY—FOR the record, the sixth—God says, "Let Us make Man in Our image."

As a mover and shaker in the Heavenly Host, I'm not enthused.

HaSatan—The Satan—it kind of means The Adversary—represents more than just my name. It's my job description. My calling to keep it real.

God can be one tough customer. (That probably should be Tough Customer.) The King of Kings has a rep as a Drama Queen. Anger management issues. But don't be misled. God's always been something of an innocent. A wearer of figurative rose-colored glasses. All blue skies and green lights.

"Maybe You want to give Man a little thought," I say.

He humors me. "The Devil's in the details."

I flash a figurative grin at His inside joke. There's no Devil among the Heavenly Host or anywhere else. It ticks me off, the image some circles make for me—a red-skinned freak with a six-pack, horns, hooves and a tail. Hell, like all the Host from top to bottom, I don't have a body. (If I did, sure, the six-pack would be cool.) Given that the rest of God's kitchen cabinet is basically just a bunch of yes-beings, what I *do* have is a moral obligation. Not to mention a ton of street cred.

"All due respect," I say. "Man's gonna bite the Hand."

God's response? "No way."

"Way," I counter. "Man's gonna bust Your Chops. Break Your Heart."

He scoops up a Handful of dirt and blows into it.

I know He's in for buyer's remorse.

He puts His new toys into this garden. Choice real estate.

I figuratively point to the Tree of Knowledge of Good and Bad with its Michelin three-star fruit. "The humans, they'll ignore Your instructions."

"You think?" he asks.

"It's a lock," I answer.

God offers a friendly wager.

I feel bad taking it. It's a sucker bet. But if a little pain is required to teach the Holy One, bring it on. Also, I know this serpent.

Eve's all ears when the serpent chats her up and sells the fruit (no, not an apple). Closes the deal by pushing women's empowerment.

She bites. Then without hesitation, she passes the fruit to Adam.

The schmuck chomps down.

Goodbye Eden.

And so it goes.

Eventually, God counters with this humongous flood. He spares only Noah and his family. "Just debugging Man," He says.

I raise a figurative eyebrow.

In time, God sees something righteous in this guy Abraham. He performs a fire-and-brimstone act on Sodom and Gomorrah then focuses His attention on this small family of Hebrews. Generations later, He makes Moses His front man to free them from bondage in Egypt. To do it, God slays all of Egypt's first-born males—boys, men, cattle. God can be a real hard-ass. (Hard-Ass?)

Then He comes up with a bright idea. Gives the Israelites these ten commandments. Not just orally but in writing. For the record. "Now, they'll get it," He says. He figuratively smiles like He's off for a month to figurative Florida.

I say nothing.

The Israelites (with a little help from yours truly) say it all with the Golden Calf.

God steams.

At the risk of repeating myself, if it takes pain—

One day I get back from a business trip.

He calls me over.

"I found one," He chirps.

I'm at a bit of a loss. "One what?"

"One perfect human being."

I shake my figurative head. "No way."

"Way. Have you seen my servant Job? No one else on earth like him. Fears Me. Shuns evil."

I know the dude. Righteous enough. Still, I express my doubts. "All due respect, but why *wouldn't* Job fear You and shun evil? He's the richest man in the East. He's gonna rock the boat? Not unless all his kids and all his wealth fall into a black hole. That happens? Job'll curse you. Guaranteed."

God gives me a figurative wink.

Who am I to turn down a friendly wager?

He sets one condition. "Do anything you want to Job but don't take his life."

Duh!

I round up my senior staff. I want ideas. Figurative asses will stay glued to figurative seats for as long as it takes. Job is going to be one tough nut to crack. But every human weakens. Eventually.

We go right for the jugular and plop Job into a shit storm. He loses all his sheep and cattle. Then his kids.

Job's wife nags her old man to curse God.

He refuses.

His friends tell him he must have done something wrong. God's getting payback.

Job lays the blame on God.

God covers His figurative Backside by reading Job the riot act.

Job concedes. He won't retract his claim that God's the Faulty Party here, but what mortal can get in the cage with the Master of the Universe?

Sonofabitch never curses God.

"Told you so," God says.

I accept my losses.

Still, I know I'm right about Man. The next few thousand years make my case.

God backs off. Mopes. Mutters regrets.

And then.

Now

I return from another road trip. God's in a great mood, whistling under His figurative Breath. He asks, "Have you seen my servant, Anatoly Abramovich? No one else on earth like him. Fears Me. Shuns evil."

If I had a tail, shock would send it flying off. *"Everyone* sees Anatoly Abramovich," I say. "All due respect, but You've heard of the internet?"

God raises a figurative Eyebrow.

For starters, Anatoly Abramovich is "The King of Tel Aviv." He arrives in Israel from Russia as a six-year-old and grows up in a hard-scrabble development town in the Galilee. Full of rage, he barely makes it through high school where he establishes A rep as, to say the least, contentious. Enters army service. Becomes a commando. Engages in several important but never-announced missions in Gaza and Lebanon. Relishes the burst of a flash-bang grenade. The torrent of fire from an Uzi or M4. The stiffening of a prisoner's body as a hood slips over his head. The release of a final breath as a knife severs a windpipe. Ultimately, he goes nose to nose with his commanding officer. Release from active duty follows. He skips the veteran's ritual trek across India and Thailand. Opts for another agenda.

Six-two, two-twenty, ripped like Michelangelo's David with a soul as hard as marble, Anatoly Abramovich becomes a bouncer in a Tel Aviv nightclub. Buddies up with unsavory characters. Works his way into Israel's criminal underbelly. Strong-arms shopkeepers. Runs women, gambling, drugs. Keeps the wives of several homicide detectives bitching about never seeing their husbands.

David Ben Gurion wanted Israel to be a nation like all other nations, criminals included. A hundred-to-one, he never had Anatoly Abramovich in mind.

Crude but bright, Anatoly Abramovich launders every shekel and invests in legitimate businesses. Skims cash to reduce his tax load. With it all, he's not a guy to shy from the spotlight. He frequents hip clubs and rock concerts, a beautiful woman on each arm.

Even if God's not into social media, He knows this.

God also knows that out of the blue, Anatoly Abramovich falls under the sway of a big-time Rebbe from Brooklyn. The Rebbe's a tzaddik—a righteous man. Tens of thousands of devoted followers proclaim his piety in every corner of the earth.

Anatoly Abramovich sells the penthouse in Tel Aviv, the beach house in Caesarea and the apartment in London. (In New York and L.A., he partied in $2,500-a-night-and-up hotel suites.) He unloads the Bentley and the Porsche. The cash from these and all his other discarded assets goes to a foundation run by the Rebbe.

The notorious Anatoly Abramovich becomes a baal t'shuvah— someone who returns to God. An ultra-observant Black Hat.

A miracle? You Know Who begs off. Says He champions free will. Always has.

But He's pumped.

I'm (almost) speechless.

The Rebbe finds Anatoly Abramovich a wife. Not the kind of beauty with whom he's familiar but young and healthy enough to fulfill the commandment to be fruitful and multiply. The newlyweds move into a rundown apartment in Jerusalem. The building's owned by the Rebbe's foundation. A small stipend from the foundation added to national assistance puts bread on the table. Anatoly Abramovich spends his days laying t'fillin, davening and studying Talmud in one of the Rebbe's yeshivas. His wife looks after the four children—two boys, two girls. Anatoly Abramovich dotes on them. The family is small by the community's standards, and they want more little ones, but Mrs. Abramovich develops "female" problems. They count on the Rebbe to reverse them. They're disappointed when he can't but never lose faith. God's will and all that.

I shake my figurative head.

Meanwhile, God can't stop bending every figurative ear in the Heavenly Host about how much He loves Anatoly Abramovich. God has a certifiable soft spot for repentant sinners although, as I point out with no little frequency, they inevitably disappoint.

Of course, a question makes the rounds among the Host. What about Anatoly Abramovich's past crimes? Are the books cleared? God references Talmud. The Rabbis teach that for offenses against Him (Anatoly Abramovich racked up plenty) God can forgive. But He cannot forgive sins committed against people. Only the victims can forgive. This raises my hopes.

Anatoly Abramovich dashes them. He reaches out to as many of those who suffered at his hands as he can. Covers the rest with a public confession at the Western Wall alongside the Rebbe. Becomes the new poster child for Ezekiel's declaration that it isn't the death of the wicked that God seeks but that they should turn from their evil ways.

Disclaimer: Ezekiel and I theoretically are on the same page, but we don't see eye to eye regarding the situation's practicality. I uphold my faith in Man's lack of faith.

I also maintain my sense of duty. "Anatoly Abramovich?" I say to God. "I hear You, but I don't buy it."

Like an accomplished stage actor, God takes a beat pause. Then he uncorks His big offer. "Double or nothing?"

I can't pass on this action. Talk about easy money. Although everything in the Celestial Kingdom runs on a kind of Celestial Bitcoin.

My staff and I noodle the possibilities. None of us doubts that ultimately, Anatoly Abramovich can be prodded to curse God. But how do we reach a guy like that? Take away his toys? The apartments, the beach house, the cars, the women, the Italian suits, the Rolex watches, action at baccarat tables around the world, part-ownership of that football powerhouse in London? Already gone.

But no way does any of us believe that Anatoly Abramovich compares with Job. It dawns on us that maybe we've been overthinking the deal. We figuratively dust off our figurative playbook.

Long story short, one Friday morning Mrs. Abramovich goes shopping for the Sabbath at the Machane Yehuda market on Yafo Street. She rides there in one of the women-only buses run by the Rebbe's foundation. At a crowded intersection, the brakes fail. A dozen passengers suffer minor injuries. One becomes a fatality.

Anatoly Abramovich buries his wife then, along with his children, sits Shiva. During their week of mourning, his closest friends—each a baal t'shuvah like him—come to the apartment to offer comfort.

As if.

They observe the customary silence, waiting for Anatoly Abramovich to speak first. After he does, they each chime in, "God's will."

"Bad brakes," he responds. Who says a man of faith can't also be pragmatic?

"No," they respond without hesitation, "you must have done something wrong."

It's not that they're bad people, but their theology remains uninformed. Bad brakes? True that. And why a mechanical failure at that particular time? My staff and I know that Anatoly Abramovich won't chalk up the loss of his wife to God's will, but we're only getting started.

Meanwhile, as we anticipated, the police investigate. They find that the foundation's garage failed to perform scheduled maintenance. But releasing this information will cook up a political hot potato. The police bury their report.

Rome—the same for Jerusalem—wasn't built in a day.

Here, let me get something off my figurative chest. I take no pleasure in Mrs. Abramovich's death. But I adhere to a simple philosophy: Any means necessary.

My crew and I move on. God's about to see Man with figurative Eyes wide open.

If not now, when?

The Rebbe's foundation runs a school. Actually, two. One for boys and one for girls. In the same building. One Tuesday, a winter storm causes the rain-drenched roof to collapse. All the children survive—except the brothers and sisters Abramovich.

The friends rejoin Anatoly Abramovich in his now-empty apartment for another round of Shiva. "You've done something," they advise him. "Something wrong. Something terrible. Why else would God punish you?"

"Such a rain," Anatoly Abramovich responds. "A rain like this you get once every twenty-five years. Maybe fifty."

This time the matter goes public. (We've planted the right bugs in the right ears.) A balagan—an uproar, a commotion—develops. Secularists pressure the government to investigate. They suspect that the foundation's construction company cut corners.

The authorities face more pressing concerns. They agree to study the matter then delay. Indefinitely.

Anatoly Abramovich remains tight-lipped.

But we're headed in the right direction. And now, it all comes down to the poster child himself.

Not that it's going to be easy. The guy's a hard case, and rules are rules. I can't take Anatoly Abramovich's life just like I couldn't take Job's. But I *can* make him, like Job, very uncomfortable.

I convene my staff. One member, off the top of his figurative head, suggests boils. I reject that out of hand. So yesterday. I direct the staff to undertake extensive research. Find a rare affliction that will cause Anatoly Abramovich severe pain while leaving him alive but difficult to treat. It should motivate him to curse God and leave him able to do it.

A handpicked crew with major credentials, the staff delivers a winning proposal.

Game on.

One chilly day a month or so before Passover, Anatoly Abramovich experiences mild discomfort. He shrugs it off.

Like drizzling spicy sauce on falafel, we add a bit of an edge.

He prays.

Might as well ask the sun to stop in the sky. (Wait! The Lord of Hosts let Joshua do that.)

No question, God is sympathetic to Anatoly Abramovich's plight, but His figurative Hands are tied.

Anatoly Abramovich's discomfort lingers. Increases. Bursts into pain.

His friends remain convinced that even after returning to God, he's sinned in the worst possible way. They stop visiting. Then stop calling.

He checks into a hospital run by the Rebbe's foundation. Gets a private room. A team of observant and quite competent doctors runs tests. Nurses—all men—check in on him around the clock.

The pain mutates into agony but stays three steps back from the edge over which he would plunge into the Valley of Death.

Awake almost twenty-four hours, Anatoly Abramovich can barely move his lips. But unlike Job, he doesn't call God on the carpet. Doesn't threaten to sue. Just praises.

We're cool with that.

Then we bring him one step closer.

Some doctor or nurse or orderly fails to scrub his/her/their hands.

Anatoly Abramovich contracts an infection. Medication can't clear it up. His pain soars off the charts.

I'm stoked.

Then dejected. Does Anatoly Abramovich finally curse God? Fuhgeddaboudit!

I wonder if I'm being conned. It comes to me that God's not about to let me win. He's yanking my chain.

My top assistant cheers me up. She's been nosing around Brooklyn. The media, she says, would kill to know what she knows. But they won't have to. She's made arrangements.

The plan is diabolically clever.

We dial things down. Anatoly Abramovich's infection clears up overnight. His pain level recedes to chronic but bearable. Three days later, he returns to his rundown apartment now as quiet as—well, a tomb.

The next day, Anatoly Abramovich wakes just as the sun peeks above the mountains of Jordan across the Dead Sea. He shuffles to his tiny living room, faces in the direction of the Temple Mount, lays t'fillin and prays.

God chants, "Amen."

I shrug my figurative shoulders.

Mid-morning, someone knocks. (The doorbell hasn't worked for over a year; the maintenance man can't be bothered.)

Anatoly Abramovich opens the door.

A neighbor, tears turning his graying beard soggy, holds out a newspaper. It's a secular rag. Under normal conditions, neither the neighbor nor Anatoly Abramovich would give it a glance.

Anatoly Abramovich figures there must some reason to look at this trash and takes it.

The neighbor sobs, spins on his well-worn heels and trundles down the hall.

Slumped in a stiff-backed chair, Anatoly Abramovich glances at the front page. He studies the prominent photo of a face as familiar as his own. His lips silently utter the headline: BROOKLYN COURT INDICTS REBBE—LOOTED OWN FOUNDATION.

Anatoly Abramovich reads the story. Every word. When he finishes, he places the newspaper on the small table next to his chair.

At noon, a nurse—a man, of course—brings chicken soup and a small challah. Checks Anatoly Abramovich's pulse. Leaves without saying a word.

Anatoly Abramovich remains in his chair. The soup cools, goes uneaten. When the time comes for afternoon and evening prayers, he races through them, mumbling as usual. It's not so much the words that matter. It's the act.

The sun sets over the Mediterranean, which caresses that pit of evil, Tel Aviv. Jerusalem falls under a dank chill. Another nurse brings dinner—boiled chicken and vegetables. Checks Anatoly Abramovich's pulse and nods. Removes the unconsumed soup from midday. On his way out, he turns off the light by the door.

Anatoly Abramovich sits in the dark, his dinner untouched. Never rises from the chair. Not even to go to the bathroom. Give credit. The man has a will of iron and, after all he's gone through, a bladder of steel. (Or some new composite material Israel's defense researchers would sell their first-born to discover.)

But the laws of physics apply as God intended. Put something under increasing pressure—

Just past midnight, Anatoly Abramovich goes to the bathroom. Then he turns on a lamp in the living room and picks up the newspaper. He searches the Rebbe's eyes. Even on newsprint, they sparkle. His soul shattered, Anatoly Abramovich crumples the paper as if he was eliminating a member of a rival gang. He wails, "I gave everything up for *him*?"

Unlike God, Anatoly Abramovich concedes what he learned as a child. The human condition lies beyond redemption.

He curses his Creator.

I can't bring myself to reveal the expletive.

Recovering my wits, I approach God. No way am I gloating.

Himself is figuratively blubbering. Yes, He explains, He created the capacity for evil. Not because He wanted to but because he *had* to. Man would be worthless without free will. Still, He's offered so much guidance. Provided more than one how-to manual. Yet Man refuses to make the right choices.

God pays off with a figurative stiff Upper Lip.

But I know. It kills Him.

The Laughing Room

No QUESTION, MILTIE called it a full month before the government declared the ban on men and women—*married* men and women—shopping in the same stores and supermarkets. As we sat at Peet's waiting for Miltie's no-frills espresso and my Caramel Caffè Latte, I couldn't help thinking how when it came to information, Miltie was way ahead of the curve. Miltie, of course, was not his real name. I can't name names. That aside, sometimes I thought Miltie had a crystal ball. Unfortunately, possession of a crystal ball would get you in trouble. A woman I knew kept reading palms at parties after the government prohibited telling fortunes, astrology included. That was just before they outlawed parties. She disappeared.

Miltie didn't need the occult. As a news editor at one of the Bay Area's three authorized radio stations, he had access to stuff the authorities didn't want people to know—until they wanted people to know. Sure, I was curious about what might be coming down the pike, but I never asked. For our mutual protection. Still, Miltie often gave the word to his close friends who, like him and me, were stand-up comics. Birds of a feather and all that. Rare birds, actually. An endangered species. Anyway, the word according to Miltie was that soon, my wife wouldn't be able to drag me shopping with her. I couldn't complain. Still, when Miltie told me after we sat at a small round table two other guys had just left, I said, "That's a bit over the top, isn't it?"

The question was rhetorical. The new edict was like all the edicts that came out of the Silent Revolution. Which, actually, had been pretty noisy, it being about religious freedom. Before long, the media devoted most of their attention to the marches and speeches and then the demands. The revolution's leaders manipulated people's guilt buttons. Liberals and progressives went for it. Conservatives bought in, too. What were the protestors asking that was so wrong? Separate schools for boys and girls would focus kids on education rather than premarital sex and the abortions that would follow. Gender segregation on buses, subways and trains would protect women. Religious law replacing secular law in local communities would strengthen the principle of self-government. One nation under *God*, right? And who could complain about shutting down porn on the Internet? Well, a lot of people. *Rimshot*. But a whole lot more believed that the First Amendment went too far. Like shouting "No more booze" in a crowded bar.

In San Francisco, we took it all with a smile or a smirk.

The morning after California adopted its new constitution—following Vermont and barely ahead of Oregon and Washington State to avoid coming in dead last—my radio alarm went off. There was no music, just static. Something like a smoke alarm with a dead battery. Maybe a month later, Miltie warned us that they had a registry of everyone's digital devices and would be cleaning them up. They'd also be coming for our old CDs and vinyls.

Next on the agenda would be stand-up comedy.

Miltie smiled that crooked smile of his. His face was asymmetric. If you saw Miltie from one side and then another, you'd think he was two different people. Needless to say, his face wasn't like that when he was on TV presenting the news. Anyway, we sat at a table far from the window. We met at this particular Peet's downtown twice a week. Each week on different days. I'd take the bus into work half-an-hour early. Miltie would be on his lunch hour. He worked at the radio station from three a.m. to noon. He'd kept a night-owl schedule when he performed stand-up, preferring midnight and after-hours shows. None of us could keep up with him. His wife disliked his schedule and a maybe few other habits, but she couldn't do a thing. Not now.

At the radio station, Miltie not only edited and wrote stories but also went on the air when someone called in sick. Or disappeared. From time to time, newscasters vanished. No announcements or farewells. You couldn't help but notice. Newscasters were familiar, because listening to the news was all but required. You never knew when a Cimby—a member of the Committee for Moral Behavior—might stop you and ask a question. What repeating the news had to do with morality no one knew. What we did know was that they didn't want you asking questions. They just wanted answers. All pre-packaged.

I had no answers as to why Miltie disappeared a year earlier, which ended his TV career. We were scared. We wondered who'd be next. Stand-ups—we all had day jobs; no one could make a living doing comedy—were not among the government's favorite citizens. Then three weeks later, Miltie showed up on the radio. He never said anything to me. I never asked. I did wonder if the government felt bad about mistreating him since the station made him assistant news director.

Not that Miltie as a news guy was singled out. I worked in a bank. One morning, our branch manager didn't show. Someone else simply sat at his desk. People say they're used to this sort of thing. They're blowing smoke. Disappearances unnerve you. When someone you know dissolves into the ether, you wait for the steel rods to rap on your own door.

But life goes on. Miltie and I sat with our coffee in the men's section looking around for Rodney. Looking around wasn't the slickest thing we could do, because a patron—or a barista—might have been on the government payroll and fingered us for conspiracy. The government had a thing about conspiracies. It started as one.

Miltie sipped from his espresso. When we occasionally met at night, he sipped espresso, as well. Wine, beer and liquor were all verboten. Napa and Sonoma Counties exported raisins. Miltie's eyelids descended as if little weights dragged them down. He stuck out his thick lower lip. His lips were fleshy. So were his eyelids, nose and cheeks. His neck, too. His whole body. People think of comedians as jolly fat men. Miltie was just short of fat and way short of jolly. For that matter, none of us were jolly. Happiness doesn't make for great comedy.

Miltie pursed his lips as if he was thinking about an upcoming government proclamation or maybe a woman. If the latter, he was taking his chances. The sword whooshing down on the back of your neck and all. He glanced at the clock above the entry. "Obviously, Rodney's not coming."

Rodney met us every now and then. He'd show up unannounced within five minutes after we arrived. At least the buses ran on time.

"Can't blame Rodney," I said, "We're like a club. And *I* wouldn't want to join a club that accepted *me* as a member."

Miltie buried a smile his eyes failed to conceal. The joke was a classic. If a joke gets a laugh—a hint of a chuckle will do—it's worth stealing. At least, that used to be the case before jokes became riskier than the stock market.

"Sorry," I said, acknowledging Miltie's heads up about a proposed ban on humor in public, which potentially included friends cracking jokes in cafés. The ban wasn't in effect yet, but if the Cimbies wanted to get a head start on enforcing the law, there wasn't much you could do.

Miltie licked the rim of his cup. "I told Rodney," he whispered. "About you know what."

Miltie definitely was pushing the envelope. Obviously, he would never pass on information about a law, edict, directive or whatever on his cell phone. Still, we were registered stand-ups. Miltie had balls.

"That Rodney," I said.

Miltie shook his head "Those one-liners."

"Look," I said, surprising myself in the process. "There's no announcement yet, right? How about one of us calls Rodney, and we go for a walk on our next day off. The three of us. Just for l-a-u-g-h-s."

Rodney and I strolled Spreckels Lake. Golden Gate Park was filled with men chatting in twos and threes. Three was the maximum number of men or women allowed to get together. To maintain that restriction, each small group stayed ten paces apart. Rodney grabbed my elbow and led me to an empty bench. We sat. He ran his right hand under the slats that formed the seat. "Clear," he said softly, as if we were in an old spy movie. Or a new one in which American renegades holed up in the mountains or underground in the cities plotting evil deeds. Rodney's eyes darted right and left, up then down. Maybe the bench didn't hide a microphone, but one or more might have been planted in the trees. He nodded. "So, Groucho," he said. "No Miltie?"

"Sick kid," I said. "He's helping his wife out. Cooking, dishes, stories at nap time."

"Dangerous stuff," Rodney said. "A man doing woman's work." He lit a cigarette. Like coffee, cigarettes were cheap. They counterbalanced the cost of groceries, which rose sky-high along with the price of fuel now that the U.S. was a major energy exporter. Smoking dulled Rodney's appetite and kept his weight down. He'd once had Miltie's heft. Now, he struck me as near skeletal given his sunken cheeks and knobby shoulders. I thought of Sid Caesar, a pioneer of TV comedy, who changed his diet after he left the small screen and emerged half his former size—the opposite everything America once stood for. Rodney said that smoking soothed his nerves. Smokers had doubled since the revolution. Rumors abounded—Miltie never confirmed them—that cigarettes now contained some kind of mood stabilizer. If they did, you'd have thought pot would be healthier, but the government only liked the drugs it liked. Still, a mood stabilizer might have been okay in Rodney's case. A man who tosses off one-liners the way other men exhale tends to be tightly wound. Knowing that comedy in public would soon be banned would be hell on his blood pressure. Not that smoking would help.

"So a duck, a pig and a rabbi go into a bar," I said.

Smoke shot out of Rodney's nostrils. "It's not a rabbi. It's a *rabbit*. A duck, a pig and a *rabbit*, for God's sake."

"There are two versions," I said. "So okay, a rabbit."

Rodney shrugged. "It's an old joke. The one with the *rabbit*. The one with the *rabbi* came from the government. Ask Miltie. Maybe if there were still bars, it would be funny."

"The old version or the new?"

Rodney's yellowed upper teeth pried a piece of tobacco off his tongue. "That's a dangerous question."

Two men approached. Two veiled women followed them. From literally behind a bush, a Cimby, who looked like he was in his twenties, popped out. His left hand stroked his reddish beard. His right wielded a steel rod. He flicked it.

The women dropped back to the mandated six paces. This eliminated the possibility of holding hands or any other public display of affection. Private affection, however, was encouraged. You couldn't listen to the radio or watch TV or read a newspaper or go online—they had a stranglehold on the Net—without being bulldozed by statistics about the birth rate and encouragement to raise it. In fact, you couldn't go anywhere without seeing banners and posters featuring Uncle Sam exclaiming, I WANT *YOU* TO PROCREATE!

My wife and I had three kids. That was the mandated minimum for every man between thirty and forty. Three more kids, and we'd be eligible for a bigger apartment, maybe a flat or even a house from which a low-child family would be evicted. We'd also earn a cash bonus, which we could use to buy a car. With a car, you could pretty much go anywhere. Kind of. A sensor would reveal where you drove and when you got there. Also, you can't easily stuff a wife and six kids into a small sedan, which was all that was available. Still, every street corner displayed a banner advising, THINK 6! or 6—YOUR LUCKY NUMBER!

I eyed Rodney.

The Cimby eyed me.

Rodney and I stared at our shoes.

The Cimby tapped his steel rod on the paved path.

We looked up.

The Cimby raised the first two fingers of his left hand to the corner of his eye then pointed them at us. He must have seen that bit in an old movie before pre-revolutionary movies were banned.

Rodney took another drag on his cigarette. If it contained some kind of downer, you'd never know by the way his arms and legs twitched.

The Cimby thrust out his jaw then moved on.

"You think he thinks we're suspicious?" Rodney asked.

"Why should he?"

"Two men. No women."

"You have your wallet, right?" The wallet of every man twenty-five or older contained an up-to-date photo of his wife and children.

Rodney inhaled then exhaled slowly as if this was the last cigarette he'd ever smoke. "Too bad Miltie couldn't make it."

"Sick kid, remember?"

"Given that, I thought maybe you'd have called George."

"George B. or George C.?" I asked.

"Either. Obviously not both."

"I tried. Fat Jacky, too, but he's under the weather. Same with Robin."

"Richard? Henny?"

"Other obligations."

Rodney shrugged. "One day, I beat all my kids at wrestling, so I yelled out, 'Who's your daddy?' I got five different answers."

We sat in silence until the Cimby made it halfway around the lake, the steel rod in his hand swinging back and forth like a scythe. "So," I said. "A duck, a pig and a rabbit… a *rabbit*… go into a bar."

Miltie, Rodney and I arrived separately at a nondescript café two blocks from Peet's. Only half the tables were occupied.

"I'm spooked," Rodney said. "My wife said she spent yesterday afternoon supervising the gardener. We live in an apartment." He raised his macchiato to his lips then put it down. "Give it to us straight, Miltie. What are we doing in *this* joint?"

Miltie smiled. "You show up at a place once too often, they could be waiting for you."

Rodney lit a cigarette.

"What about the new you-know-what?" I asked Miltie.

Rodney looked at me. "We're safe. We may be three guys, but only two of us are funny."

I frowned. "About stand-up." I mouthed the words.

"Or sit-down," Rodney cut in. "A friend cut himself working around the house. I took him to the emergency room. It was crowded with guys, so we sat on the women's side. *Both* of us ended up with stitches."

"Needs work," Miltie said.

Rodney flicked an ash. "Not a joke."

I looked from Rodney to Miltie. "So?"

Miltie bent forward no more than two inches to avoid attracting attention.

Rodney and I avoided leaning in even that much. Appearing to pay more than a casual interest to a conversation could be waving a red flag.

Miltie smiled. "We'll be announcing you-know-what in three days."

Rodney shook his head. "I bought a watchdog. They told me he was ferocious. The mailman bit it."

I reached for a napkin at the empty table next to us as an excuse to check the room.

Rodney flicked another ash.

Banning stand-up might not make sense to some, but we all got it. The people at the top don't like being hated, but they can deal with it. They just ratchet up the fear factor. What shakes them up is being made fun of. One more joke, and maybe the country reaches critical mass. Still, details of the new law wouldn't be published. You'd get a summary but not the actual language. That way the security agencies and the courts could interpret any law however they wanted.

"We can't let them get away with this," I said. I don't know why. I'm no hero.

Miltie stared into his cup as if he was threatening the law against diviners. "You're not alone. Andy said the same thing yesterday. We have an idea."

I couldn't help leaning forward.

I was the first that evening to arrive at Andy's flat off Fulton Street. A bolt clicked. A chain clattered. The door barely swung open. I squeezed into the small, darkened entry. My feet scuffled over the hardwood floor. All I could hear were Andy's breathing and the pounding of my heart. Andy's wife and kids were at his in-laws across the park. Andy was a proud daddy, although he married only after the edict mandating hanging for homosexual behavior. Rumor had it someone volunteered to father his two children and the third on its way. Which of course constituted adultery punished by stoning. He closed the door and opened his arms. Andy was a big man with a belly that leaped out over his belt like a muffin top and an Abe Lincoln beard he grew at City College and hid behind since the revolution. "I'm glad you're here, man," he said in a gravelly voice that masked a gentle soul. "It's a risk, man." We hugged.

I took two steps into the living room. The drapes were drawn. Every apartment, flat and house in the city covered its windows with thick drapes or heavy shades to gain a measure of privacy. Naturally, everyone waited for the decree banning window coverings. I blinked a few times. The dark green walls—paint stores sold a limited variety of colors; green was the most common—absorbed much of the light coming from a single table lamp with a low-wattage bulb.

Andy went to a stack of books with green covers and handed me one. The books would provide our alibi in case the Cimbies came. If Andy's flat constituted a public venue—the Cimbies could always find a tortuous way of coming to any conclusion—we'd counter that we'd gathered for religious study. Hopefully, we'd endure nothing more than a lecture.

Knuckles rapped on the door. Andy held a finger to his lips.

Leaving the initial greetings to Andy—guys clustering in a doorway invited scrutiny from suspicious neighbors—I dropped onto the sofa. It threatened to collapse like a soufflé cooled too quickly. Half an hour later, a dozen anxious but exhilarated comics, including Rodney, who'd squeezed in between Miltie and me, filled Andy's living room. The air grew warm and close. I kept brushing my hand across my forehead and pulling my tee shirt away from my skin.

Miltie stood.

Rodney turned to me. "I met my wife in high school. She said she was hot to trot, so I took her to an expensive restaurant. Then we parked at the lake. That's when she told me she was on the cross-country team."

I cleared my throat.

He shook his head. "I'm still working on that one."

I nodded. A great stand-up makes an audience think it's easy. But a joke people remember can take days, weeks and even months to hone.

Miltie held up his right hand. "Welcome to Andy's living room. Although tonight it's a laughing room. Even if there isn't much to laugh about." He clapped his hands together. "*Especially* since there isn't much to laugh about."

We were thirteen altogether, counting our host. Miltie laid out the ground rules. Each of us would do eight minutes tops. Miltie would time us. There'd be a short break after the first seven sets. "If you have to laugh," Miltie warned, "hold your hands over your mouth. A pillow if you need it." After Miltie closed the show, there'd be no sitting around schmoozing. We'd tiptoe out together and scatter. In a few seconds, each of us would be by himself. No one would be breaking the law. Unless we'd run afoul of some law we didn't know about.

As far as our emcee went, Andy had proposed Moms, but Miltie advised against it. A woman in a flat with a dozen men? Even a study group?

Miltie wrote numbers on small pieces of paper. We drew lots. George C. opened. Before the revolution, George C. skewered politicians of both traditional parties and all leanings. The Cimbies watched him for two years. Every month or two they picked him up at the garage where he worked or at his studio apartment. Rents South of Market went way down after the social media techies lost their jobs. The Cimbies would blindfold George C. and take him somewhere in the city. At first, he tried to figure out where, but they made frequent turns and often doubled back on their route. After the third or fourth trip to one or another windowless cell for a two- or three-hour interrogation, he gave up.

"You know the difference between a Cimby and a sack of horseshit?" George C. asked. "Don't worry about it. No one else does, either."

The joke produced a few muffled laughs and one or two cleared throats. Frayed nerves combined with the heat made the room particularly tough. So did egos. Comics can be nastier than starving cannibals in a vegan restaurant. In fact, the cannibal thing was my opening joke. I'd put a lot of effort into my set, but I couldn't keep my right leg from shaking as Jonathan went into one of his wild improvs. Everyone in the room had more experience than me. My career consisted mostly of open mics. Drawing the ninth spot in the lineup offered some relief. After eight other stand-ups warmed up the crowd, everyone might be in a good mood.

We broke for coffee, tea and cookies baked by Andy. Rodney opened the second half of the show. "In college, I took this hot girl to a motel. We tore off our clothes. She looked at me and said…"

Andy's front door exploded.

The month or so that followed is still hazy. I do remember them packing us into a van. Other images bounce around my head like pinballs. Unyielding brick and concrete walls. Fists. Feeling my face contort as if I were the subject of a painting by Edvard Munch. Worse, actually seeing my face contort without a mirror.

The present comes into sharper focus, so a few things I know. For starters, I do not want to go back to religious education camp. Also,

Stockton, California is a far cry from San Francisco, although cities and towns have grown increasingly alike in their drabness. I live in a halfway house and work in a convenience store. They sent my wife and kids south to Victorville. I can't go see them. My papers are stamped NO TRAVEL.

I miss the guys, too. I haven't heard from Rodney or Andy or Henny or anyone else dragged from the laughing room that night. I never will.

I'm also pretty certain about a few other things. For one, Miltie landed on his feet. He's back on TV—the same eleven o'clock news everyone in Northern California gets. They shoot his right side. Miltie's very relaxed in front of the camera just like he used to be. He's gained weight.

Also, Miltie was the Judas. I put that together as soon as I saw him on TV. What bothers me is that I'm not sure I blame him. Of course, none of us saw it coming just like we never saw the revolution coming. Saying we should have, that's hindsight. It was too outrageous. If we'd gotten the picture, we would have made more jokes. Put together whole routines. But we were asleep at the wheel. That's why I kick myself. I can't guarantee that comedy would have made a difference. It didn't in Nazi Germany or the Soviet Union or Egypt after the Arab Spring played itself out in a heartbeat. But I have to believe it might have.

One last thing. I'm still alive. I often ask myself why. When I do, I know I'm only avoiding the truth. The truth hurts. It hurts worse than everything they did to me in religious ed. I can't shake it. I never will. And it's so simple. They just didn't think I was all that funny.

"The Laughing Room!" appeared in PacificReview (2015).

In the Path of Totality

WINE FIRST. THEN pot. No relief. The second prescription, some. The medium contacts Robby. His soul's still in transit. No worries. Can *we* speak with him? She shrugs.

Six months later, we're up in Oregon. Small-town B&B. Smack in the path of totality.

Breakfast comes with eclipse glasses. We brought our own. Stomachs fluttering, we go outside. Locust-like, a crowd devours the earth to the horizon.

It's hot. We can't drink enough water. Then! The moon-disk caresses the sun. Nibbles. Gobbles. The sudden chill provokes shudders. They are not unfamiliar. On with our jackets.

Light returns. The crowd cheers. We remain mute. They go off to old routines. We endure our new normal.

Janice blinks. Hard. I thought I heard Robby's voice, she says. I respond, You think? Warmed like the morning's muffins, she slips out of her jacket.

I can no more shed my jacket than my skin.

Really, Do We Have to Know Everything?

"REALLY, DO WE have to know everything?" I ask.

"I'm just saying," Greg says. He studies his beer—his second—like he's examining a legal brief. "You know, with everything kids get into these days. Would *we* have done what these kids do?"

"No idea," I say. I glance at Mikey asleep in his stroller. The top shades him from the warm late-March sun, one of the advantages of living in the Bay Area. He stays down despite the conversation on the patio at the restaurant where Greg and I meet on his monthly Fridays off. Earlier, I took Mikey to toddler swim. I enjoyed it. Maybe not the "swimming" part, but all those young mothers. Definitely. I admit it. When you have three kids—two teenagers and a toddler—your household gets a little crazy. Things between you and your wife tiptoe south. You notice how attractive younger women are. Even if they're mothers. When we finished, we had time to kill, so we walked around downtown with its calm, leafy streets. Mikey pushed his stroller most of the way. Mikey has energy to burn. "We didn't have cell phones, remember?" I say.

"Technology," Greg says. "Makes kids crazy. Could be the radiation. So anyway, you hear about Kelly Henry?"

Kelly, Greg's Madison and my Sarah are all juniors at Foothill High. I also have a freshman, Danny. I thought I knew teens—what they were capable of. Even the best. Kids like Sarah and Danny. And Greg's kids. He also has a son, Andrew. Hormones kick in. Things go haywire. *We* had hormones.

Mikey babbles something.

I look down.

He ignores me and settles back into his snooze.

"God knows what they'll have when Mikey's in high school," Greg says.

I shrug. No point rushing things, although Mikey becoming a teenager offers lots of advantages. For starters, Sarah and Danny will be out of the house. Well, you hope. Mikey will be in high school. On his own for the better part of the day. Except for vacations. Summers, he'll be in camp. Sleep-away camp would be great. Or he'll have a job. Either way, I can get a lot done.

Greg raises his glass.

I struggle not to cringe.

"Dad of the year," he says.

I raise my glass in relief. I'd expected the usual toast.

"I don't know how you can do it all over again," he says. "Not that Mikey isn't the cutest little guy in town." He winks. "Here's to surprises."

You'd think two well-educated people could do a better job with family planning. "So Kelly," I say.

He shakes his head. "Texted photos of herself to half the fucking boys in the fucking school."

"That surprises you?"

"Naked."

I peer into my beer. Yes, back in the day we had sex on our minds. Our folks had sex on *their* minds. But sexting?

"So hey," Greg says. "You think you know what your kids are doing, but—" He looks at Mikey. "He's what? Two?"

"Closing in," I say.

"They're small, they're innocent."

I fight off a grimace. I don't want to believe the springs will uncoil when Mikey hits adolescence. I know they will.

"Fuck it," Greg says. He raises his glass again.

I nod.

"To Al and Phil," he says.

Al, Phil and Greg were partners at a heavyweight law firm in San Francisco until the Great Recession put them through the ringer. The survivors billed hours like juniors to keep the firm afloat. One midnight, Al put a gun in his mouth. Three weeks later, Phil drove his Mercedes into a tree. The firm decided that every remaining partner and associate—as long as they didn't have a court date—would take off one Friday each month.

I appreciate the guy time with Greg. Once, I'd been a project manager at a tech company. A behemoth ate us up and spit half of us out. The job market wasn't kind. The economy may have recovered, but it passed me by.

Fortunately, Kimberly is a Certified Financial Planner®. Capital letters. The circle "R" is a registered trademark. Being smart and personable, she grew an impressive client base. She has an office near where Greg and I are eating. Not that she spends much time there. Most of her clients and prospects want to meet in their offices or in their homes. I admit to having a few concerns in that regard. I can imagine plenty of men working up an interest in more than retirement strategies and tax-advantaged investments. Her business keeps her running days, nights, weekends. No complaints on my part. We're a modern family.

We drink to Al and Phil.

"What I'm saying is," Greg says, "you never know. This sexting thing? Tip of the iceberg. How do we know where our kids are when they're not in school or at home? How do we know what they're doing?"

"Sarah and Danny?" I say. "I trust them."

Our waiter—or waitress—or waitperson—arrives with our burgers.

Mikey's sleeping like a champ.

I order another beer.

Greg makes a face.

"What?" I ask. "I'm eating. And we'll walk to the car."

He shrugs. "Anyway, we're too old to fool ourselves about these things."

"What things?" I take a chunk out of my burger.

"My father used to say that no one gives you trust in this world. Trust is something you earn."

I pick up a shoestring fry. "You don't trust your kids because of something someone else's kid did?"

Greg lowers his burger. "It's not about trust."

"Then what?"

"It's about *knowing*. Where your kids are. Just in case."

"In case of what?"

"In case, say, Madison or Andrew gets kidnapped."

I raise an eyebrow.

"It happens."

"And the odds are what?"

"It happens. So I did something."

"Did what?"

"There's this app. You download it into your kids' cell phones. It tracks them. Anywhere they go, you see where."

"They let you do that?"

"They had a choice?" Greg leans forward. "This app. I could have downloaded it into their phones while they were asleep. They'd never have known. You can do that and hide the app. Actually hide it. But I *wanted* them to know."

"Because?"

"Because now they know *I* know where they were. And that should— could—keep them from doing stupid stuff."

"Like getting kidnapped? What if the kidnappers take their phones?"

"That can be a good thing."

"Kidnappers taking their phones?"

"I check the app. I know right where my kids are. Or where the kidnappers are."

"Then what? You call the kidnappers?"

"I call the police." Greg raises his glass, swallows, sets it down and picks up his burger. "It's not like I'm losing sleep. What are the odds, right?"

I shrug.

"Anyway, sometimes kids go places you don't want them to go because they'll do things you don't want them to do. They don't plan to do anything wrong, but they go someplace— Shit happens."

"Or maybe they do," I say.

"Do what?"

"*Do* plan on getting into trouble."

"I rest my case."

"Really, do we have to know everything?" Kimberly asks. She plumps her pillow for the umpteenth time. Her nose stays buried in a book on new approaches to tax strategy.

"Look, you know what kids do," I say. "It's on TV. The radio. The Net."

"And you think this makes sense? Snooping on your own children?"

"Snooping is a loaded word."

"So you call it what?"

"Parenting. I call it parenting."

She takes a very audible breath. "And if they say no?"

"Who are the parents?"

"But can't they disable the app or something like that? Kids know all about this stuff."

I close my eyes. I'm beat. I took Mikey to gymnastics that morning and his playgroup that afternoon. I broiled chicken for dinner because Kimberly was meeting with a client. Or was he *not* a client and I was just fooling myself? Anyway, we'd run out of leftovers and Kimberly left specific instructions not to order another pizza. I figured that cooking dinner, including a green vegetable, was easier than going at it about what I fed the kids. Or didn't. After dinner, I read to Mikey and settled him down. Then I made sure Sarah and Danny got started on their homework. As soon as I collapsed in front of the TV, Mikey started fussing and kept at it. "Disable the app?" I say. "Not if they want to keep their phones."

"You're sure about that?"

"Who *pays*? I mean, *who*? If I say— If *we* say we're doing this tracking thing so Mom and I will know where you are—"

"Don't drag *me* into this. I don't want to be the bad guy here."

"It's a matter of safety. Safety is what it is. And if it'll make you happy, *I'll* be the bad guy."

Kimberly nestles the book on her stomach like it's Mikey as an infant. "Scott, get real. Business is nuts. I don't have time to snoop on the kids."

"Track them," I say. "Your own children?"

She pulls the blanket up to her chin like it's some kind of armor then picks up the book. "I've got a lot on my plate."

"Your plate's full. I get that. You put bread on the table. Wine in the rack. Thank you for your service."

Kimberly closes the book. "I took on three new clients this month. Do you know how much work it takes to get the ball rolling with these people?"

"I can imagine."

"Not to mention servicing all my other clients."

"Honest, I appreciate everything you're doing. So do the kids. Even Mikey. Or he will when he's older."

She sighs. "Not that I've ever heard any thanks from them."

I place my right hand on her shoulder. "They appreciate everything. You know they do. The house. The clothes. The trips."

"Sarah hated Maui. Who hates Maui?"

I fight off a grin. She's just given me what I need to close the deal. "Sarah's sixteen. What sixteen-year-old girl likes hanging around with her parents and her kid brother and her baby brother on top of that? They want to do stuff with other sixteen-year-olds. The way *we* wanted to do stuff."

Kimberly opens the book. "Fine."

"Really, do we have to know everything?" Sarah asks. We share a rare few minutes alone after school since Danny's at a photo club meeting. She paces around the island in the kitchen like a shark circling a seal. Not that she cares about eating. Getting Sarah to eat is a chore. We wonder if she's borderline anorexic. "Really, Daddy, if you always get to know where I am, shouldn't I get to know where *you* are? And Mom? Mom's always somewhere."

"We're the mom and dad," I say. "You're the daughter. Danny is the son. For now, Mikey's out of this one. Just do the math." That's not-secret code for *Parents get more votes than kids.*

Sarah texts someone.

I keep talking. "Mom and I think it's important that we know where our children are. Just in case."

"In case of what?" she says while her thumbs beat on her phone's keyboard.

I peer into the family room. Mikey sits contentedly in his playpen. It has six sides—two red, two yellow, one blue and one green. All those colors are supposed to stimulate his brain. What's stimulated now is my thirst. I open the fridge and take out a bottle of Pinot noir, half of which I put away the previous evening after the kids went to their rooms and Kimberly retreated to the guestroom, which doubles as her home office.

Sarah looks up.

"It's just wine," I say.

"Aren't you supposed to wait until after five?"

"That's less than an hour off. Forty-eight minutes."

Sarah collects her backpack. "I'm going to Emily's."

"I thought you and Emily weren't speaking."

"Once I get my license, I can drive to Madison's."

"But Emily?"

"*Duh!*" We're writing up our physics project.

"*Duh!* doesn't strike me as an appropriate thing to say to your father. If there's anything I don't need right now, it's attitude." I pour a glass of wine. "How do I know you'll be at Emily's?"

"You just installed tracking on my phone, remember?"

"That's my point."

Sarah rolls her eyes. "Well, I hope it makes you happy snooping on me. Knowing when I'm at Emily's or volleyball practice—"

"Volleyball season's over."

"Or Madison's when I get my license. They live in a nicer neighborhood, you know."

"We're not exactly living on the wrong side of the tracks."

"That's racist."

I have no intention of touching that one, whatever it means. "Be home for dinner," I say.

"What are we having?"

"Changing the subject?"

"I'm trying to find out what we're having for dinner. *Duh!*"

I figure Mikey and I will pick up something at Whole Foods. Or at the gourmet deli. I like shopping with Mikey. He draws lots of attention from women. Good-looking women. Sometimes I wonder what it would be like to be divorced. Or widowed. A single dad tragically left alone with a small child. Obviously in touch with his feminine side, but still a man's man. However that works. Just a fantasy. We all have fantasies.

Sarah flips her hair and hoists her backpack. "I suppose you'll be tracking Mom soon."

"Really, do we have to know everything?" Dr. Benjamin muses. "What do you think, Scott? *Do* we?"

I cross my legs. I uncross them. I started seeing Dr. Benjamin before Kimberly got pregnant with Mikey. I'd been out of work for a while, which led to Kimberly and me discussing my taking over the household chores. Then she—we—added the baby chores after we decided that while we supported a woman's right to choose, an abortion wasn't for us.

"Why *do* we, Scott?" Dr. Benjamin asks again.

My mind goes blank.

"Have to know everything," he says.

I take a breath. "Oh right. Well, not *everything*."

"Fine. *Some* things."

"Your kids, they're not *some* things. They're the most important things in the world, right?"

"Are they?"

I force a smile.

"So, Scott. You downloaded this tracking app. It's been what? A month?"

"Five weeks."

"And it's working?"

"It's an app. Technology."

Dr. Benjamin nods. "What I mean is, how is it working for *you?*"

I take a moment to sort things out then respond. "Well, Danny's not a problem. Not yet. He's just a freshman. But who knows? Any day, look out!"

"And Sarah?"

"Sarah's fine."

"Do you think she's being more careful?"

"About what?"

"Where she goes. Who she sees. What she does."

"Because of the app? Maybe. No. I mean, no, she's a good kid, she wouldn't do the wrong thing."

"So the app is doing what? Reinforcing your confidence in your children? Sarah in particular?"

"Maybe."

"Then there's no problem."

I feel my face scrunch up.

Dr. Benjamin stares.

I sigh. "It's just— Sometimes Kimberly seems so distant. Her head, it's always in the business."

"Which perhaps means she's still working and you're still looking after the kids, the house."

I'm tempted to answer, *Duh!* Instead, I say, "I've been thinking. If I track her cell, it'll kind of keep her closer. *Us* closer."

"Track your wife's cell? Really?"

"I've been thinking is all."

"Have you done it?"

I shake my head.

"But you'd like to."

My fingers clutch the armrests of my chair. "Sometimes, I—"

"You what? Sometimes."

"Don't trust—"

Dr. Benjamin raises an inquisitive eyebrow.

"She could be anywhere doing anything, couldn't she?"

"And why would that be?"

"Because look who she's married to. A guy who looks after the house and the kids."

"A house-husband?"

"You could say that."

"Would *you* say that?"

"I thought I *did*."

"And with this tracking app, you'd always know where Kimberly is."

"I guess."

"But would you know what she was *doing*?"

I shrug. I haven't really thought about it that way. "Anyway," I say, "it feels like I'd be betraying our vows or something like that. Does that make sense?"

"Does that make sense to *you*?"

"I don't know."

"Because you think Kimberly has betrayed your vows?"

"I don't know. Maybe. It happens."

"And you haven't?"

"Haven't what? Betrayed my vows?"

"Installed the app on Kimberly's phone."

I shift my weight. "I thought I said that."

"Really, do we have to know everything?" the female TV co-host asks. It's a woman's show. Not all that many men stay home watching TV on a weekday morning. But the male co-host is an ex-NFL linebacker.

The female co-host turns to their guest, a woman who wrote a book about the relationship between technology and human behavior.

The ex-linebacker smiles. I wonder if his mouth contains more than the normal quantity of teeth.

The author answers, "Why *wouldn't* people want to know everything?"

I glance at my cell phone on the coffee table.

"Our curiosity," the author goes on. "Our desire to know. Our innate *need* to know. *Everything*. That's what makes us human."

"It's like— Basic," says the former footballer.

The studio audience applauds.

Right on the money, I think. A few nights earlier I went online after Kimberly went to sleep and found out how to download and install the tracking app—and disguise it so she'd never know. It was simple given that she leaves her cell on her desk in the guestroom/office to recharge and I know her code.

After I slipped into bed, I stared at the ceiling for at least an hour. Ultimately, I consoled myself that while now I *could* track Kimberly that didn't mean I *had* to. If I ever did, it was because secrets destroy a marriage. I did it for *us*.

The co-hosts continue chatting with their guest.

I wonder where Kimberly is and then look at my cell. I remember what Dr. Benjamin says: We owe it to ourselves to be honest with ourselves. I check back in with the TV.

"If there's anything we've learned," says the author, "it's that technology is empowering."

The female co-host announces a commercial break.

The ex-linebacker tells the TV audience not to go away.

Mikey stirs in his playpen.

I cock my head. I'm afraid that looking over will wake him.

He quiets down.

I glance at my cell again. I think, what if I check on Kimberly? It's mid-morning, so wherever she is, it'll be an innocent thing. Except that no one suspects anything unusual goes on in the morning, so what better time for a quickie? But really? Mid-morning? Kimberly? I'm a damn fool to be jealous. But why not see where she is? It's not like I'll be snooping. Knowing where she is, in a way it'll seem like we're together. Like having coffee. When was the last time we did *that* on a weekday morning? I pick up my cell and click on the app. A map appears. I click again. She's in her office downtown.

Mikey calls out.

I go to his playpen, pick him up and hoist him onto my shoulder. He needs a change, a cup of juice and a walk. Then lunch. After his nap, a trip to the playground to make a mess in the sandbox followed by a little gentle roughhousing before a bath. Or after a bath. Then we'll settle in. I'll pour a glass of wine and read from the cloth picture book he loves—a book stained for eternity with baby food and real food and spit-up. He needs all of that.

And what do I need?

Maybe it seems strange, but I was disappointed to find Kimberly in her office. That sounds counterintuitive, but it's not. Because if I *had* caught her somewhere suspicious—say a motel—that would explain everything. I'd have a right to be disappointed with what my life has come to because nothing is your fault when you're a victim.

Mikey settles down. His soft, innocent breathing mixes with my pulse, which clangs in my ears like a jackhammer.

I whisper, "Really, do we have to know everything?"

A Good Ol' Country Boy

I'M CRESTING THE top of Strawberry Hill in Golden Gate Park when my ex, who I haven't seen in years, steps out from behind a tree. It's spooky, because this is where we first met—above what used to be a reservoir or pumping station that I fantasize once served as a swimming pool in a resort long abandoned. She's wearing this big, floppy straw hat like the one she wore that day. I take it as a sign. God knows, I need one.

She tilts her head. Obviously, she sees me. I stop in my tracks to consider retreating down the hill. Also to catch my breath. College and grad school are basically invisible in the rear-view mirror. But I still hike up here for the views of the Marin Headlands, the Golden Gate and the bridge heading north out of the city. Now, I regret my fondness for the place. But I can't walk away. Again. She still knows people I know. Word will spread at digital speed that I'm some kind of schmuck. Again.

I play it casual. "Hi, babe," I call out. I want her to see me as cool with seeing her after so long. That I'm content with my life. Happy. Sometimes, nothing sustains you like a lie.

She stares.

As I approach her, I turn breathless, and it's not the climb. She isn't Nicole. I stop, leaving five or six feet between us, and swivel my head in search of witnesses who can testify that no assault is taking place. All I see is a gray-haired couple a hundred feet off looking south towards the Sunset District. They don't notice me. Notice *us*. Although there is no us.

The woman takes off her hat. Her long brown hair is thick and wavy—lush like Nicole's when we met. After we got married Nicole cut it short. She never said why.

I take a small step forward.

The woman holds her ground. She's either a good sport or has a black belt in karate.

"Sorry," I say. "I thought you were someone else."

She squints. I read her eyes hurling a message I've been hit with more than once. *Is that your best line?*

It's not. Although *Hi, babe* might be as good a pickup line as I've ever used. Which admittedly is odd. My profession is all about words. I'm a poet. And a teacher. Of poetry. I help students digest and analyze complex, meaning-laden words, phrases, lines and stanzas. Deconstruct deep thoughts, ideas and emotions. Strip away the layers of self-deception that condemn us to stumbling endlessly through the dark maze that is life.

Definitely a crappy metaphor.

I've been in a slump.

A long slump.

Not that my life would be much different if I were being published regularly. Poetry never pays the bills. You place something with a big commercial magazine, you get a kind of reasonable check. Doing that once a year represents an accomplishment. A book? You probably pay the publisher. Break even? Probably not. So you submit to small, esoteric publications and treasure a skimpy contest prize or honorarium. More often than not, you welcome the free copies as ocular proof of your being published. For a few weeks, you can pretend you've earned what passes as prestige while the poets you know flash their claws behind your back. I never minded playing pretend, so I milked every published poem. Then I told Nicole we had no future together. I packed up my books but left an expensive silver bowl from my aunt with her. Also my muse. I fell out of editors' favor the way ancient mariners feared falling off the edge of the earth. *Here be dragons.*

If I'd had a photo of my muse, it'd still appear on milk cartons. But it strikes me that maybe I've found her.

I inch forward until I'm close enough to touch the cheek of a woman who resembles Nicole, although now not so much. The woman's nose is longer. Her lips thinner.

She nods almost imperceptibly as if maybe she's one of my former students and recognizes me. Then she removes her earbuds.

This is awkward.

"Do I know you?" she asks.

I'm tempted to answer, *Well, you do now, and lucky for me,* but I pass. Some guys get away with shit like that. They're a lot younger. They say forty is the new thirty. I have my doubts. "Sorry," I say. "I thought—"

"I'm someone you knew once," she says. "An old girlfriend?"

"Well, now that I've gotten a better look, you're probably too young."

"Depends on how old your old girlfriends were."

My right foot paws the dirt. "Thanks for not screaming."

"I wanted to see who it was. I broke my glasses this morning, and you walked towards me like you knew me."

"An old boyfriend?"

"I would have run." She shrugs. "Just a friend."

"I should be so lucky." That, I reflect, is a pretty good line.

"So, I guess you're not a serial killer or anything like that."

I pass on a wiseass comeback like, *Not lately.* Instead I say, "It's odd seeing anyone up here on a weekday who's not a senior citizen. February's not exactly tourist season."

"I have today off."

"You work weekends?"

"Some. It's not easy finding a decent job in San Francisco if you're not in tech."

"Tell me about it," I say. I have *two* jobs. Together they don't add up to full-time. No benefits, either. Colleges save money by hiring adjunct professors, which is a bullshit title for part-timer. I manage to cover rent on a studio behind someone's garage out on Forty-third off Fulton. The notable features of life in the Avenues are wind and fog. On the plus side, the park's half a block away. And the 5-Fulton runs on time some of the time.

My new possible-but-don't-bet-the-farm friend smiles as if to say, *This has been pleasant but nothing more and thank you but I'd just as soon head down the hill to the boathouse for tea or maybe to the band concourse and get some lamb samosas at the Indian food truck and be by myself the way I was before you maybe not quite so much intruded as interrupted me—or maybe intruded after all.*

I feel impelled to preempt that. "What are you listening to? Or *were*."

"Music," she says.

I nod. "What kind?"

"Country."

I discern neither twang nor drawl. "Where'd you grow up?"

"Santa Monica."

"That's surfer territory."

"My folks loved the Beach Boys. Me, I'm my own woman."

I see an opening. I grew up in New Jersey but once taught for a year at a small Catholic college in San Antonio. "You know what I like about country music?"

"What's that?"

"The lyrics. Every country song tells a story. Country lyrics are meant to be heard. Like poetry."

She nods.

I point to my right ear.

"Merle Haggard."

"Okie from Muskogee" is the only Merle Haggard song I know and I like it, although I don't identify. "Wasn't he from California?"

"Bakersfield. But his family was from Oklahoma. Okies."

"Like the Joads," I say.

The reference to *The Grapes of Wrath* escapes her. I'm okay with that, because what intrigues me is that she's cute in a maturing post-post-college way. I'm guessing she's ten years younger. Forty and thirty? Nothing wrong with that.

"Know what I love most about country songs?" I ask. I don't wait for an answer. "The titles." I draw a blank. There's "Okie from Muskogee" and then what? I figure I've got nothing to lose bluffing my way. "And the— Hooks, I think they call them. The line in each song you can't get out of your head?" One's stayed with me for years after I heard it driving through the park in the rain. When I had a car. When I had a wife. "Sometimes you're the windshield. Sometimes you're the bug."

"Mary Chapin Carpenter," she says. "'The Bug.' I love that song. You must have a good ear. Or a way with words. Or both."

"I'm not sure about the ear, but I like to think I have a way with words. I'm a poet."

Her eyes brighten. "Really?"

My stomach flops. She'll want to know where my poems have appeared. I doubt she'll be impressed.

She throws me a curveball. "Ever tried writing songs? *I* write songs. Country."

I know a set-up when I hear one. She's about to tell me she not only writes songs, she's got a contract with a record company. She goes on tour. She's in San Francisco to play some club or maybe the arena in Oakland or the one down in San Jose. If I'm not tongue-tied, I'm close. "*You* must have a way with words."

"I like to think so."

This won't be the first time I've been humbled, but I'll feel like a bigger fool if I make some lame excuse and slink away. "Do you perform? Sing your own stuff?"

"Working on it. Bar gigs now and then. A dozen people on a good night. Ten drunk. Pass the hat. Maybe make enough for a beer and Muni or BART fare."

Schadenfreude lifts me off my feet me like a sneaker wave when your back's turned to the ocean. I struggle to regain my sense of civility. I don't want to be one of *those people*. "Still, that's impressive."

"I bet *you* could write country songs," she says. "I mean, you being a poet and all."

My response should be simple and straightforward: *Oil and water.* But I'm attracted to this woman in the floppy straw hat and sense that her being my muse may not be all that far-fetched. "Probably," I say like a ventriloquist's dummy. The words can't be mine but whoever or whatever is manipulating me has a stubborn streak. "I could probably write some pretty damn good country lyrics if that was the road I was taking."

She smiles. Her teeth are perfectly white except for one in the lower front. "I bet you could whip something up in a hurry. We could meet here day after tomorrow. Same time. You don't need a melody. I can handle that. Just the lyrics. I bet you could teach me a lot."

What I say: "Okay."
What I think: *Idiot!*

The sun has abandoned the Lower Forty-Eight, so I turn on an old gooseneck lamp humped over a corner of my child-size desk. It's the only light on. Keeps my PG&E bill down.

Although I rarely drink beer, my preferred adult beverage—as fatuous a euphemism as exists—being wine, specifically chardonnay, I pop the top off a can of Bud Light. I hope beer will summon the muse who abandoned me. The muse that the woman in the floppy hat may be channeling. We're meeting in less than forty-eight hours. She expects lyrics. Country lyrics. And what gets country juices flowing better than beer? Getting drunk is what country singers sing about. Guys, at least. I could have bought a bottle of whiskey, but I don't drink whiskey. For that matter, I don't chew tobacco. But I'm like a method actor preparing for a role. Although I know nothing about acting, method or otherwise.

These days, I'm not sure I know anything about poetry.

Ten minutes into the Bud Light, I sense that my muse is refusing my invitation. Maybe she doesn't care for the neighborhood. Too foggy.

Half an hour later, I've only finished half the can and not a word to show for it.

Then a thought hits me. A sequence of thoughts. In the world of country music, life is a torment to be endured and overcome. And where do you hear about enduring and overcoming? In church. *If* you go to church. Which maybe you do Sunday morning after getting drunk Saturday night. This suggests an interesting theological discussion, but I'm entering the world of music where life is raw.

I bring the can back up to my lips. The beer is bitter but the possibilities are sweet. Every country song tells a story. Every story involves suffering. Ergo, suffering's what I'll write about.

So what comes next? The title? It strikes me that if I have a title, the rest will follow. I drum my fingers on the desk. No particular rhythm. I'm not particularly musical. But my fingertips sing to me: "A Good Old Country Boy is a Suffering Man."

I type those nine critical words into my laptop. Doesn't look right. Of course not. Country people don't talk that way. I edit. I replace the ending "d" and "g" with an apostrophe. "A Good Ol' Country Boy is a Sufferin' Man."

I'm on fire.

I chug the remainder of the beer, cough then re-read my title. Clever, what with the contrast of *good* and *suffering*— by which I mean *sufferin'*— *boy* and *man*. A concept easy to understand without an MFA.

That's more than I can say about a lot of the stuff I've been struggling with. Dark, moody pieces. Fashionably opaque. Or more like out of fashion. I read drafts to my students. They look up at me—*when* they look up at me—glassy-eyed. I throw them the same lifeline: *A good poem offers many meanings. Think metaphor. Think beauty in the eye and all that.* Sometimes this lubricates a class discussion.

Mostly not.

But I'm a budding country songwriter now, and I have a job to do.

I also have to pee. The bathroom's only ten feet away, but I hold it in. I'm on a roll. And as an adjunct professor of poetry, I understand my responsibilities to my art. So I take hold of a pen and a yellow pad—a cowboy with a laptop?—and make notes on all the impossible-to-hit curveballs life throws at a good ol' country boy.

- *DRINKIN': The night before church—the mornin' before—in church—after church for sure—at work—at your boss's daughter's weddin'—your own daughter's weddin'—*
- *WOMEN: Wives who cheat—girlfriends who cheat—wives and girlfriends who cheat—maybe with each other—probably with a good ol' boy—your brother—no, that's creepy—your bes' frien'—*
- *JAIL: Public drunkenness—or beatin' up a cheatin' woman—or your bes' frien' your woman cheated with—maybe bank robbery (everyone hates banks)—prob'ly beatin' up your bes' frien' since beatin' on women is unmanly—unless you shot him—and her—*
- *MAMA: She's doin' poorly—better, she just died—heartbroke while you was in prison for killin' your bes' frien' who cheated with your wife and/or girlfrien'—*
- *DADDY: Mean ol' sumbitch—better, the image of kindness— Christian kindness—his life taken at the plant or down in the mine*

or by an actual mean sumbitch who cheated playin' Texas Hold'em and fired at point-blank range when Daddy called him on it—

- *RENT: You got fired by your sumbitch boss for drinkin' on the job— couldn't support your family though you never really did—stress led your wife/girlfrien' to cheat with your bes' frien' who you killed in a drunken rage after your bank robbery only brought in a few hundred dollars in marked bills and your daughter saw it—five years old, blonde hair, blue eyes—lives with her mama who went to live with her mama a long ways off—you're outta prison, no job—live in your truck with your dog, faithful all those years, you behin' bars (out early for findin' Jesus and exhibitin' good behavior), only now he's standin' on his last (four) legs—*

- *THE DEVIL: Not that a good ol' country boy ain't tryin' to be a new man, but the Devil just won't let go his soul!!!*

I run the back of my hand across my forehead to wipe off the sweat then toss the empty can towards the wastebasket on the other side of the desk. It makes a hollow sound as it bounces off the rim and onto the floor. I stand to go to the fridge. Just one beer? Not for a good ol' country boy.

I sway. Maybe I drank too fast. No. Has to be the late hour. No. It's barely past ten. When did ten become the new midnight?

I take a breath. Try to clear the cobwebs. I've got plenty to write about, not to mention a great title. All I need now is to get down a couple of lines. Build momentum for tomorrow.

I consider a short sprint to the bathroom. I'm not sure I can do it. That's good. I'm sufferin'. I sit. Country boys never quit. I'll begin by drawing—drawin'—on my own life experiences.

- *ALCOHOL: I've gotten what might pass for drunk twice. Once during high school at a friend's house on a Saturday afternoon. I conked out in his basement. The other time at a bar when I tried to show some fellow grad students that I could drink like Dylan Thomas. Joyce. Bukowsky. All I remember is someone calling me an asshole.*

- *WOMEN: I'm encouraged here. There's the divorce. Nicole wasn't the most grounded woman. She hated children, which I found out only after we were married. She had frequent nightmares and screamed in her sleep. Every few weeks, she'd go out at midnight and wander the streets. Admittedly, I didn't have much going for me, either. Maybe except for ambition of a sort. Right after I got my BFA, I entered an MFA program. This put me on the career path to write and teach. It also freed me from having to find a job. Right off, I earned bragging rights and free drinks with acceptances from a few small journals, but the New Yorkers and the Georgia Reviews ignored me. That shot down any chance of a tenure-track position at a major university, which condemned me to academic genteel poverty. That and I have a bit of a cleanliness fetish. Also, I snore.*

- *JAIL: I'm way to timid to risk that. You know what happens to educated men who go to jail.*

- *MOTHER AND FATHER: One each. Dad passed in his sleep a year after I married Nicole. Mom still lives in Jersey. She threatens to move to Florida. Why is that a threat? Anyway, she's thriving. Dad left a lot of life insurance, impressive assets and a paid-off home. I call every week. I fly back twice a year. Summers, she takes me to her tennis club to watch her play. Doubles. No one attempts to return a ball hit more than two steps away. We have lunch with her girlfriends. They know I'm divorced. Several tell me they have daughters in California. And tell me. And tell me.*

- *RENT: Finally, a good ol' country boy and I have something in common. Or not. I'm always paid up. Granted, my studio doesn't look out on Lover's Mountain or Heartbreak Creek.*

- *THE DEVIL: A non-starter. I grew up Jewish. Not religious. Just Jewish. Jews aren't into the Devil. Still, it's a great image. Look what Milton did with Satan/Lucifer. I tried something like that once. I'm no Milton.*

Past midnight, I finish processing these and related thoughts. Still, the screen beneath the title remains blank. But I'm right on the edge. Unless it's a precipice. I call it a night. I have a class at nine. I'll let my subconscious do the heavy lifting while I sleep.

I thrash around until three.

Early the next afternoon, I return home and scrunch up to my desk. I have little more than twenty-four hours before meeting the girl with the straw hat and dark wavy hair. I visualize wearing a cowboy hat. Me, not her. Country stars wear cowboy hats, even inside arenas and TV studios. Probably to the bathroom. To make a statement, I guess. What that statement is I'm not sure. I make my own statement. I go to the fridge, take out a can of Bud Light and pop the top.

As I scour the list of troubles I assembled the night before, the truth bitch-slaps me. The closest I've ever come to being a cowboy is eating Tex-Mex in San Antonio and listening to that old band Kinky Friedman and The Texas Jewboys. Kinky was the only actual Jew.

Bitch-slap number two drives into my head that the woman in the straw hat isn't my muse. Not that I don't want to get to know her better. I do. But someone else will have to write "A Good Ol' Country Boy."

I go to the sink and empty the beer down the drain. Then I pour a glass of chardonnay from a bottle opened the week before. It's a bit stale. I don't mind.

Damned if I haven't earned the right to fail on my own terms.

All the World's a Stage

THEY TELL ME I don't have much time to express my gratitude to this wonderful audience, so I'll just focus on the Exalted Leader. I mean, everyone else walks in his shadow, which is what all the winners said at last year's annual film awards, but it's worth repeating. Even when you go in front of the camera alone—naked is a good way of looking at it—no actor succeeds by himself.

Of course, this would be a good time for me to mention all those small-minded people back in Los Angeles who never gave me a shot, but that was another world. Another time. I owe everything to the Exalted Leader.

I see heads nodding. Of course. Every film during the seven years I've been here in the Democratic People's Republic, you can see the Exalted Leader's golden touch. Look at his incredible writing and directing skills. His dazzling set design and cinematography. His eye for casting. Even if he's had no direct contact with a movie, every movie in the DPR is better because of him.

Not to mention he's a genius nuclear physicist.

So, you can see how when I saw that ad in *Backstage*—an unnamed East Asian film company looking for an American to play a major role in a big-budget film and offering corresponding financial rewards—it was like the great god Hwanung was guiding me.

I didn't know what kind of character I'd be auditioning for—an American probably—so I uploaded a monologue from a friend's adaptation of Dickens' *A Tale of Two Cities*. The end where Sidney Carton is on his way to the guillotine. Who knew?

You can imagine how thrilled I was to receive my contract, although the English was a bit mangled But the first-class ticket through Tokyo clinched the deal. The day I landed is all a blur, but I remember waking up in my cottage on top of the hill here in Pyongyang next to this woman— very pretty, beautiful, my wife only two months later—who said, *This is your home now. It is a gift from the Exalted Leader.* Three bedrooms, two baths, fantastic views of the city dazzling at night until the lights go off at nine because as the Exalted Leader reminds us, Changsega created the world with its own lighting system. Oh, and the fridge. Stocked with Stella Artois as well as Taedonggang. How did they know?

Yes, I'm hurrying, but just let me say that when you've struggled through a decade of rejection in L.A., and you know you're a better actor than at least half the stars and co-stars working regularly, you appreciate someone giving a shit.

Can I say that? Does it matter now?

Anyway, I was so pumped—that means excited—when I got my first script, *Doomsday of Freedom*, written by the Exalted Leader himself. I celebrated with a Stella. Two.

In the States, the first thing you do is talk things over with your agent. But in the DPR, no one *needs* an agent. Or a manager. Or headshots or a website. The Exalted Leader was my agent, my manager, my everything. He personally chose me out of all the actors—and there were lots—who answered that ad.

Naturally, I emailed my agent in L.A., especially since he released me two weeks before. Asshole!

Can I say *that*? What the hell, right?

The asshole, all he did was send me running to auditions for five-and-under TV roles. I'd have killed for twenty words of meaningful dialogue.

Oh, and I refused commercials. I'm an artist.

Anyway, you do a scene and the casting director tells you how great you were, only you never get a callback. Or you get a callback along with a herd of other actors. It's obvious you're not the type they're looking for. Too old. Too young. Wrong ethnicity.

Except here in the DPR, I was the *right* ethnicity and a star from the get-go. I'm appreciative. Honestly.

So you remember, in *Doomsday*, I played this Russian scientist. For years, he helps the DPR build these big rockets that can reach San Francisco, Los Angeles, New York, Washington. Only I'm really an agent of the CIA sent to blow up the engineering lab where all the research takes place and rape the chief engineer's daughter played by my soon-to-be real-life wife who went on to star in so many of my films.

Anyway, the role required me to go into a really deep, dark place. All those classes—everything from Shakespeare to improv—paid off. Of course, I'm found out and killed. That's a given. But I'm proud as hell I did all my own stunts. Thank God for that summer course in stage combat.

Can I say that? Thank God? Although given the situation—

I'm getting the sign to cut it short. But let me take just a moment to thank the Exalted Leader again.

And my wife. No hard feelings. She was right to go to the Minister of Security. A personal friend of ours, I'd like to add. Thinking about it, which I've had however-many months to do—it was hard keeping track of time where I was—I can understand her concern about what I said one night at dinner. Although in my defense, I was speaking a second language. I said, *I don't want to be immodest, but I've earned the right to go back to L.A. I have more than thirty principal roles under my belt and kind of celebrity status.* I said, *I know I can land big roles in big-budget Hollywood films and cable shows.* I thought it was innocent enough—at the time.

On the other hand, I suspected that going back to L.A. wasn't an option. I mean, how is Washington letting me come back? Not that I've done anything wrong here. I've never been political in my life. In America, I only voted in one presidential election.

Can I mention elections?

Anyway, the White House probably takes a dim view of the roles I've played—basically the American bad guy. Honestly, they don't get artistic expression.

There's that finger-across-the-throat-sign again. Okay, here's the wrap. I'm grateful for my career here. Also that my wife will be released from the reeducation camp next year. They say her stay will be a lot shorter than most.

Let me leave you with this. All the world's a stage. That includes the scaffold I'm about to drop through. So no regrets. Really.

All I ever wanted to do was work.

Two Suitcases by the
Side of the Road

YOU THINK YOU'VE seen it all in San Francisco—the homeless, the addicts, the people who dress for Halloween year round, the people who don't dress at all. So what stops you in your tracks on your Saturday morning walk among the towering eucalyptus in the Presidio National Park?

Two suitcases by the side of the road

Black. Battered. Stylish though. The kind that flaunt PRIORITY labels when they drop out of the chute at airports in world capitals or on tropical islands with five-star resorts.

Both open—and full of clothes in what might be called disarray.

The suitcases made me nervous. Maybe that's a function of age. But studying them from what I assumed was a safe distance offered the opportunity to catch my breath and cool down. I'd been walking uphill since leaving my house. I kept my jacket zipped though. The fog was sprinting in from the Pacific like it had a plane to catch.

I moved closer. At critical moments like this, detectives in the PBS and BBC America mysteries Evelyn and I watch whip out a pad or a notebook. I suspect real detectives talk into their phones, but I don't feel comfortable doing that, so I often carry a small notebook of my own. I searched my pockets. Not this morning. I started making a mental list.

The obvious: It was a quarter past eight. So far so good. Also, one or more people had left two open suitcases on a hard-packed dirt trail overlooking the Golden Gate, the Marin headlands on the other side and the ocean. In full view.

A little further digging: Nothing appeared to have been taken. Not that I could be certain. Life doesn't lend itself to certainty.

A guess: The bags were left during the previous evening, after sundown but before midnight.

New observation: Some or all of the clothes had been scooped out of each bag when they were tossed aside then thrown back in. I ruled out raccoons. Raccoons don't put things back.

Supporting theory: No one packs without making at least some attempt at folding stuff to make more room.

Rebuttal: Someone in a hurry would do exactly that.

I kneeled. My knees ached. At seventy, you accept that as inevitable. I looked closer at the contents that were visible: A white blouse. A teal sweater. Two skirts, one navy, one brown. A pair of shoes—basic black. A plastic bag with underwear. Women's.

Theory: The bags belonged to the same woman. Curious as I was to know more, I refrained from touching anything. I knew from TV not to disturb or contaminate evidence—if this was evidence. Also, I was developing a hazy image of the woman, and I didn't want to invade her privacy. I suppose she didn't care—she'd abandoned her things for anyone to see—but I did.

I stood and gave thanks that my joints didn't go snap, crackle and pop like that old breakfast cereal. I may have been a little spooked, because I looked around for signs of a body. Nothing suggested foul play. I figured it was time to move on, but I stood rooted to the spot.

A foghorn bellowed, and it came to me. Sometime last night, *She* stuffed two suitcases full of clothes and left home in a hurry. No, not *She*. Grace. The name just popped into my head. Did I know a Grace? No. Had I ever? I didn't think so. But I had to connect the suitcases with a real human being, and when I did, I saw what happened the way you turn on the light in a dark room and everything is clear as day. Hours earlier—I now speculated just before sunrise—Grace tossed two suitcases by the side of the road then, for whatever reason, opened them. She must have been searching for something. What she looked for, I didn't know. What I *did* know was that all was not well. I was sure because Grace now seemed as real to me as Joyce and Maria.

I knew them.

Clarity, kind of: The trail runs alongside a road winding from the Golden Gate Bridge to Twenty-Fifth Avenue, which heads south into the west side of the city. Grace would never *walk* all this way hefting two suitcases. She was driving. From where?

Theory number two: From Marin County, just across the bridge. Grace was headed to a friend out in the Avenues where fog is a way of life. Someone on Twitter even gave the fog a name: Karl.

Theory number two refined: Grace was heading further south but staying off Nineteenth Avenue, which is Highway 1, to disguise her route to Pacifica or Half Moon Bay down the coast. Or, she was heading further south to Santa Cruz or Carmel. Carmel would appeal to a woman of means, which obviously described Grace. Or had. I don't know much about women's clothes—as Evelyn informs me—but what I saw looked stylish. So Grace was heading to Carmel. And who was waiting for her? A friend? A boyfriend?

Key question: Why did Grace run away from one of the wealthiest counties in the United States?

Clear answer: Donald.

Look, it was still early morning and I needed to create a story to make sense of it all, and if Grace's husband Donald popped into my head, no worries. Grace and Donald then. Everyone's perfect couple. The kind that sends Christmas cards with their perfect portrait, which draws one of two comments from every recipient: *My God, Grace and Donald never age* or *Jesus Christ, why don't they show their age already!* But any detective will tell you that appearances can be deceiving.

Donald was a bastard.

Maybe I'm overreacting because I felt closer to Grace, but that only made sense. Whose suitcases and clothes were laid out in front of me? Grace's. Further, it was about time Grace ditched Donald. Not that he wasn't a good provider. (Grace was a poet—not much money in that.) Donald practiced dentistry. *Practicing 'til I get it right*, he loved to joke. Not funny. Like when your dentist is about to fill a cavity or stick on a crown and holds up the kind of needle your mother used to knit with. Mine did.

Correction: Strike my remark about Donald being a bastard. He didn't drink to excess. Maybe to take the edge off after a day at the office, but who doesn't? He didn't snort coke. Never had. Weed? A few times in college. Very important, he never cheated on Grace. I can't say the same about my relationship with Joyce. With Maria, it was different—in a way.

Pointing the finger: Donald is dull. When he isn't peering into people's mouths he runs model trains for hours on end. His set's a ginormous work of art and passion, which probably earns him points in some circles. Still, how long can you watch miniature trains run around miniature tracks past miniature trees and miniature houses? And miniature people, who are just about as exciting?

I also point out that Donald still loves Disco.

Confession: Joyce and I went through the Disco thing, but it peaked when Jimmy Carter was president and died when Ronald Reagan took office. Times change. You keep up. Anyway, I was two years out of college when I met Joyce—the sister of my friend Arnie. I knew her in high school but tangentially. A few years later, she tagged along when Arnie and I met for drinks in the city. People who grew up in Queens like we did called Manhattan *the city*. These days, Manhattanites dismiss Queens as one of the *outer boroughs*. These same people grew up in Ohio or South Dakota.

So Joyce and I reconnected, and sparks flew. Three months later we moved into a studio apartment above a bodega in Jackson Heights. The studio was small and dingy. The steam heat was iffy. Finding a parking spot for my Corolla took half my free time. In bed, we'd hear the 7 train. It ran on elevated tracks that kept Roosevelt Avenue in constant darkness. Joyce took the 7 into the city to her job as an administrative assistant at a publishing house.

More on the 7: Its roar and rattle blended with the sounds we made having sex. I'd say *making love* but on reflection it was just sex. Not that I'm griping. I liked the sex. We both did. I also liked living in a dump. Loved it. I was writing my first novel, and living in a dump enables young writers to break free from their bourgeois upbringings so they can enlighten the world about Truth with a capital T.

We split the bills. My share came from teaching English nearby at Newtown High School. The position wasn't easy to get, but my parents knew someone. I looked at it strictly as a day job. In a year, maybe two, three tops I'd finish the novel and find an agent who'd sell it to a major publisher who'd make me a household name. At least in households where people read serious fiction. I'd start a new life in the city. Joyce and I might get married. That we weren't married was no scandal. Ten years earlier maybe, but this wasn't your father and mother's America. Not in New York. Still, each of us thought, *Yes, she/he might be the one.* Our parents did. They let us know every chance they had. We got engaged. It seemed like the right thing.

Until Amy.

Amy taught history at Newtown. She never revealed who got her the job. We ran into each other at faculty meetings, the teachers' cafeteria, school dances. Amy had long dark hair and a slim figure. Actually, she was kind of skinny. Ordinarily, I'd never have given her a second look—or not much of one. I was engaged, right? Sex with Joyce was still pretty good. Then after winter vacation, Amy came on to me.

Not that she said anything. A woman doesn't have to say anything. It's the way she looks at you. Or takes your arm. The way she clings to you says, *You want it? I want it.* In spite of my being a writer and seeking Truth with a capital T, this was out of character for me.

Reminder: I was engaged to my friend's sister.

But a sense of masculine power and what you think is animal magnetism can set your head spinning faster than a Long Island Iced Tea.

One day after lunch, I called Joyce and told her I had to stay at school for a basketball game. A certain number of teachers had to be at each home game to keep order. And there *was* a game. But I went to Amy's place. She grew up in Huntington out on Long Island and shared an apartment with another girl in Rego Park where my parents still lived. The danger turned me on. The sex was so-so, but I got off on the idea of having an affair. Writers have affairs. You can't be a writer unless you live like a writer. Or so I thought.

After a couple of weeks, I wondered if real writers felt guilty about having affairs. I figured they did. Writers need to suffer. I suffered.

Guilt consumed me. Not that I was about to confess to Joyce. You save confessions for Yom Kippur.

Confession number two: To ease my conscience, I stood the situation on its head. I found fault with everything Joyce did. She screwed up boiling pasta. She got up too early on Sunday mornings—ironic since now I'm an early riser. She preferred the Beatles to the Stones. Stupid stuff. There's a term for putting your own guilt off on someone else. I don't know what it is, but there has to be one.

Two days after the spring term ended, I threw some stuff into the Corolla and took off for San Francisco. I never saw Joyce again, although I heard she got married two years later and lived not far away in Kew Gardens. Her husband was a dentist.

I stared at Grace's suitcases and thought, *Grace is heading to Carmel, but why did she leave her suitcases and her stuff at the side of the road?* Then it struck me that the question resembled the old joke, *Why did the chicken cross the road?* You look for a complicated answer when it's all so simple. Grace tossed away her old clothes because they reminded her of her old life with Donald and maybe with the kids, although I couldn't picture Grace having kids with Donald.

I saw Grace's logic. She wanted to create a new life from her underwear up. I could relate. I had a credit card and a decent balance in my checking account, so I packed a minimum of clothes for San Francisco and several cartons of CDs and cassettes.

My guilt followed me. I kept the pedal down hoping to outrun it. Talk about youthful folly. But San Francisco represented new beginnings. Scott Fitzgerald wrote, "There are no second acts in American lives." But California is filled with people who reinvented themselves. Unlike Jay Gatsby, many made it work.

Enter Maria.

I rented a studio not far from where Evelyn and I live now. I felt like a writer again. Teaching? Out of the question. It took ten weeks and a not-inconsequential drain on my savings until a small ad agency took a chance on a neophyte copywriter. This was before Arnie, a hot agency art director, moved out from New York. I still thought of it as a day job but a natural fit. Every copywriter wants to write novels, plays or screenplays. Poetry not so much. Poetry encompasses a different sensibility—like Grace's.

Maria was assistant marketing director at Golden Pacific, a small savings & loan, which happened to be our biggest client. It took my boss Jack a year to allow me to meet her. Like all agency owners, Jack was paranoid. Some bigtime agency owner once said, *Every evening, my inventory goes down the elevator.* The next morning that inventory could go up a different elevator along with major accounts.

Maria and I hit it off to the point where Jack let me take her to lunch as often as I wanted to talk up the agency. We did lots of lunches. Then we added breakfasts. Jack was a happy camper until the morning I told him Maria and I were opening Gelberg and Gonzalez. Our initial client? Golden Pacific. I still laugh at the consonance.

The consequences not so much.

Eighteen months later, Golden Pacific got gobbled up by a competitor. G&G went under like the Titanic. So did my relationship with Maria, although I only cheated on her that one time in Reno when I was shooting a TV commercial.

I found an agency job in Sacramento and doubled down on writing short stories. One night, I tossed my stack of rejection form letters into a metal garbage can followed by a match.

Not long after, I read in ADWEEK that Arnie had come to San Francisco. I called. I was that desperate. He wasn't thrilled, but Joyce had met the dentist, so Arnie tossed me a few referrals. He'd only been in San Francisco a few months, but he knew more people than I did.

On my own, I landed a job with the marketing department of the S&L that swallowed up Golden Pacific. I met Evelyn. We had a kid. We bought a house.

I stopped writing.

I used the sweatshirt under my jacket to wipe the moisture off my glasses. The fog also dampened Grace's suitcases and clothes, but I left them untouched. Not that I thought she'd come back to retrieve them. Grace is the kind of person who, once she makes up her mind, never turns back. That's another way she's different from Donald.

I hoped Grace would settle into a very nice life in Carmel. Or head further south. I couldn't see her in L.A., but maybe Santa Barbara. She'd land on her feet selling real estate or working in an art gallery.

I looked up at the bridge now totally obscured by fog. Sometimes, it unnerves me that something is right in front of you and you can only see it in your mind. In your mind you can see anything. Create anything. Like all those lives in my stories and the three novels I wrote before I bought my first Macintosh. The manuscripts are moldering in my garage, laid to rest in the boxes the paper came in. Cardboard coffins.

As far as Evelyn and I go, the fireworks burned out a while back, but we're content.

Old guy's insight: Grace is still relatively young and maybe clinging to a few last illusions. I hope things work out, but the future tends to set its own agenda. We try to write the stories of our lives, but life writes us.

Picacho Pink

I'D BEEN PISSED at the world-famous artist Garrett White on and off for years. I usually got over his shit because we go way back. Which is why on a crisp mid-October day we sat at in a deli on Queens Boulevard a block from the synagogue where we'd both been bar mitzvah boys. We each dug into corned-beef on rye. Gary drank orange juice. Who drinks orange juice with a corned-beef sandwich? The kind of guy who devotes himself to letting the world know he's a different breed. When you're worth however-many millions of dollars, you can do that. Respecting tradition—in my way—I contented myself with a Dr. Brown's cream soda.

Then came words from the great man. "Arnie," Gary said, "for the hundredth time already, get your act together." He still calls me Arnie—usually Arn unless he's making a point—although I sign my paintings with Arnold. I call him Gary because I knew him when he was Gary Weisbrod.

Regarding my act, our careers ran on separate tracks. Not that I judged myself a failure. My paintings hung in homes and offices in and around San Francisco and parts of the West. Every now and then a Bay Area newspaper does a small story on me. But I'm no Garrett White. You can count his peers on the fingers of one hand. Two if you're a generous type.

Gary projecting a major gravitational pull in the art world, I'd flown back to New York, which I'd done twice a year when my mother was alive. After breakfast she'd watch her soaps, and I'd take the subway into

Manhattan to keep up with the galleries and museums, knock on a few doors. I'd often get together with Gary, who'd be free with advice but drew the line at referrals. *Don't take it wrong, Arn, but I send you to someone, it's my reputation. Besides, you make it big with my help, you'll end up hating me.* He did call a gallery for me once, but the owner was an asshole. Still, Gary felt that my failure to make the required impression reflected badly on him.

Now, a chunk of potato knish stuffed into his mouth, he provided familiar words of wisdom. "There's art for art's sake, but only if you're in fourth grade or a schmuck who loves poverty. Art is a business."

"I get that," I said for the umpteenth time. What I didn't get was why my career, humble to begin with, had stalled. Was it because I limited my subject matter to the nearby hills in Marin County while Gary painted everything from cityscapes to nudes to abstracts? Or because acrylic remained my sole medium while he churned out work in acrylic, oil, watercolor, and pen and ink with forays into collage, sculpture, jewelry and light installations?

Gary pointed a finger the way he did during one of his interviews on Charlie Rose before Charlie Rose got the boot from TV. "You've got some talent, sure, but your horizons are too close. Those hillsides? You're painting postcards." He picked at a piece of corned beef wedged into his teeth. "Why do I have the loft in Chelsea? A whole floor, obviously. Okay, the neighborhood's mainstream now, but I'm sentimental. And the house in the Hamptons and the place in Boca? And yes, Boca's a bourgeois joke, but when I'm there I get away from it all. And no, I'm not looking to buy another home in London. I take a suite at The Dorchester. Anyway, why? It's all about getting your hands around the market at its highest level. Being a businessman." He flicked the bit of corned beef onto his plate. "Screwing, not getting screwed."

I could argue? No question, Gary had tremendous talent, but so did plenty of artists who never became household names. I'd read the stories and listened to what he called his confessions. He'd clawed his way to the top, slipping out of more tight spots than Houdini or David Copperfield. You could see it coming in ninth grade when we barely escaped that episode with Diane Rubin. A hallway in a junior-high basement is not an appropriate place to conduct a rudimentary exercise in sex education. I have a daughter. I support the #MeToo movement. No excuses. But if I can offer a shadow of perspective, it's that everything took place above the waist and was consensual. And fourteen-year-old boys suffer overdeveloped hard-ons and underdeveloped brains.

For me and Diane Rubin, that was it, although keeping my distance did nothing to deter regular fantasies of our going below the waist. In high school, Gary lived out those fantasies, but that's another story—and one that pains me.

As we finished our sandwiches, I thought about what else rankled me. I didn't require much of a search to arrive at an answer. Gary's success represented an inversion of natural forces.

In high school, I got better grades. Also, I was a better baseball player. Gary gobbled up every ground ball at second base but barely hit .200. I played third and outhit him by a hundred points but never received a scholarship offer let alone had my name called in the baseball draft. The military draft was something else. I spent most of my two years at Fort Bliss in El Paso, Texas. Steve got deferred for teaching school. Gary and Jeffrey ended up with medical deferments. How did that work? Anyway, Gary talks baseball every now and then to impress the media that despite being acclaimed a genius, he's a man of the people.

After college—I went to Syracuse, studied graphic design and took the occasional studio course—and the army, I landed a position as a junior art director on Madison Avenue. Hard work and, yes, talent produced better jobs until I took off for San Francisco, the end of the rainbow.

Gary stayed home and went to Pratt, dropped out after a few years and holed up in a ratty basement in the Village to do *real art*—basically doing real drugs and starving.

At thirty-five, I had a picture-postcard house in Sausalito with a picture-postcard wife and daughter. I painted on the side.

Gary, who'd cleaned up his act and somehow pressed all the right buttons, had just split with his second wife, Keoku, and was the darling of *The New York Times*.

By forty, I'd burned out on advertising. We had money in the bank and Carla was an administrator at Marin General Hospital, so I said fuck it and left to paint fulltime. I placed my work into a gallery in Mill Valley then into another in the city. My paintings sold enough to keep me hanging on the galleries' walls, but I didn't make in a year what Garrett White made off a single piece.

My own confession: Gary's success tormented me. Maybe that wasn't so bad because it also pushed me. On and off—and never all at the same time—I placed my work in Reno, Carmel, Vail, Park City and Santa Fe. I received occasional commissions. When the economy went south during the Great Recession, so did my market. Not Gary's. His collectors didn't skulk away because their portfolios dipped ten or twenty or fifty million. Toughing it out, I continued painting my trademark Marin landscapes—golden hills with shades of vermilion, green oaks and brilliant blue skies dotted with cotton-ball clouds. Sucking it up, I exhibited at local art shows. A few pieces sold. The price tags wouldn't cover Gary's lunches in Manhattan—when he ate alone.

Carla stuck by me.

Gary ditched his fourth wife, Galina, once a fashion model in Moscow.

I pushed my plate away, leaving part of my sandwich untouched. Dr. Marcus was always on me about cholesterol. "I have an idea," I said. "A new approach to my Marin hillsides."

Gary held up his right hand. "Don't tell me."

"All I'm asking—"

He shook his head. "Arnie, we've been through this. When you get to where I am, people always try to pick your brain. That's a euphemism for *steal*."

"I'm not *people* for God's sake."

He rested his hand on my left forearm in a display of what might be interpreted as compassion. "What the hell. If Garrett White can't offer a childhood friend a little advice, what's his success about?" He raised the hand and brought his palms together as if he was engaging in some form of esoteric contemplation before revealing hidden secrets. "I love your hillsides." He held up the pinky of his right hand—an old New York sign setting bullshit aside. "But Arn, you've worked that mule to death."

I had no idea where he came up with the mule imagery, but I feared he was right. How much longer could I argue with my bottom line? My work—my ornery, stubborn mule—needed to be turned in a new direction. What direction that might be, I had no clue.

One of the countermen dropped our check on the table.

Gary pushed it towards me.

* * *

Something I learned: Smalltime buyers of art like landscapes of where they live or visit. That's why my sales were close to home.

Another lesson: I wasn't satisfied with building a regional reputation. Gary's accomplishments ate at me, condemned me to be a lifelong also-ran.

Then I went to Arizona.

Ted Locke, a buddy from San Francisco agency days, invited Carla and me to Tucson for a long weekend in early March. One of the hottest creative directors in the country, he started his own shop, amassed shelves of Clios, sold to a conglomerate and never looked back.

Why Tucson? Ted's wife Valery wanted to be close to her aging parents. They built a home in the Santa Catalina foothills. *Architectural Digest* and *Dwell* ran spreads. An art guy himself, Ted welded scrap metal into sculptures. He sold locally. He was happy.

As the sun melted into Saguaro National Park, Carla and Valery put together a salad. Preparatory to steaks hitting the grill, Ted and I sat by the fire pit sucking down margaritas. "The light," I said. "Fantastic. And the mountains. Wow."

"Want to see something special?"

"There's more?"

"Tomorrow we'll drive up to Picacho Peak."

Wow was the operative word. The mountain wasn't all that high—maybe two thousand feet—but it stood fairly isolated, and the last few hundred feet soared straight up. At sunset, Picacho Peak turned colors drawn from the palette of a painter on an acid trip.

I took photos. Even before we pulled into Ted's driveway, I was on a mission. I had to show Picacho Peak to the world.

One wall of my studio covered with photos, I started on small studies. I conceded that my subject was a mountain in southern Arizona, but it was magic. I saw the opportunity to make art that inspired. Also big bucks.

I practically abandoned Carla, who still missed Sophie, in grad school at Northwestern. Much to my chagrin, Sophie was a big Garrett White fan. They'd never met, but he sent her a loose pen-and-ink self-portrait as a bat mitzvah gift. He couldn't attend since he had to be in Paris. "Sorry," he wrote on the back, "the bitch-goddess calls." I stashed the drawing in a safe deposit box. Someday, it could help Carla buy a house. Also, I wouldn't have to see it.

Not that I discarded Carla like Gary dumped Galina for Ashley, who would never be wife number five. During a radio interview with Terri Gross, Gary publicly swore off marriage. I give myself points for Carla and I having dinner together every evening before I'd go back into my studio. Later, she'd usually pop her head in the door and cluck. Not a scolding but more of a mother-hen thing. One night she asked if I was re-enacting the movie *Close Encounters of the Third Kind*. "You remember how Richard Dreyfuss became obsessed with what's it—Devils Tower? Wyoming, I'm thinking. Or is it in one of the Dakotas?"

I remember Richard Dreyfuss' character sculpting a mountain out of mashed potatoes. He couldn't help himself. Neither could I. I had to make sense out of what I experienced at Picacho Peak. The power of the colors, particularly the purples and pinks. Pinks mostly. It was a compulsion.

One April afternoon, Carla came home from work early and nudged the studio door open cradling a bottle of a Sonoma Chardonnay we especially liked and holding two plastic cups. Her face turned from expectant to puzzled. "Didn't you once say gallery directors hate pink?"

I grinned the way you do when you can't refute an accurate observation but can't stop doing what you're doing. "I hear you," I said, "but I've got this."

Carla slipped out the door.

A week later, I lobbied Gary for a preliminary show-and-tell in New York.

As we followed the lunchtime hostess at the Modern, heads turned. Conversations dulled into whispers. I sensed myself displaying a smile of self-importance and summoned an expression blending confidence with modesty. The confidence part shattered when we sat. Our table faced the sculpture garden of the Museum of Modern Art.

The garden displayed an iconic piece by Garrett White. Two eight-foot-high arcs made from steel tubing stood side by side. Each was painted red, yellow, blue, green and black. A length of steel tubing painted white pierced each horizontally.

"*Africa in Agony*," Gary said. "Remember my World in Agony period?"

No agony for Gary. The museum valued the piece at seven million.

A waitress approached the table. Like all the staff I'd observed, she was attractive. More than attractive. I assumed getting hired demanded movie-star looks and accompanying figures. She tendered Gary a broad smile. "So wonderful to see you again, Mr. White."

He winked and ordered a Negroni. Twist of lemon.

I placed a small leather folder at my right hand and asked for Chardonnay. Whatever she recommended.

"I thought," Gary said, "we might take in the Mets game tonight for old time's sake, but I'm tied up tonight." He slouched in his seat.

"Tough going?"

"We're firming up the move to the new gallery. You can't believe how complicated these things get in New York. And they want a major show this fall—all-new stuff—to coincide with my retrospective here."

"What'll you do?"

"We'll see. I've got my crew to churn out enough pieces. Santa's little elves." He licked his lips in anticipation of his cocktail. "Anyway, business is good, which is more than I can say for my personal life."

I leaned forward.

"Ashley. Disillusioned, she says. Says she's leaving me."

A basket of rolls and a dish of olives appeared followed by our drinks.

"L'chaim!" Gary offered.

"L'chaim!" I responded, the occasional uttering of a Yiddish word the extent of our adult Jewish practice—other than eating deli. "You never told Ashley marriage was a non-starter?"

"I did."

I offered a smile of encouragement. "You'll find another beautiful woman."

"I did. A few months ago."

I nodded in recognition of the situation.

Gary studied a black olive. "So what's the story, Arn?"

I unzipped my leather folder. "I've been exploring some new work myself. I haven't been this excited in years."

"Jesus, not again!"

I thought my jaw might bounce off the table.

He laughed. "Arn, lighten up. It's me and you. A couple of kids from Queens."

I took out half-a-dozen photos—my favorite studies of Picacho Peak.

Our waitress approached.

Gary waved her off.

As he riffled through my proposed masterpieces, I sat like an accused man in a courtroom knowing he's innocent but unsure as to the jury's verdict. He handed the photos back and looked up.

My cheeks felt as if a hot iron was pressing the creases I'd accumulated.

The waitress gave it another try.

We ordered lunch and a second round.

I placed the photos on top of the folder.

After fresh drinks arrived, Gary peered into his Negroni for what seemed like a longer time than he'd checked out my studies. "Is that a real mountain or something in your head?"

"Picacho Peak. Near Tucson."

"Which is where?"

"Arizona."

He sighed.

Not knowing what to say, I fell back on a trick I'd learned in the ad game. I remained silent.

"The subject is maybe interesting," he said. He shot a glance out to *Africa in Agony*. "But pink?" He sighed again.

A shock of resentment rippled through my body. Did he expect an explanation? An apology? Artists don't explain. Artists don't apologize. I'd come to him for advice. A kind word. And sure, approval. I needed that. In response, he played the critic. The thing about critics is, they love to scoff. They *have* to find something wrong to reinforce their bona fides. "What about Picasso's Pink Period?" I asked.

"*Rose* Period."

"*The Actor*. That's a lot of pink. And *Acrobat's Family With a Monkey*?"

"Jesus, that's *Picasso*. All I'm saying is, maybe if you worked on some mountain people recognized, although that's a stretch. And pink?"

"Pink!" I shot back louder than I intended.

The room hushed.

Gary grimaced. Then the mask he usually wore—even with me—fell away. "Arnie, from the heart, okay? You exhibit these out there in the Wild West, you sell a painting now and then, but you're right back where you started." He glanced around the room. "On this level?"

Pralines of foie gras terrine arrived for him. Greens for me.

He patted my hand. "I've got lunch."

Back home, I filed away the Picacho Peak studies and turned to researching the New York and Los Angeles art markets in depth. London, as well. Not that I intended to leap onto someone else's bandwagon, although that was hardly uncommon. What I wanted was an accurate picture of what major collectors were sinking chunks of their fortunes into. I also came to grips with the small but rankling financial burden I'd dumped on Carla's shoulders. We were hardly struggling, but I wanted us to maintain our lifestyle and keep putting money away for the future. Guilt-ridden, I made calls and landed freelance jobs. I wasn't quitting on doing art, but having reflected on my recent lunch with Gary, I decided to take a sabbatical, shuck off my self-absorption and align myself with the marketplace. I'd pick up a brush after I got my head straight.

Ted and Valery Locke invited us out for the July Fourth weekend. We accepted. Tucson gets hot but not as hot as Phoenix, and from time to time, the monsoon cools things down.

The night before the Fourth, we stretched out on chaises by the pool. Nature seemed to have ripped off Van Gogh's *Starry Night*. Ted popped the tops off a local craft beer. "You ever finish your studies of Picacho Peak?" he asked.

"I never emailed photos?"

"No, but I didn't want to push. In case it was a bit of a struggle."

"Something like that," I said.

"We could drive up there tomorrow. Summer light's different."

"Thanks but no. I've put Picacho in the deep freeze."

"Tough sledding, the art world," he said. "Me, I just piddle."

I sipped from my beer. "Lucky you."

By Labor Day, I let go of any vestige of anger I'd felt towards Gary. If anything, I'd turned a one-eighty. When I was ready to paint again—and I felt myself getting close—I'd be focused on the top of the market, the heavy hitters. Gary had revealed a simple if painful truth: To satisfy my ego, I'd have to rein it in. Kind of a Zen thing.

In early October, an agency asked me to go to New York to help present a TV campaign. The trip would enable me to get together with Gary on the client's dime. I wanted to thank him in the flesh for ripping the scales off my eyes.

I left messages on his cell for three days.

I was sitting at the gate at SFO when he called back. "Arn, how long will you be in town?"

"I have a meeting tomorrow morning, but I'm staying over. I thought we might get a drink tonight. Do dinner tomorrow."

"Oh shit, I'd love to. Either or both, but the new gallery— The opening's tomorrow night. It's balls to the wall."

"I imagine."

The phone went silent.

"So meet me there," he said. "I'll leave your name at the door. There'll be plenty of food and an open bar. And I'll introduce you around. I'll text the address."

When the gate agent called my group to board, I floated down the jetway.

After the morning presentation, I joined the agency team for a celebratory lunch. Then I walked up Fifth Avenue to the Guggenheim to check out Gary's "White on White" exhibit. You entered this square room with white walls, a white floor and a glowing white ceiling. Nothing more. Maybe Gary was commenting on a void in life that only the artist can fill. Maybe not. The Times had run a piece on some nine-year-old girl's comment. It wasn't positive. Still, I had to wait on line to get in. When I left, the line was a lot longer.

Following a nap, I took the subway downtown and headed west on Twenty-Sixth Street. Gallery windows offered seductive glimpses of their wares. Some pieces appealed. Others left me cold. Beauty is in the eye and all that. But I got it that all the artists shared a key trait: While they'd never admit it, they'd subjugated their so-called integrity to impress the critics who influenced the one-percenters—and their pricy consultants—searching for another hot investment or a future tax deduction based on the considerable appreciation of a donated asset.

I crossed Tenth Avenue and approached Gary's new gallery. Rather than a sampling of his pieces, the windows displayed several large caricatures of the artist. No name. If you didn't recognize Garrett White, you didn't belong here. At the door, a very young blonde in a very tight black dress revealing impossibly long legs checked her iPad. I feared my name wouldn't appear on the screen. She smiled and waved me into a small anteroom.

A waiter offered champagne. He exhibited the good looks of an aspiring actor not currently in production or rehearsal but taking classes religiously. I checked out a display spanning Garrett White's career, including a video of Gary in his studio—elves hidden—and another of the famous Charlie Rose interview with titles instead of sound framed by two panels of copy lionizing his impact on the art world.

I took one step into the main room and froze. I reassured myself that I was in Chelsea on familiar ground, but part of my brain screamed that I'd been teleported to another dimension where everything I thought I knew proved to be an illusion.

Nearly two-dozen canvases displayed the unmistakable, if stylized, shape of Picacho Peak. Gary's palette included every imaginable hue and shade of pink.

A hand shook my right shoulder.

I spun around.

Gary pressed his palms against my cheeks and kissed me on the lips.

I flashed on Michael Corleone kissing his brother Fredo goodbye in *Godfather II.*

"Arn, you're my inspiration. I'd offer you a percentage, but the gallery already has my balls in a vise."

An attractive woman stood over his shoulder. She seemed vaguely familiar and possibly our age, although I couldn't be sure given the apparent effects of one or more nip-and-tuck jobs. Her low-cut black dress revealed a considerable quantity of tanned flesh. The diamonds and emeralds around her neck must have run fifty or even a hundred thousand dollars. She stepped forward and smiled. Her teeth gleamed a white that would leave a copywriter stuck for adjectives.

"This lovely lady," Gary said, "just bought two of my pieces."

The woman gazed at me with an air of expectation. Did she think I was another of Gary's collectors? Or was I supposed to recognize her? If the latter, I drew a blank.

"I've collected Gary for years," she said.

I thought it odd that she hadn't called him Garrett.

Gary drew her close in a way that suggested a comfort with each other bordering on intimacy.

"I live on Park Avenue," she said, "but in Boca, we're practically neighbors."

I struggled to establish whatever connection I might have had with this woman—if I'd had one.

Gary grasped the back of my neck with his free hand as if he feared I was about to run out on him.

I was tempted to do just that—maybe after decking him with a roundhouse right.

"Isn't Gary incredible?" the woman asked.

He gave my neck a slight squeeze.

I felt like a mouse trapped in the jaws of a snake, a victim that concedes the futility of resistance and ceases to struggle. The woman was right. Gary *was* incredible. He did whatever he wanted—screwed whoever he wanted—and in his world, no one would call him on it.

Gary lowered his hand and kissed the woman on the lips.

Her eyes shone.

Still, I struggled to put a name to her face.

"Arn," Gary said, "enough with the joking. You remember Diane Rubin."

"Picacho Pink" was a finalist in Glimmer Train's
November 2013 short story contest for new writers.

Empty

Schwartzman glances up at the ner tamid above the ark enclosing the synagogue's Torah scrolls. The eternal light mocks the finitude of life.

His eyes drop to the casket. Top of the line. A massive and equally opulent assault vehicle engineered to propel Cohen through heaven's most impenetrable defenses.

A prickly heat assaults the back of Schwartzman's neck.

It's all about illusion, he thinks. No, self-delusion.

The casket lies empty.

An explosion at a huge chemical plant reduced Cohen to molecules. Atoms. Elementary particles.

Rabbi Fine fashions words of impressive bulk to give Cohen a presence. To Schwartzman, air projected across vocal cords. Empty as Cohen's casket.

No harsh judgment. He knows Cohen.

Knew him.

Sometimes envied him.

Still, Schwartzman considers himself Cohen's opposite. Small. Usually invisible. An actuary for an insurance company. Not much to talk about. The interesting guys investigate fraud. Particularly murder. Great stories.

Cohen was big and not just physically. An executive VP with corporate clout. Appetites to match.

The rabbi knows.

But disgrace the dead? In front of three wives and seven children? Possibly a mistress in the far corner? All those donors?

The rabbi's words register at gale force.

Schwartzman anchors his thoughts.

Cohen filled every room. Sucked the air out. Congregants said they liked him. Bullshit. Can you think *bullshit* here? Regardless, well-upholstered asses smother the pews' cushioned benches.

One of Cohen's sons speaks. Words shuttle between the walls like bats suffering failed sonar. Does the Law require placing the dead on a pedestal before lowering them into the earth?

Schwartzman sighs. People pass. Truth dies with them. At two hundred-thirty pounds, Cohen was a lightweight.

The rabbi chants *El Male Rachamim*—God filled with compassion. The family recites *Kaddish*. The blessing for the dead makes no mention of death. Coping through avoidance?

Schwartzman again raises his eyes to the ner tamid. The elaborate glass fixture conceals an LED bulb. Eventually the bulb will need replacing.

Will he experience the ner tamid's inevitable moment of darkness?

Running on fumes, he's experiencing his own dark moment. The return of light remains a matter of conjecture.

Prescribed Burns

I TAPED JONAH's ankles then wrapped his hands before helping him slip on his bloodstained gloves. The roar of the crowd exploded through the thin walls of what once was an office space inside what once was a warehouse in West Oakland near the old Oakland Army Terminal where my father came back from Vietnam. It served as the locker room. Gunmetal gray partitions formed cubicles to separate the waiting combatants. Jonah's opponent occupied the second cube over. He, too, was silent. Theoretically, the partitions would keep fighters from beating the shit out of each other before they beat the shit out of each other in the cage. People paid good money to see these kids fight. As to light, a couple of small windows dotted the far wall, but it was dark out. Six fluorescent tubes hung from the ceiling. Three worked. There was no shower.

For that matter, each cubicle was empty except for a single low metal stool and a small metal table the size of a large nightstand but without a drawer. Jonah sat on the table. Like the walls when the crowd grew intense, he seemed to vibrate.

As I finished with Jonah's hands—each human hand contains twenty-seven bones, all capable of breaking when delivering a blow—I became aware of individual voices in what might be called the arena. Most were men's, although I heard women, too. They sounded like beasts in the wild shrieking for meat.

Jonah didn't seem to hear anything. I suspected he heard voices sometimes but not those. And not now. He was too focused to hear anyone but me, although I had to work to keep his attention. The way things were, he didn't hear me very often and certainly not once a fight began. I'd long wished he were the kind of person who *did* hear others, who listened intently, who thought before he acted, who controlled his impulses. They say that as people mature they learn to do these things.

At sixteen, Jonah hadn't come close.

I knew Jonah was a little off-kilter early on. Shari had her suspicions, but it took her longer to admit it. "He's just a child," was her mantra.

There are children and there are children.

By the time Jonah turned five, the mantra yielded to troubled silences between us. We knew we had a problem, but we couldn't agree on how to solve it. Worse, we couldn't agree that it *could* be solved.

Not that I condemn us for our doubts and hesitations in the early years. Who wants to think there's something wrong with his kid? Jonah *looked* normal. Except for his eyes. They were a beautiful blue like you might find in a painting. Some people find a lot of symbolism in blue eyes—gentleness or maybe intellect. They think dark eyes indicate passion or danger. It doesn't work that way. At any rate, not for Jonah. What I saw in those eyes always sent a chill knifing down from my shoulder blades to where it twisted itself between my legs the way you might debone a ham.

I caught on to Jonah a good two years before Shari did. Was that because he was a son and not a daughter? I have no idea other than this: Maybe fathers are more critical of their children than mothers are. Particularly with sons. I base this thesis not only on Shari and me but on other couples we know.

Knew.

Before long, other parents wouldn't let their kids go anywhere near Jonah. That went back to pre-school.

At first, friends and relatives offered the usual advice. *Just be there for Jonah. Love him unconditionally. Give it time.* We were, we did and we tried.

You wouldn't think a five-year-old would beat the shit out of another five-year-old. And then a seven-year-old. What are the odds?

Our pediatrician referred us to a therapist. More than one, eventually. Jonah went through talking, role-playing and behavior therapy. We even slogged through parent education. Sometimes Jonah would just sit, staring daggers. Other times he'd scream. And keep screaming. He'd play with toys in a sandbox when that was part of his treatment. For a minute. Then he'd throw them around the room or break them.

Jonah broke Dr. Glasser's nose. She didn't sue but only because therapists don't do that. She *did* tell us that as intriguing a client as Jonah was, she'd have to refer him elsewhere.

Elsewhere might have defined more exotic approaches to dealing with Jonah, but our healthcare benefits extended just so far, and every penny we saved went into our two-bedroom house on a leafy street in the Oakland flats. Thank God we bought before the hordes fled San Francisco's hyper-inflated real estate prices. We thought about a second mortgage, but Shari lost her job. Then she started having migraines.

So elsewhere came down to medication. Methylphenidate made Jonah more irritable and aggressive. Risperidone left him drowsy and even less able to focus. Needless to say, his schoolwork suffered. That was a disappointment because in spite of it all, Jonah was and is a bright kid. Valproic acid made him dopier. Nauseous, too. Still, he kept gaining weight.

So what's a father to do? And a mother?

In eighth grade, Jonah knocked down his English teacher, Mrs. Folsom. I give him this: He didn't mean to. She was trying to break up another of his fights. She broke her arm.

The principal said that even if Jonah was given a diagnosis of ASD—Autism Spectrum Disorder—the district couldn't afford additional resources. We had no diagnosis, and they couldn't kick him out. All she could suggest was a certain private school, which we couldn't come close to affording. It offered something of a track record with disturbed youngsters. That's how she described Jonah. Disturbed. Neither Shari nor I took her evaluation personally. We'd read a good deal of what literature seemed to apply. We didn't see ourselves as the bad guys other than in maybe unknowingly carrying some genetic time bomb. How can you be responsible for that?

Disturbed? Parents who can't cope, *they're* disturbed.

Thank God my dad passed when Jonah was four and didn't see him at his worst. Dad spent the summer between his two years at City College of San Francisco as a U.S. Forest Service firefighter with the Shasta Hotshots based north of Redding. This was when a lot of California still hadn't been mapped. He'd been an Eagle Scout in San Francisco, and he jumped at the chance to get out of the city. He had plenty of stories to tell. They included flying to a fire in a tiny helicopter. His job was using a shovel to scrape the earth and clear an eighteen-inch-wide swath of vegetation.

The job was important because California has a fire season, which has only gotten worse. It delivers a lot of hell-on-earth scenarios. For obvious reasons, fire season coincides with dry season. Most of California's rain— like its snow—falls from November through March. Used to be, by late summer the state would turn into tinder. Now it could be May. And rain might not fall until December. Lightning starts some fires. Dry lightning is the worst since the ground contains so little moisture, and there's no rain to help out. People start fires, too. And PG&E's equipment fails. A hundred thousand acres or more can burn to a crisp.

The policy regarding fighting fires when Dad was out there was pretty much what it seems now: Don't let anything burn if you can help it. Given all the people who live in the mountains and forests these days—all those houses and cabins and barns, all those horses, and dogs and cats—and all the wildlife, the perfect fire season is one in which no fire ever starts. Or if it does, gets smothered in hours.

That's like envisioning the perfect child—one who never gets angry and violent. Or if he starts up, you stick a pill in his mouth and he stops.

So every year, a big chunk of California goes up in flames.

Dad thought things should be done differently, and he never stopped saying so even though he only spent eight or nine weeks up north and became a mechanic at the United Airlines facility at San Francisco International. Today more and more people agree with him.

See, if you always protect wooded areas, the underbrush grows dense. You keep accumulating more and more fuel. When a fire starts, it ends up being way more intense, way more dangerous and way more expensive to control.

So, you let some fires burn themselves out while you keep them from spreading. You even *start* some fires. Prescribed burns. It's a preemptive thing. There's a cost, sure. But when you do away with a lot of undergrowth, you get rid of a lot of nasty fuel. And the plants and flowers come back. So does the wildlife. The forests get healthier because more sunlight makes its way in. You end up with less area containing fuel for a really savage fire and less erosion during the next rainy season.

Nature has handled forests that way forever.

As Jonah grew, Shari and I reached the point where we were barely holding on to our marriage. I started seeing prescribed burns in a whole new way.

I checked Jonah's gloves. They have holes in the fingers so fighters can get a grip since they wrestle as well as punch. Feet are left bare except for ankle wraps, because legs are more powerful than arms and a shoe can really do damage when a fighter launches a good inside leg kick or a switch kick to the ribs.

Gloves and bare feet. Basically, those were the only rules. What else would you expect? There was this network of underground fight clubs all over Northern California. All illegal. I mean, the fighters were teenagers.

Still, Americans love their mixed martial arts. That's a euphemism for blood lust. Cable features cage fighting practically every night. But you have to be eighteen—an adult—and licensed to fight for real money. Although Jonah didn't fight for money at all.

So Jonah went at it with other teens like him. The kind of boys— young men—who beat up other boys—young men—on the playground or at the rec center or near school or outside the multi-screen or the mall because that's what they did. It wasn't fun for them. It wasn't cruelty. It was a compulsion.

Better mixing it up inside a six-sided steel cage in a smoke-filled, gutted warehouse with a winner's purse of fifty dollars or a hundred if you'd built a reputation than a fight in the exercise yard at Folsom or San Quentin or Pelican Bay.

Only once, fortunately, did we have to deal with the police. Freshman year in high school, Jonah and another boy pretty much his match got into it. Since Jonah was passing his classes, and we were looking for a new medication the way a drug addict looks for a hit, the matter stayed out of court.

Give Jonah credit. He got the point. He was smart enough to take his anger elsewhere. He'd hop on a bus or BART to another part of town or somewhere else in the East Bay as far north as Vallejo and south to San Jose. Sometimes he'd go across the Bay to San Francisco or Daly City. He'd find kids online who burned up inside the way he did. He won more than he lost. Either way, he felt better. He'd be bruised and cut, and he got his nose broken more than once, but the violence would calm him for a few weeks. Sometimes a month. He brought home passing grades. Nothing to brag about but passing. For the first time, no one called from school or emailed. We'd enjoy a mild sense of relief.

Then he'd go hunting again.

What kept me up at night? Anything can happen on the street, like someone pulling a knife or a gun.

"God moves in mysterious ways, His wonders to perform," says the old hymn written by William Cowper. I was having coffee at a place in the neighborhood one Saturday morning when I overheard two men talking about underground cage fights. I inquired.

Someone rapped on the gray metal door. I saw the blurred silhouette of a man behind the milky wire-glass panel cracked in several places but not broken.

Jonah's eyes betrayed anticipation.

I zipped up the small orange duffle that contained Jonah's clothes and shoes, his jacket, his wallet and a small first-aid kit. There was no locker or storage box. You wouldn't leave anything in the cubicle even if there was.

Jonah kicked the stool aside and banged his right fist into his left palm.

After his opponent went out, I counted to ten before opening the door. I got hit with the usual smell of beer mixed with cigarette smoke. We walked down the aisle formed by sections of metal folding chairs. I stared straight ahead.

As we approached the cage, someone in the crowd howled like a wolf over a fawn with its throat ripped open. I bit my lip. It stung. *That* pain, I could handle.

The First Fashionistas

"OH MY GOD!" Eve shrieks as she eyes the fig leaves covering her top and bottom. "I can't leave the house looking like this."

"We sleep under a tree," says Adam. He checks his own fig leaf then offers a thumbs-up. "You look great in anything."

"Duh, like my closet's empty!" Eve scolds.

A voice interrupts. "Where are you wild and crazy kids?"

Adam gulps. "Do you think He knows?"

"We'll lay it on the serpent," Eve says. "Just don't say anything stupid. For a change."

God's image appears.

Eve flutters her eyelashes.

"Where'd you learn to do that?" God asks.

Eve stares.

"Oh, these," says God. He holds up two suits of clothes he's sewn from animal skins.

Adam flashes another thumbs-up. "All I need now is a brewski."

Eve throws eye-darts. Of all the men in the world!

Adam offers his what-did-I-say-now shrug.

Eve rolls her eyes and takes her new outfit to the pond, holds it in front of her and checks her reflection. When she returns, she flips her long, dark hair—she's toying with going blonde—and says, "Master of the Universe, the outfit's really cute, but I'm a two. Of course, it has to fit in the hips. And this color doesn't do much for my eyes. And the hem— So last year."

God shrugs. "Creation's only a few days old."

"And where," Eve continues, "do I find shoes and a bag to match? And you don't really expect me to wear the same outfit two days in a row!" She smiles. "The day-and-night thing. You're so clever." Her lips purse. Her eyes narrow. "A girl can never have enough fun outfits and accessories. And jewelry. Can we talk?"

Adam steps away, picks up a stick and draws in the dirt—a beer can. He frowns then draws an opener.

"Spare the rod," God mutters. "Look," he tells Eve, "Eden isn't the real world. And it's not all about shopping."

Eve's eyes widen then narrow again.

"I was thinking," Adam interrupts, "that it might be cool to have a pocket. Something big enough to hold a spare brewski while I'm out and about."

Eve relaxes her face, pats her cheeks and smooths the skin around her eyes.

Adam strokes his chin and addresses God in a respectful whisper: "You think maybe Eve's putting on a little weight?"

"Don't get me started about kids," God counters. "Anyway, I'll give it to you straight. You want beer? I'm sending you to a place where you can grow barley, malt and hops. But you'll have to sweat for it. And you'll want to keep the water clean out there."

"Out there?" Adam asks.

God turns to Eve. "You want a new outfit?"

She gives God what Adam calls "the look."

God shudders but refuses to back down. "Help your husband round up some sheep. You'll want to go wool this winter."

"Winter?" the first couple ask in unison.

"Wool's warm. And for those who care, it offers plenty of fashion opportunities. Put in the effort, and you'll find plenty of snails and vegetables for dye."

Eve places her hands on her hips. "You expect *me*—?"

"On you, I see teal," God says, "but it's your call. *Vogue* won't come out anytime soon." He glances at Adam and back to Eve. "I'm just saying, it's all on you two now. Use your imagination and make good choices."

Adam looks down at his feet. "God, I could use a brewski."

Eve looks past Adam, who scratches a now-private area, and spots a pool of black shiny liquid near a date palm. "We're empowered, right? That means we can do anything. Like learn chemistry with that sticky stuff over there and create plastic. Then turn all the oil we sell into money and *use* plastic."

God points eastward. "Wait till *you* become parents."

Twins Under the Skin

DREW SMALL'S INSIDES quiver sympathetically with the vibrating linoleum floor as Lester Moore clomps into the far end of the canned fruit and vegetables aisle at three-fifteen on a January morning.

Not that Drew expects Lester, graveyard manager at the 24-hour Biggie-Mart and totally a company man, to accuse him of shirking. While acknowledging the standard shortcomings of the average twenty-three-year-old and perhaps a few additional failings, Drew does not see himself as one of those caricatured Millennial slackers. Over the past eighteen months, he has gone out of his way to meet Lester's demands because Drew Small gets it. California's big cities generate impressive employment statistics, but the job market up and down the Sierra foothills and throughout the Valley for the most part remains tethered to the Great Recession. Like his previous gig as a kind-of apprentice for a non-union heating and air-conditioning company, which short-circuited when the owner disappeared along with two weeks' pay.

Lester's footsteps boom like artillery rounds in a video game.

Drew's heart thumps. Still, determined not to be caught off guard, he slices open a carton of canned Hawaiian pineapple. Not that Drew holds any fondness for stocking grocery shelves. For one thing, his position forces him to contend with Lester, who regularly boasts of his A.A. in business from Gold Country Community College where Drew has taken a few classes—deserving of props given his learning difficulties. Also, Drew continually endures the fallout of Lester's relentless determination to manage the daytime shift before the new year gives out. Then there's the wage Biggie-Mart pays. Minimum. And that they offer him fewer than thirty hours a week employment, which reduces his benefits package to zero.

Drew grasps three cans in each hand and places them in the rear of the shelf, nudging the old cans forward. Then he aligns the labels, each facing out to best inform and entice consumers. For some people, cleanliness is next to godliness. For Lester, godliness relates to orderliness, which relates to shelf appeal. Drew sees no choice but to acquiesce. He stands little chance of finding another job that isn't even shittier. Not that he would ever become a pathetic lifer at the Biggie-Mart. Drew has big dreams of which Lester, now half-way down the aisle, can never conceive.

Only Joni-Jo Pflugermann (née Wojciechowski), his mascot twin at GCCC football and basketball games, understands that Drew's night job is his *day job*, the term with which people in show business emphasize the temporary nature of their humble circumstances. Drew believes with all his heart that his talent as a sports mascot harnessed to unwavering determination will enable his escape from the town that chokes his hopes like a boa constrictor squeezing a poodle.

Lester waddles closer. His forty-four-inch waist enhances the suggestion of a bear shambling towards its den before a winter's hibernation, stuffed and satisfied. Alternatively, Drew thinks, an avocado with legs.

Drew peers into the carton and spots a can marred by a dime-size dent. Lester talks incessantly about empowering "his people." Now, Drew will have to determine whether someone—not a mother but probably a single guy in his early twenties like himself—will link a seemingly harmless dent to the risk of tetanus or some other disease. His thoughts trace the pineapple back to Hawaii. He hopes to own a home there someday—a large house with a vast lawn, gardens filled with exotic flowers, a pool, maybe a tennis court—although he doesn't play tennis—and sweeping views of the Pacific. He loves to imagine swimming and surfing in warm tropical waters, although he rarely goes to the beach. The water off San Francisco is frigid. The warmer waters at Santa Cruz require a longer drive and even more gas money. He has his priorities.

Drew places the can on the rear of the shelf out of Lester's view.

The pounding of footsteps segues to Lester standing over Drew and sucking a straw poking up through a box of apple juice. "Working hard there, Small?" he says.

This strikes Drew as a barely disguised accusation. He looks up, determined to respond without confrontation. "Pineapple," he says. "From Hawaii."

Lester resumes sucking. His puffy cheeks contract to coax out the juice's residue, the box making a sound intimating slabs of granite abrading each other. His thirst quenched, he grins. "You're a big asset to the company, Small," he says with a startling sense of conviction. Lester regularly declaims against flattery. "Just the kind of guy I need what with the weekend coming up."

Drew freezes.

"Which is why I need you here Friday night," says Lester.

"*Next* Friday night?" Drew asks, troubled but hopeful.

Lester crunches the juice box in his fleshy hand. "*This* Friday night. As in *tonight*."

Drew turns more labels towards the aisle. The busier he looks, the more weight he'll give to his protest. "But it's already Friday," he says. "It's also night."

Lester chuckles. His belly jiggles. He knows what he looks like when he laughs but no longer cares. He's a man on the way up. Moreover, he resigned himself to his girth after failing to lose more than five pounds during the many weight-loss programs in which he enrolled. "Close but no cigar," he says. He glances at the eighteen-foot-high wall of plate-glass windows defending the front of the store from the darkness just beyond. "Night, yes. You got that right but only kind of. To most people, this is the morning. I mean, sunrise is what? Maybe four hours off? Ask anyone what time it is, they'll say 'quarter after three in the morning.' The way people look at it, before midnight it was Thursday night. When they wake up, it'll be Friday morning. When the sun goes down again, then we'll have Friday night. So, this is Thursday night or Friday morning. Take your pick."

"Okay," says Drew, refusing an encore of his previous brushes with authority figures.

"Okay then," Lester says, flaunting a self-satisfied smile. "Felipe came down with this major flu and Mary is getting married this Saturday which, FYI, is tomorrow. It'll be at St. Matthew's, and I'll be attending. So, like they say, *you* the man."

Drew drops several cans of pineapple back into the carton and stands. "I can't."

Lester rises on his toes as if he's examining the top shelf, a minor difficulty given that at five-feet-four, he stands an inch shorter than Drew. When he lowers himself, his rubber-soled shoes make a squishy thud. "What part of major flu and getting married don't you understand? Because you're not sick, and I know Mary didn't invite you to her wedding."

"We have a deal."

"Deal?"

"I don't work the night after a game. Not when I'm coming down off the high."

"High? You're a mascot which, I'll say it for the umpteenth time, is kind of a weird hobby."

Drew stifles a frown. He's explained countless times that being a mascot involves way more than wearing a coyote costume. His world is theater. He's a performer. An actor. An artist answering his calling. A role as a mascot provides an opportunity to get out of his skin and create a whole new personality. Like Joni-Jo, he maintains the faith of a religious devotee that a place awaits him in the entertainment industry. He reminds scoffers—including his mother on their monthly calls—that movie superheroes like Iron Man wear costumes. Granted, those actors have lines and usually reveal their real faces. They also get paid millions. The thing to remember is, if they can work their way up, so can he. He concedes that stardom represents a challenge, but one he is determined to meet with the holy trinity of talent, hard work and persistence.

Also, acting involves more than dialog. This stands as one of his core beliefs, since his learning difficulties make it difficult for him to read, let alone memorize, a script longer than a page or two. Stage characters like Nana in "Peter Pan" require an actor in a dog costume who has no lines but plays a critical role. In fact, a musical based on the writing of the original play "Peter Pan" appeared in New York and toured the country, including San Francisco. He wished he'd seen it. And what about mimes? They were big in the 'seventies and maybe some other time in the distant past, but who said they couldn't come back? He could go on forever. TV commercials with Mr. Peanut. Big Bird. And all those mascots entertaining people in amusement parks. Disneyland wouldn't be Disneyland without them.

Lester's mouth hints at a scowl.

Drew grins. Despite barely keeping his head above water, he sees green lights where others see stop signs. If he and Joni-Jo have a long haul ahead to reach Hollywood or Broadway, they keep each other's spirits up. Friends since kindergarten, they appeared in shows together in middle school and high school. Joni-Jo read to him so he could memorize scripts. They would appear on stage at GCCC, but the powers-that-be dealt with major budget cuts by granting classes in business and the trades precedence over the arts.

Lester's right foot taps the linoleum floor.

Drew balls his right hand into a fist. Work after tonight's basketball game is non-negotiable. "The thing is, Lester, I have to be in Sacramento tomorrow, which yes, is Saturday. In the morning. Ten-fifteen."

Lester scratches his head. He views himself as a reasonable man in a demanding profession what with the industry's narrow margins. "You get off at seven tomorrow morning. It's gonna take you what to reach Sacramento? An hour or so? And then what? Another half-hour at most to get wherever it is you're going? That's a problem?"

"I need to be rested," Drew says. "I have an audition. The River Cats. A new mascot."

"They're cutting Dinger?"

Drew shakes his head. Two weeks earlier, a web site for mascots posted that the Sacramento River Cats—top farm team of the San Francisco Giants—would hold a general audition for a second mascot, Dinger Junior. Drew immediately googled. Researching characters is part of an actor's craft. He learned that *dinger* is baseball slang for home run.

Lester takes a deep breath. He seems to expand into one of those blow-up characters that floats above Fifth Avenue in New York's Macys Thanksgiving Day parade. He releases the breath and descends to eye level. "The way it is," he says, "we're short-handed tonight. So, what you do is, you skip the basketball game and take a long nap then come to work then nap again for maybe an hour then head over to Sacramento."

"I have an audience waiting," says Drew." And I get *paid* for basketball games."

Lester's eyebrows rise in disbelief that anyone would challenge his heartfelt approach to career advancement. "You get paid to work *here* and a lot *more.*"

Drew presses his lips together. He feels for Lester. No one ever accuses Drew Small of being insensitive. Foolish? Now and then. Heartless? Drew understands that Lester has his own dreams. He doubts those dreams will be shattered if Saturday-morning shoppers find the Biggie-Mart's shelves not entirely filled.

"Have I made my point or what?" Lester asks.

Drew places the toe of his right shoe against the half-filled carton of canned pineapple and nudges it towards Lester. "This audition's important. And you don't get cast unless you come to an audition fully prepared."

Lester lifts his arms away from his body to balance then nudges the carton back. "You want to work at the Biggie-Mart, you play by the rules. That's how I got where I am."

Drew scratches his right arm where the flesh beneath his sweatshirt bears the tattoo of a rattlesnake. Its giant fangs rest on his neck. At Sutter High, he and Joni-Jo performed in matching Rattler costumes, each with pronounced foam fangs. They gave each other matching tattoos as graduation presents. Hers was the only gift Drew received. In moments of dejection, he gazes down at the snake and feels uplifted. "I'm going home," he says.

"Can't roger that," counters Lester. Forced to play his trump card, he says, "You walk out, you keep walking."

Drew, who hasn't uttered a word of dialogue in the five years since high school, whose art consists of movement and gesture, nudges the carton back towards Lester, raises his right hand and extends his middle finger.

Fifty minutes before tip-off that night, Drew and Joni-Jo arrive at their dressing room in the GCCC gym. It primarily serves as the janitor's closet. Inside, a fluorescent ceiling fixture casts a greenish glow. *I know you'd like lighted mirrors like I guess they have in the school theater,* Jock Ball, the director of athletics, once explained, *but at least I got you folding chairs to replace the wooden bench that collapsed.* Mr. Ball often reminds Drew that he and Joni-Jo should be grateful for their roles as Mr. and Ms. Coyote. Their tenure as students has been, to say the least, questionable given that Drew last attended classes the fall of his second year. *But you two are real good, and that partner of yours? Won't take no for an answer.*

Drew sits and stares at a knot in his shoelaces. "This morning," he says, "I told Lester to fuck off."

"Oh God," says Joni-Jo, still standing. "I hope you're not thinking of going back to you-know-what. Not that you don't have bills and all."

Joni-Jo appreciates that making ends meet is tough. After her marriage to Juan-José Pflugermann fell apart like an overheated casserole in a microwave oven, she worked the counter at Donuts & Stuff. When the position of shift supervisor went to Laurie Clarke with her new A.A. in business, Joni-Jo left to work the register at Burger Barn. It paid an added twenty-seven cents an hour and offered one free meal a day, soft drink or shake included. Overcoming her reluctance, she moved back in with her parents to build her savings preparatory to fleeing the house, the town and the county. Re-entry came with a price. Her parents required contrition. She performed impressively, tearing up during her mea culpa. She also accepted her parents' demand that she take one business class at GCCC each semester.

Drew pulls a water bottle from his backpack. He'll hydrate enough to counter sweating but not so much he'll have to pee before the first half ends. "I guess things were easier for *you* when you were married to Juan-José," he says.

"It wasn't about his money," she says. "Not just."

Joni-Jo still confides everything to Drew, the occasions always tear-filled. Drew always offers the same response: *No offense, but what girl coming off a break-up wouldn't fall for Juan-José?* Even Drew admits that Juan-José looked like a leading man on network prime time. More impressive, the rolls of currency he flashed included large denominations. He also drove a new Chevy Silverado. And they both had J-J names, which Joni-Jo took for more than a coincidence. Left out of her explanation but clear to Drew was her opportunity to turn a bad boy good. Still, Joni-Jo and Juan-José married for even more compelling reasons. She thought she was pregnant again. Her parents threatened to go to the police, since she was still south of eighteen and Juan-José was twenty-three.

She miscarried.

That represented the least of her problems. Their first Christmas, Juan-José rendered the left side of her face the color of Santa Rosa plums and assorted other California fruit. Despite her parents' objections, Joni-Jo kept Juan-José's name. This freed her from hassling with the DMV, Social Security and all those other government bureaucracies. Also, Pflugermann struck her as more professional sounding than Wojciechowski.

"Anyway, it's not like I have a choice," says Drew, referencing his sketchy employment record prior to the Biggie-Mart, including the failed heating-and-air company. His junior year at Sutter High, he started dealing weed and prescription drugs to weather the storm darkening his horizon. The day after graduation, his mother took off to Modesto with her boyfriend, a used-car salesman named Don Nixon. "There's six days of rent still paid and a fresh half-gallon of milk in the fridge," she told him. "In six days, God created heaven and earth. You'll figure things out."

Joni-Jo touches the tattooed Rattler fangs on Drew's neck.

Drew believes he and Joni-Jo understand each other's deepest emotions, although they are years from being involved romantically. No question, he needs to make rent on his studio apartment in a 'seventies redwood-and-stucco four-plex restored to sufficiently livable condition after a major fire. He also has payments on his used 2009 Toyota Tacoma in which he's had unfortunate run-ins with a utility pole and a recycling truck. Raising the water bottle to his lips, he takes stock of the closet's brooms, dust mops, garbage can liners and translucent spray bottles filled with cleaners in more colors than the bottled fruit juices at the Biggie-Mart.

Joni-Jo shimmies out of her jeans.

Drew re-focuses on his shoelaces. He could have looked up at Joni-Jo, but why? He sees her in her underwear all the time. Occasionally, in moments less of passion than desperation, he sees her without her underwear. As artists they reject middle-class constraints. He tugs. The knot comes undone.

"So anyway," she says, "we've got an audience out there."

They stuff their clothes and shoes into their backpacks then slip into their costumes. The bodies feature yellow faux fur with brown, rounded bellies. The heads exhibit large yellow eyes with black oval pupils. Tapered snouts with black noses protrude above mouths flashing toothless grins out of which flop pink tongues. Their long ears, Joni-Jo often notes, stand erect like men in heat.

Five years earlier, they convinced Mr. Ball that twin mascots offer sports fans more entertainment than one lone and lonely performer. *Okay,* he responded, *but they have to be a boy coyote and a girl coyote and not those in-between jobs like they get away with in San Francisco.* Drew's costume features a blue ball cap, Joni-Jo's a pink bow between its ears and matching pink micro skirt. *Short's okay,* said Mr. Ball regarding the skirt. *Mascots don't come with genitalia, if you know what I mean.*

Completing the change into their costumes, Drew and Joni-Jo resemble something of an old married couple. Acquaintances since kindergarten, they became close in middle school and closer as freshmen at Sutter. Their relationship created the teamwork required to make people laugh and applaud and say, *I tell you what, those Rattler mascots are a hoot!* Junior year they came closest, after which the Wojciechowskis took Joni-Jo to an abortion clinic in Rancho Cordova. This placed a stumbling block in front of Drew and Joni-Jo's out-of-costume relationship which, after her divorce, morphed into friendship with occasional benefits.

Henry Chan, the basketball team's manager, knocks then opens the door. "Fasten you guys up? Gym opens in a minute."

Drew nods.

Joni-Jo slaps Drew on the back. "Showtime!"

As fans trickled into the gym, the P.A. system plays the Bee Gees' "Stayin' Alive." Lacey Quinn, a second-year marketing student, puts together play lists to entertain older people because few students attended games, particularly given that GCCC boasts only three victories with the basketball season at its midpoint.

Drew and Joni-Jo perform dance steps made famous by John Travolta and Karen Lynn Gorney in *Saturday Night Fever.* Both are certain that neither Lacey nor anyone else in town can identify Karen Lynn Gorney as Travolta's co-star. They continue as the visiting team from Shasta College takes the floor and begins their warmups. When the song ends, applause rises from the three-dozen people already seated. Drew turns and sees the GCCC Coyotes run onto the court. He prefers to think the applause salutes the Coyote Twins' dance routine.

As players shoot baskets, Drew and Joni-Jo run through their favorite shticks. They imitate fans walking from the entry to the grandstand, exaggerating the swing of their arms or the way portly fans—people run heavy here—list from side to side like ships bumped by ocean swells. Drew's Mr. Coyote puts one arm around a middle-aged woman with a figure suggesting Lester Moore. His free paw makes curving motions signaling she's hot. Joni-Jo's Ms. Coyote approaches a man, sways her hips then takes his hand. He pulls away. Both muss children's hair. The boys smile. The girls squint and screw up their lips. Then Drew makes a show of patting Joni-Jo's costumed butt. She stands indignant, paws on hips. He drops to one knee. Paws clasped, he begs forgiveness. She helps him rise then kisses him, snout to snout.

Half-a-dozen fans applaud. One man whistles.

During the first half, they run through their standard routine. Fist pumps rouse the crowd. When a referee's call goes against GCCC, they run towards him with arms outstretched in protest. During time-outs, they dance with the five-woman pep squad.

The buzzer ending the half sounds. As two youth-league teams run out onto the floor, Drew and Joni-Jo retreat to their closet dressing room. They keep their Coyote heads on to stay in character.

After closing the door, Drew helps Joni-Jo slip out of her costume.

Joni-Jo lowers herself onto the small portable RV/marine toilet she will have to empty and clean at home.

Drew sits on his folding chair. He prefers staying in costume and thus in character.

"Ready for the audition in Sacramento tomorrow?" she asks.

"You're auditioning for Dinger Junior?"

She shoots him a look of disbelief. "I go to the same web sites you do."

Taking a measured sip of water, Drew reflects that there's no reason why Joni-Jo wouldn't audition. Of course, he'd do anything to help her live her dream. He's still fond of Joni-Jo. More, he feels protective. Still, the River Cats are offering just one role. And while Drew believes he's better than anyone else who might possibly audition, he concedes that Joni-Jo is pretty much his equal. Added to that, she's just as obsessed with stardom. No question, this makes them twins under the skin.

Drew shifts his weight on the chair, causing his coyote backside to slip off the seat. He rights himself. The situation, he knows, is precarious. Being Joni-Jo's primary competition makes him uncomfortable. He owes her. Their second year as the Coyote Twins, Joni-Jo convinced Mr. Ball to let them entertain at birthday parties and store openings. For pay. After conferring with the Dean of Something or Other, Mr. Ball reported back, *Deal's done. You'll be ambassadors for the school. But you get your costumes cleaned on your own dime.* Drew and Joni-Jo celebrated with pizza at Don Giovanni's. They'd just put the *business* into show business.

Joni-Jo wipes herself with a Kleenex and stands. "So anyway," she asks, "what time's your call tomorrow?"

"Ten-fifteen," says Drew.

"No shit. Mine's ten."

"We can drive to Sacramento together," he says. He wants to rise above any potential hard feelings when he lands the role. "On the way, we'll pick up coffee, but not at Donuts & Stuff. Heading back, we can get lunch at IHOP."

Wriggling back into her costume, Joni-Jo looks pensive. "You're sure you want to audition? Really? Because I'm thinking you'll feel kind of strange after I finish whatever business they want us to do and they say, *That's it, Joni-Jo, you're Dinger Junior and everyone else can go home.* I mean, rejection's tough. You're sure you have the balls?"

Drew takes a breath to still the flow of his competitive juices. Artists compete just like athletes. The stakes are that big. Leveraging the Sacramento connection, the artist playing Dinger Junior might move up to playing Lou-Seal, the Giants' mascot. That means performing in front of crowds of forty thousand. But reaching the heights demands a will of steel. Maybe a touch of ruthlessness.

Joni-Jo holds out a paw. "No hard feelings tomorrow?"

Drew waits a beat. "They'll audition everyone. Then they'll look at video. It'll probably take a week. More like two." He intends to let the matter drop there but can't contain himself. "Besides, *I'm* gonna get that job."

Joni-Jo cocks her head. "We'll see about *that.*"

"But Dinger Junior is a *guy.*"

"In a *costume.*"

Henry Chan knocks.

They put their heads back on.

Walking to the gym, Drew feels something akin to repentance for insisting he'll get in Joni-Jo's way. Twins, he believes, share souls. "So anyway, we'll save on gas if we go together." He places a paw on Joni-Jo's shoulder. "And we'll be rooting for each other, right?"

Joni-Jo pats his paw. "What do you say, after the game we get a beer at The Well? We'll still have plenty of time to sleep."

Drew hesitates then answers, "Sounds good."

A country tune plays over the P.A.

The Coyote Twins two-step across center court.

Twenty-five minutes after Shasta College finishes routing GCCC, Drew and Joni-Jo enter The Well. Joni-Jo suggests a pitcher.

Drew responds with two human thumbs up.

They find a table, its wooden top gouged with initials, hearts, several mysterious symbols and a penis—circumcised. The table wobbles. Drew makes a shim out of a Sierra Nevada coaster.

When the pitcher arrives, they toast each other's success the next morning.

Forty-five minutes later, Drew realizes that Joni-Jo has poured only a single glass for herself and has left half.

The pitcher stands near empty.

With nothing left to lose, he drains the tasteless dregs.

"Whoa!" says Joni-Jo, her timing exquisite. "How're you gonna be on your game tomorrow?"

"It's just beer," says Drew. "Anyway, adrenaline burns alcohol."

Joni-Jo's hand finds his knee and crab-walks up the inside of his thigh.

Drew draws a deep breath. Joni-Jo is his friend. Also, his partner. Also, a competitor. The breath rushes out. Also, a woman.

"My place is closer," she says. She prefers something of a euphemism to *my parents' place*. "I'll drive."

"You think I *can't*?"

"I think there's lots of things you *can* do."

"What about your folks?"

"Reno. We'll leave your truck out back here with Mr. Coyote safely locked up then come by in the morning with my costume, and you can drive us to Sacramento."

"I don't know," he says.

Joni-Jo runs her hand up to where it dead-ends.

Still seated, Drew slips into his jacket, grateful it descends half-way to his knees.

Ten minutes later, Joni-Jo unlocks the door to her parents' house, drops her purse on the kitchen table and pulls Drew into her bedroom.

After Joni-Jo comes with a soft, high-pitched howl, she turns on her lamp and reaches towards her clock-radio.

Drew studies her Rattler tattoo. He wonders if her fangs are bigger than his.

"I'm setting my alarm for six-thirty," she says.

"I use my cell."

"I don't."

As Drew tries to doze off, Joni-Jo says she feels a little weepy or a maybe it's just nerves or a little of both and needs to talk. She launches into the same monolog Drew has heard too many times to count since no one, she insists, understands her like he does. "So anyway," she says, "I hope you appreciate we'd never have been allowed to stay on as mascots at GCCC if I hadn't had that sit-down with Mr. Ball, which became a lie-down, and to give Mr. Ball his due, not all that bad since he *is* an athletic director, but the real thing is if you want to make it in our business you do what you have to do. At any rate, I'm leaving town before they parole Juan-José out of Folsom."

Drew grunts.

Joni-Jo continues. "Which is why I'm trying to figure how much money I'll need if I don't get the role as Dinger Junior, so I can get by in Hollywood for three months or six or a year at the outside before I get my big break because you know how people are always saying how I should go down to L.A. to be in the movies or on TV or maybe to Vegas which is why I live here with my folks and only pay token rent although I make my own truck payments."

Wind rustles the white fir outside the window.

Joni-Jo yawns, which sounds something like the wind. She drifts off and gently snores.

Drew falls into a sleep so light it borders on wakefulness. A sort of YouTube video loops in his head: Joni-Jo performing a routine with someone acting the part of Dinger or maybe the actor who plays Dinger. Everyone applauds. Then a voice announces the end of the audition before Drew gets his turn.

He opens one eye. Joni-Jo's clock-radio reads 5:26.

An epiphany follows, although Drew does not relate it to St. Paul's on the road to Damascus, a story with which he has only the vaguest familiarity. It occurs to him that Joni-Jo will wake herself at something like six while he supposedly is still asleep. Ninja-quiet, she'll take his truck keys from his jeans then use her folks' bathroom to pee, put on make-up—she'll want to make an impression out of costume—and dress. Given that he has no friends left in town, she'll leave him stranded.

Joni-Jo mumbles in her sleep.

Drew thinks he hears something like, *I'm ready for my close-up now.*

Joni-Jo resumes snoring.

Drew counts to ten then swings his legs out from beneath the blanket, lightly plants his feet on the carpeted floor and circles over to Joni-Jo's side of the bed. If she wakes up, he'll say he's going to the bathroom. He turns her alarm off.

She snores on.

He dresses in the kitchen. Then he slips Joni-Jo's keys from her purse, takes three steps to the counter next to the fridge and removes the spare set she keeps in a red and green tin box that once held Christmas cookies. His shoelaces untied, he tip-toes out the door.

After swapping trucks at The Well, Drew heads to his apartment for a quick clean-up at the bathroom sink. Skipping a shower will counter the risk of Joni-Jo waking early and calling a friend—not Juan-José, thank God. She might even call the cops, but he'll take that risk. Outside Sacramento, he'll stop to shave and change into fresh clothes. As he shuts the door, his heart flutters. His career—his *life*—lays ahead of him.

Halfway out of town, he stops at the Biggie-Mart to give one of the cashiers Joni-Jo's two sets of keys, secured in a Ziploc bag. Passing through the sliding glass doors, he changes plans. The cashier could be a witness against him. He goes to the canned fruit and vegetables aisle and sets the keys behind the pineapple someone else finished stocking. He'll call Joni-Jo after the audition. Having had time to think things through, she'll understand. She'll even laugh. And she'll admit, he has balls.

Approaching the highway, Drew battles second thoughts. In the past, he's done bad things, but he doesn't think of himself as a bad person. What's more, Joni-Jo holds a special place in his heart. The *only* place in his heart except for that cavernous space where he stores his hopes for the future.

He enters the highway. His cell rings. He hits the gas.

Chutzpah

ROBERTO APPROACHED MY table as if all the years filled with maybe-he-is/maybe-he-isn't came down to—unbidden on my part—maybe-we'll-put-this-to-rest. The bar was dark and highlighted by browns and rust like the portrait of an old woman attributed to Rembrandt but probably painted by an apprentice. Either way, worth big money. Other than the commercial aspect, the portrait hardly represented my taste. Ditto the bar. I prefer the transcendent natural light that fills afternoons in the Bar Room at the Modern in Manhattan—which happens to look out on the Museum of Modern Art's sculpture garden and, generally, one of my pieces.

That noted, Roberto hovered over me and smiled.

I nodded.

He sat.

We ordered drinks.

That covered, let's hold off a moment on my meeting my son—or the young man who might have been my son—for the first time. When Garrett White comes to town, it's a big deal. I'd flown in from New York to donate a wall-size triptych I painted to San Francisco's Museum of Modern Art. Before he died, Andy Warhol called me a polymath. I had to look it up. But what can I say? Years back, *Vanity Fair* wrote that Garrett White defines contemporary American art for people with discriminating taste and the money to prove it. The triptych represented a kind of alchemy—paint transmuted into media play transmuted into gold through the museum's valuation, which created a very attractive tax write-off.

Okay, Roberto. I permitted myself to sit in that nondescript bar that afternoon because I figured it would be smarter to deal with what might loosely be called a family matter in private—a relatively rare occurrence for someone who lives his life in a Bohemia crystal fishbowl.

Not that I failed to acknowledge my duty to the museum. I left my personal assistant at the hotel to toss tidbits to the hungry media types who love to sink their glistening fangs into a juicy story. We'd feed them this one—meat, fat, gristle and bone—once we rendered it from undercoating to highlights. Garrett White always provides because media coverage— good or bad—always pays. I refer you to that legendary moment in 1939 when Salvador Dalí shoved a bathtub through a holiday window at Bonwit Teller because the mink that lined the tub—he'd designed Bonwit's windows—wasn't one he'd chosen. The New York press had a field day, which was right up Dalí's alley as a world-class self-promoter. Of course, that happened long before I was born, but the lesson registered once I emerged from my angry-young-artist-turns-his-back-on-the-media- because-they-don't-know-shit phase.

Roberto again. It's not like I invited him to meet me, although I knew he lived in San Francisco or at least did as a kid. He found out which hotel I was staying at—I make no secret of my whereabouts—and left a message. That caught me by surprise since he'd never made any effort to contact me before. Here, let me state that Garrett White is nothing if not honest. No way would I pinky swear that I was thrilled to see him. But at this point, it made no sense to let the matter drag on.

So, Roberto and I sat facing each other, me sipping a Negroni, twist of lemon, him fondling a Diet Coke.

"You're how old now?" I asked.

"Thirty," he said.

I studied him as if I was back in my portrait class at Pratt. His dark hair was shaggy and so badly cut I half-wanted to have the hotel concierge recommend a stylist. My own hair's still dirty blond underneath—I have it all, by the way—but years ago Sasha on East 53rd suggested I go for a Kenny Rogers silver to communicate wisdom and dignity while emphasizing what JFK called—witness his screwing Marilyn Monroe among others—vigor.

As to Roberto, he had his mother's caramel skin. Also her big, dark eyes. The nose, the chin—a toss-up. Could have been mine. Could have been the mailman's. Aside from the hair, a good-looking kid. Also slender. I'll call it lanky, which sounds better than skeletal. His clothes were eye-rolling hideous. I wasn't expecting a $2,000 suit, but he dressed like a cross between a hipster and a faux bohemian unsure of the concept. Gray zipper jacket with stains from God knows what. Black tee shirt. Didn't that fad ever end? Jeans with a hole in the left knee. That really passes for style? Still, the eyes.

"You've got chutzpah," I said. "You know what chutzpah is?"

He shook his head.

"No, you wouldn't. Not with your stepfather."

"Father. He adopted me."

"Father, right. Sean. Irish. My point."

Roberto's face remained impassive. If he played poker, he didn't have much of a tell.

"Does your mother— Do your folks know I'm here?"

"Probably not. They don't go to museums. They used to read the newspapers but not for years."

If he wanted to hurt my feelings, he failed. The people who counted, *they* knew I was in town. "Okay, so chutzpah. You don't know what chutzpah is because Sean is San Francisco Irish. But your mother knows because she's Puerto Rican and Italian from the Bronx. Did she tell you she's from the Bronx? We met in the Village—a party at a walkup on Christopher Street. Did she tell you that? She struck me as exotic. I went to school with mostly Jews and some Italians, but there weren't many Puerto Ricans then in Queens. Today, exotic women are a dime a dozen, but your mother— That was before I became famous."

"When you were still Gary Weisbrod?"

I took another sip of my Negroni. A long one.

"Mom told me stuff from back in the day. Also, how you never wanted to meet me."

I countered with, "You said Sean's your father, right?"

He shrugged. "Anyway, I was too fucked up to meet you until maybe six months ago. That's when I turned my life around. Started a business."

Jesus, the kid had balls bragging about dealing drugs. He didn't look like he could do anything else unless he was one of those techies, but I didn't get that vibe. Then again, I didn't know anything about him. I didn't even know he existed until he was two. That's when I heard from Teresa's lawyer, although we never married and anyway, she was the one who walked out. She had her reasons. Those were crazy days. But my lips to God's ears, I didn't know she was pregnant. Hell, *she* didn't know until she got to San Francisco.

I didn't believe Roberto was my kid because it's not like I was the only one screwing around. And yes, DNA tests were available, but they were in their early stages and from my perspective, suspect. I refused to take one. My lawyer—a friend of a cousin—said I'd be better off acknowledging the child because it probably was mine and who was Garrett White—the name was still new and my career almost airborne but still subject to a death spiral—to get caught in a scandal? Not just your run-of-the-mill artist's scandal but abandoning his kid. Some collectors—a lot of big money flashed in very conservative circles—might balk. Not to mention, the child support Teresa wanted was relative peanuts given where we saw my income heading if the gods—I gave up any pretense of religion after my bar mitzvah—smiled on me. Not being Dalí-savvy at the time, I said okay, let's settle.

Actually, it worked out. I was freed to focus on what was important, namely my art. My career took off, and the payments amounted to nothing more than pocket change. Of course, I took on a ton of responsibilities. In the movie classic *Lawrence of Arabia*, Anthony Quinn plays this sheik who tells Peter O'Toole, *I am a river to my people*. No shit. There was the shark-infested law firm I hired a year after the settlement. My reps. Gallery owners on two then three then four continents—I'm in Tokyo and Sao Paulo. Various assistants—in-studio and out—and public relations gals. Women. You have to call them women. Also my exes, who took me for big money—the price for surrounding yourself with beauty—and assorted other women of intimate acquaintance. Not to mention my patrons and culture mavens at large.

Things worked out for Teresa. She married Sean when Roberto was four. Maybe five. That ended my child support payments. It was like Teresa and the kid didn't exist anymore. Never had.

Until Roberto found me.

"One thing I can tell you," I said. "It takes chutzpah to change your name and reinvent yourself like I did."

"So that's a Jewish word, right?"

He seemed a bit slow on the uptake, which made me wonder whether his drug business made enough so he could buy coffee in the morning—or his inventory was going up his nose.

"It means like what?" he said. "Balls or something?"

"Chutzpah's Yiddish for kind of like balls, but balls is another word. I don't remember it. I maybe know a dozen words. My parents spoke Yiddish but only when they wanted to keep secrets, since they were both born in New York. Anyway, it's more like guts or nerve."

He gave me a blank look. Was he putting me on?

"There's an old joke that defines chutzpah better than anything," I said. "This guy kills his parents then begs the court for mercy because he's an orphan."

Roberto smiled.

"So, you want a real drink?"

"I'll pass, thanks. What I was thinking was, we'll take the bus out to my business."

Wonderful, I thought. I'm going to get arrested in San Francisco for drug dealing, although any charges would end up being dropped and on the bright side, my PR people could use that. But did I need that tsuris? "Garrett White hasn't taken a bus since you were born." I said. "Since before. We can take UberLUX."

He shook his head. "You can't understand my business if you isolate yourself from regular people. That's my customer base. Besides, there's a Muni stop just a block away."

I humored him since he struck me as a little off-kilter and I wanted to minimize the risk of things getting physical. I was hardly in shape to take on a young guy seeing how after being a starting infielder on one of Queens' top high school baseball teams, my biggest physical exertion besides applying paint and cutting metal—my assistants do most of that now—became signing autographs and hoisting cocktails.

"So, this business of yours," I said as our bus headed west towards the ocean. If he was a pusher or a slanger or a skidaddy or whatever word's hip these days—for years I just called Tony—he wasn't at the top of the food chain.

"It's all about disruptive innovation," he said. "I learned that in a business class at City College after I got clean."

The kid related the problems he overcame despite passengers surrounding us. When I was a kid riding the subway, you kept your head down and your mouth shut. Anyway, it all began when Roberto was eight or nine. He decided to kill Sean. Not that Sean did anything wrong. It's just that Roberto couldn't do anything right, and Sean kept calling him on it.

"Like what?" I asked.

"Like name it," he said. "Don't get me wrong. I learned to own everything I did. But my chemistry or wiring or whatever was off. That's why I sucked in school. And why I got into fights. Even when I got the shit beat out of me, I'd keep getting into other kids' faces. Usually bigger kids. That was bat shit, right? Then at the end of middle school, I went the other way and shut the world out."

What do you say when the kid you maybe fathered tells you he's a fuck-up? If he *is* your kid, was it *your* genes or his mother's? Logic told me the defects came from Teresa. Look at Garrett White. The millions. The loft in Chelsea. The house in Boca. The adulation, including three *Vanity Fair* covers and two honorary Ph.Ds. Teresa? She married a service rep at a BMW dealership and ended up working for the DMV. Still, I wanted to be supportive. "You must have done *some* things right. You strike me as a guy most people like when they meet you."

"I guess," he said. "Some people tell me I have charm. That's probably how I got my diploma from high school. Public school, teachers let a lot slide if you get on their good side, like just showing up for classes and not making a fuss. They give you a C instead of a D, a D instead of an F. You get a diploma. I couldn't get into a four-year college so Dad—Sean—thought I should go to City, but I told him I couldn't sit in another classroom. All I wanted was time to figure out what came next. He said I couldn't live at home and do nothing. I didn't know what to do, so I went to the Army recruiting office in Daly City. There were a couple of wars going on, and the sergeant or whoever didn't know about my problems. And I had my diploma, right? I guess I charmed him a little. Or bullshitted him. Is there a difference? He said sure, the Army would take me, and that made me feel good about myself. Later, I found out they had quotas to fill. Anyway, it was the smart thing to do because it means something when you put military service on your resume. Even if it was only five weeks. I haven't written a resume yet, but if I do and someone asks, I'll say *Yes, I was in the Army, but I'd rather not talk about i*t. If they kind of push, I'll say, *No, I wasn't in Iraq or Afghanistan, but thanks for thanking me for my service."*

I saw where he was coming from. Everyone agrees that Garrett White has charm except people who think Garrett White is an asshole, because they don't relate to the persona I created. To get anywhere in the art business, you have to have a persona. So giving credit, Roberto had chutzpah. A full deck, not so much because things got worse.

After the Army, he went back home, did drugs and alcohol heavy-duty and went off the deep end. Teresa held off Sean and forced Roberto to see another therapist, who told him, *If you think you can get by on charm alone, you're delusional.*

Roberto eased off drugs and booze enough to get a job in a supermarket. He also signed up for acting school. "The way I looked at it," he said, "I already *was* an actor."

Teresa paid for his classes.

Sean called her an enabler.

They argued a lot.

"My first class went okay," Roberto said. "The instructor mostly talked about how hard acting is and how you have to have this devotion to your craft. He used that word a lot. *Craft*. The next class we tried moving like animals. Walk like a chicken or a lion or a whale. The whale thing was tough. The teacher saw I was having trouble. *Whales don't have legs*, he said, *but if whales did, how would they walk? You have to get out of yourself and into the whale. Be the whale."*

Bob De Niro is a friend. I made a mental note to ask him about that.

Class three, Roberto put a move on a girl named Jennifer.

"She had long dark hair and a great ass. During break I said, *Jennifer, you could be in movies. You really could. You have a great ass."*

Jennifer didn't see the charm in that. Neither did the teacher. There was no class four.

We walked to a supermarket in a neighborhood that, despite stucco-covered buildings painted in pastels, reminded me of where I grew up. At this point, I knew Roberto once panhandled downtown, went through a period of smashing car windows and spent a few years living in a tent in Golden Gate Park.

Sean no longer spoke to him, but every two or three months Roberto showed up at the house when Sean was at his Friday-night poker game. Teresa made him sandwiches and slipped him a few bucks. Some mothers do things like that. Mine went into a shell after my father died and never came out.

I glanced at my watch—a Rolex Cellini Moonphase. I only wear my Christophe Claret Dualtow Night Eagle when my bodyguard's with me. "So now what? It's four. The museum's hosting a cocktail party in my honor at six." Of course, I wouldn't arrive until six-thirty—the earliest. You have to make an entrance.

Roberto walked up to a yellow newspaper dispenser.

"You sell newspapers?" I asked.

He pointed to a large white plastic cup with a San Francisco Giants logo someone left on the top. A small hand-printed sign was duct-taped next to it:

HELP, PLEASE,
ANY AMOUNT.
I TRUST YOU.

Roberto looked into the cup. "Some singles and a lot of change. Eight, maybe nine bucks." He read my expression. "I used to write *GOD BLESS* on the signs, but here, that freaks people out."

"In New York, you'd get ripped you off as soon as you turned your back. Even if you didn't."

"San Francisco's different."

"And this business of yours, it's sustainable?"

He tapped his right temple. "Most people like to feel they're helping someone. But personal involvement makes them feel awkward. Besides, I can't be here all day. I have seven locations."

Old people and mothers pushing strollers went in and out of the supermarket. I thought someone would recognize me, but this wasn't the Upper East Side, Chelsea, Beverly Hills or Mayfair.

"Every morning, I put all my cups out, all in this part of the city. Just before the stores close or it starts to turn dark, I collect them."

I flashed on a room-size video installation. Seven cameras record all the cups so we see seven videos on seven huge screens. We contemplate the human condition as people come and go. Some deposit money. Others stare. Others pass by without giving the cups a second thought. All the while, the light shifts—sun and cloud; dawn, noon and dusk. Better, internet cameras provide live feeds. "And you make money?"

"Seventy-five to a hundred bucks a day. A hundred-twenty-five when business is really good. I'm always working, so that's seven days a week."

"That, my friend, is chutzpah."

He offered a sheepish grin, which failed to hide the fangs of a wolf. "I'm thinking about expanding."

If Roberto wanted someone to pat him on the back because he ran a successful scam, who better than me? Still, I wondered if he wanted something more. "So now what? Am I supposed to reward you with a job? Or money because you proved a point, whatever it might be?"

His grin disappeared as if a single brushstroke smeared it out of existence.

A cab pulled up in front of the supermarket. An old lady got out. Clutching a cloth shopping bag, she balanced herself on a metal cane with three rubber-tipped feet. I waved the cabbie to wait. "Okay, you've got a business," I said to Roberto. "I'm proud of you. Really."

A bearded young man wearing a Rasta-style wool cap—yellow, green, red, black—dropped a coin into the cup.

Roberto smiled again. "Maybe we could get together tomorrow."

You want chutzpah? I reached into my pocket, dropped a C-note into the cup and said, "I don't think so."

Searching

DANNY PRESSES HIS cell's end-call button like a terrorist detonating a bomb. Goodbye Mother. Goodbye yet another assessment of his thirty-nine years.

He fears his upcoming Skype session with the search committee will be almost as unpleasant.

At least Mother praised his applying for a *big-boy job*. He last held a fulltime position, as an associate rabbi, following ordination over a decade ago.

For two years.

Then came part-time gigs. Torah study at JCCs. Judaism classes at community colleges. Tutoring B'nai-mitzvah students. Hipster weddings at the beach or in the redwoods.

Mother disapproved.

Especially of his playing guitar in dive bars with the Verklempts. A Yiddish-named band covering Motown *and* Springsteen?

It upset her so much, she could never talk. Just sigh.

Mother does use words to tout a steady paycheck. *Paycheck* being a term from her younger days. Although she receives Social Security, the concept of direct deposit puzzles her. Healthcare coverage she gets. *For now, you can't afford to get sick again. Like after Becca.*

At this point in life, money and benefits sound good. Maybe moving up when the senior rabbi with the liver condition retires.

His application, however, includes a stumbling block.

Not the Verklempts.

True, musicians attract women, and he's had his share. Of course, as a rabbi he only slept with single women—never-married, divorced, widowed. But that shouldn't come up.

The real problem? *No* woman. As in wife. Or fiancée.

If only you could stay in a relationship, Mother admonishes.

She divorced Dad fifteen years ago.

Still, she makes a point.

He married Becca a week after ordination. They lasted a year.

He didn't cheat. He just didn't love her.

The board at the temple held back a new contract.

Fortunately, rules prevent the search committee from asking personal questions. But nothing can stop them from wondering what example a bachelor rabbi on the cusp of forty sets for the congregation. Particularly for teenage boys.

He puts on his suitcoat. It projects an image of gravitas. But too formal? Cold?

Jacket goes, tie stays. He wants to impress the committee that he's serious enough to meet their spiritual needs while sufficiently relaxed to accept their shortcomings without being a scold.

Like she whose name he will not mention.

Still, given a résumé long on creativity but short on substance, his persona needs bulk. Jacket on.

Bulk yes, but not stodginess.

Jacket off. Should he loosen his tie? He could slip on one of his old Verklempts tee shirts for balance. Or would that sabotage the interview?

Back on with the jacket.

The call appears on his screen.

Why, he wonders, would this search committee consider him? Does the shul have problems he doesn't know about? Are they that desperate?

Is he?

440 Lows

THE FIRST FIVE minutes after leaving the house were the most awkward but not the most frightening. Like a blind date, Tony thought. In fact, he acknowledged to himself, it *was* a blind date. A major mistake. Something he normally would be too careful to let himself in for.

They were waiting for the light to change by the Marina Green, just past the Palace of Fine Arts, when he finally said, "Some view." And then, without waiting for a response and the possibility there would be no response, he added, "It's even better driving west back to your house. I always liked watching the sun set behind the bridge. Then you really know why they call it the Golden Gate."

Adam shifted in the front seat beside him. "Could we get fries, too?"

Tony laughed. Maybe a little too loudly, he thought in semi-self-reproach, but at least they had broken the ice. "Sure," he said, modulating his voice so that it would not frighten the boy. "Pier 39. Food. Games. Anything you want."

A jogger darted into the street just as the light turned green, sprinted full-out past the car and ran off down the clay path that paralleled the edge of the bay. Tony watched the jogger run, absorbed in his lean, athletic grace. A horn blared. Tony raised his right hand, waved apologetically without turning around and stepped heavily onto the gas pedal.

"Can we get ice cream, too?" Adam asked, his eyes cast down at his sneakers.

Tony glanced at Adam and then turned his eyes back to the street. "Gee, I don't know. I didn't ask your mom about that. That's a lot of food for a kid."

"She always lets me have ice cream if I eat all my hamburger."

"Well sure. Yeah. Why not? How often do you get to go out with your dad anyway?" Rhetorical question, Tony thought. He withdrew into himself, then reproached himself for not making more of an effort. "They have any baseball games at the arcade?" he asked. "Monica and I . . . Monica's my girlfriend. Did your mom tell you about Monica? Monica and I go to this arcade in Westwood sometimes. I'm not into video games that much, but they have this baseball game, and it's like these little men really hit the ball and catch and throw and everything. I used to want to play baseball in high school. What I wanted more than anything else was to play for the Giants."

"Did you?"

"Well, I was a pretty lame baseball player, I guess. Plenty of speed but no power. I couldn't hit a curve ball, either."

"I don't like baseball."

Tony started to turn toward Adam and checked himself. "Yeah, well . . . I go to Dodger games now. I used to hate the Dodgers when I was a kid, but it's hard to root for the Giants if you live in Los Angeles. It's not the same though. I remember how excited everyone was when the Giants moved here from New York. Sometimes, when they'd lose, I'd cry. I go to Dodger games now, but I don't get all that involved."

"Could we get pizza if I eat all my ice cream?"

Tony shifted his gaze to his side view mirror, then braked hurriedly for a red light. "The ice cream's probably the limit. I don't want to get in trouble with your mom."

The light changed. The tightly bunched cars slowly separated themselves. Tony took a deep breath and let out a long, silent sigh.

Adam rubbed the toes of his sneakers together.

"I ran track," Tony said. "I was a lame baseball player, but I was fast, you know?"

"Were you in the Olympics?"

Tony smiled. "What do you know about the Olympics? You're only in the fifth grade."

"Fourth."

Tony tapped his fingertips on the steering wheel. "I ran the hurdles. Four-forty lows. Four hundred and forty yards, see? We still ran yards in those days, not meters. I don't think they call them low hurdles anymore, either. I mean, they're not low at all when you're trying to jump over them. The four-forty is a quarter of a mile, and you have to jump over these hurdles all the way. It's the toughest event in track."

"Did you win any medals?"

"A couple."

"You must have been good."

"Well, I ran in college for a year. It took up too much of my time, though. I was into other things. We were very politically-concerned then. Besides, I left during my junior year anyway. You have to make a real commitment to run the four-forty lows. It's tough enough sprinting for a quarter of a mile, but then you have to jump over all of those hurdles. You see the first and you thank God when you clear it and all of a sudden there's another, and they just keep coming until you think you can't clear one more. I used to get depressed . . . even during a race. I'd just be thinking how unfair it was that you could run so fast and jump all those hurdles and there always seemed to be one more in the way, and each hurdle would look higher than the last even though they were all the same size and you knew that. You get tired, see? We used to call the last hundred yards, when you really have to suck it up to finish out a race, the four-forty lows. Like in how you felt because you'd come such a long way and you still had to clear hurdles practically right up to the end."

"Do you have a girlfriend?"

Tony spotted the parking garage and sped up. "Well, Monica's my girlfriend. I told you about Monica and me going to that arcade in Westwood. I mean, it's okay having a girlfriend. It's kind of like your mom and me. Years ago, I mean. We fell in love . . . your mom and me . . . or thought we had . . . and so we lived together . . ."

"Was mom ever your girlfriend?"

"I just said that."

"Oh,"

"See, that's how you start. You meet a girl and ask her out to a movie or something like that and then, if a man and woman like each other so much they don't want to go out with anyone else, they become boyfriend and girlfriend. It usually just happens, but you have to really think about that because it's a pretty serious thing."

"Is Monica a mom?"

Tony waited for a knot of tourists to cross the street before turning into the garage. "Oh no. Monica's not a mom. We haven't known each other that long. I mean, we've known each other long enough. A couple of years. Three, I think. I had another girlfriend before Monica, but it didn't work out."

"What was her name?"

Tony took a ticket from the machine, watched the gate rise and drove up the ramp. "You aren't really going to want pizza after the ice cream, are you?

Adam wrapped the cord from the hood on his sweatshirt around his finger. "Do you live in a house or an apartment?"

Tony drove forward slowly. "A house."

"A *big* house?"

"Big enough. Three bedrooms. In Encino. In the Valley. That's over the hill from L.A. We have a pool."

"I don't like swimming."

Tony drove up to the third floor and found an empty space between a station wagon and a minivan.

Adam released the cord from his finger and got out of the car. "Whose house is it?"

They walked up the ramp and out to the pedestrian bridge leading to the pier. Tony stared out at the sailboats flecking the blue-gray bay with white, then at the rustic buildings lining the pier, built only a few years earlier but designed to create the illusion of a past that had never existed. "It's *our* house. We rent it. We've thought about buying, but that's a big decision. There's a lot involved when you buy a house together."

Adam strode ahead impatiently.

A breeze came up off the water. "We spend weekends by the pool. I love San Francisco, but you can't swim here. In L.A., you can even swim on Christmas."

Adam led them into the video arcade.

Tony coaxed a five-dollar bill into a machine and scooped up a handful of tokens. "Crowded, isn't it?" he shouted above the din of voices and synthesized sound effects.

Adam circled the arcade tentatively, found a *Commando* game and placed a token into the slot. A helicopter appeared on the screen and dropped the commando onto a scrubby patch of ground. Enemy soldiers appeared. Adam used the joystick to spin the commando around while pressing a button to fire the commando's machine gun. The enemy soldiers dropped. He pressed the joystick forward. The commando advanced, filling the screen with white bursts of automatic fire.

"Can't you just jump over them?" Tony asked.

"Over who?"

"The enemy soldiers."

"You have to go around." Adam spun the commando in a circle, dodged a flurry of enemy fire and killed three attackers before finding shelter behind a clump of trees. New attackers appeared. Adam fired straight ahead from the security of his stronghold. A stream of attackers ran past, the trees deflecting their fire. Those that crossed in front of the commando's ceaseless fire fell.

"Make a break for it!" Tony yelled.

Adam held his finger on the trigger and turned away from the screen. "Why?"

"Aren't you supposed to go somewhere? To the enemy headquarters or a fort or something like that?"

"What for? They just end up *killing* you."

"But that's how you play the game, isn't it?"

Adam frowned. "This kid, he got all the way through once. Through all the gates and everything. He set a record. But he still got killed."

Tony reached for the joystick. "But you have to take a chance. It's just a game!"

Adam blocked Tony's hand. "This way, *I* get to set the record on this machine and nobody can ever beat it. They let you put your initials on the screen, and *my* initials will be at the top of the screen all day."

"But nobody's going to know it's *you*."

Adam looked up at Tony and glowered.

Tony watched the point total pass fifty thousand. "But you never know how good you are if you don't try."

"Then I won't set the record."

"But *trying's* the fun of it."

Adam pressed down harder on the firing button. "You don't know anything!"

Tony watched Adam watching the screen. "I wanted to quit the track team in high school, but my dad talked me out of it. He said if I fought through the four-forty lows I'd feel better than I'd ever felt about anything. When I was a senior, I came in third in this big meet over in Berkeley. They didn't put my name in the newspaper the next day, but it didn't seem to matter. My dad made this wooden plaque and mounted the medal I got on it and put it up on the wall in our living room. It's still there, I think."

"Ninety-five thousand!" roared Adam. Then he pushed the joystick forward, exposing the command to a deadly burst of fire. "I'm hungry. Let's get our burgers then we can come back and I'll play 'til I get two hundred thousand. Okay?"

Tony fingered the tokens in his pocket and followed Adam out of the arcade. The sun was comfortingly warm. He placed his hand against Adam's arm and then lay his own arm around Adam's shoulders. "Burger, fries, Coke, ice cream. You got it."

They walked across the pier to the snack bar.

"You know why kids in San Francisco don't care about swimming much?" Tony asked. "Because it's too cold. In L.A., you can swim any time you want. If you visited, you'd probably really like swimming. You could come down any time, even in winter, and you'd like it. You think?"

"440 Lows" appeared in Oyez Review (1988).

Medium-Boiled

I DON'T KNOW why I pointed the muzzle of a snub-nosed Colt .38 Detective Special right between the old lady's eyes. Maybe I wasn't myself. More likely, I was. What I know is that I wouldn't have teetered on the brink if I hadn't tried to play the hero for Jocelyn. I could have left the gun locked up in my shop. There's not much crime where I grew up in San Francisco and still live. And I'm no gun nut. But can you ever be too careful?

I chose the .38 because that was the weapon of choice in movies from Hollywood's Golden Age—the '30s through the '50s. Ditto for hard-boiled private eyes like Philip Marlowe in Raymond Chandler's novel *The Big Sleep*. For an English class at UC Santa Cruz, I wrote a paper on Marlowe. Jocelyn Wong, my sort of ex, wrote one on Wolverine from the *X-Men* movie. I'm more comfortable with the past. I've always felt I was born too late. Dr. Rosenblum still finds that interesting.

As it happened, two break-ins occurred near where we lived, so I brought the .38 home. Jocelyn objected. She hated guns. Wolverine's huge metal claws, they were okay. Still, I had to protect her, and after a few days, she admitted she felt more secure. If that seems inconsistent, that's Jocelyn. That's any of us.

As to home, that's a one-bedroom apartment between Geary and Clement a few blocks from my shop. I repair chair caning. My parents like to remind me it's not what they expected from a college graduate with a degree in English. I respond that an English degree can take you anywhere.

As to Jocelyn, she left me. More accurately, Devesh took her away. Devesh was a programmer with a six-figure salary, stock options and a ton of perks at the office—where Jocelyn worked—including a full-service café and a masseuse on call. He lived nearby at a nerd commune with a gourmet kitchen, dining room seating twenty, wine storage, billiards room, two bowling lanes, sauna and Jacuzzi. Residents hashed out their problems at weekly meetings on their laptops or phones, even when they were home.

I might be bitter. Tech nerds push up rents and crowd out working stiffs. And who wants to be around hipsters?

Jocelyn, I guess.

That said, her taking off was a hella surprise. We met freshman year of college at a soup kitchen. Dr. Rosenblum suggested Santa Cruz beat the pressure at Berkeley or UCLA.

Jocelyn was exotic. She's three-quarters Chinese. Her father's mother was Mexican. Grandma sang with a band then opened a restaurant in the Mission District. At school, Jocelyn was into Chinese calligraphy, making chicken mole and smoking pot. All winter, she wore a DayGlo green raincoat.

She figured I was exotic, too, given my ginger Jewfro, which made me look taller. Also, I scrounged thrift shops for suits from the '30s and '40s, the ones with the wide lapels. I still do. I told her about my month before freshman year at an institution highlighted by green lawns, smiling faces, calm voices and the dispensing of varied pills and liquids. That can be scary stuff, but some women are impressed.

They say opposites attract, and I believe it. Jocelyn was the social type who chugged margaritas. I was a loner who preferred martinis—dirty, two olives. How long that kind of attraction lasts, they *don't* say.

After graduation, we drifted apart.

I saw Dr. Rosenblum a lot.

Years later on a winter night, I ran into Jocelyn at the Balboa Theater, an old neighborhood movie palace struggling to hang on. She still wore that DayGlo raincoat.

Three months later Jocelyn moved in. Not long after, I proposed. Jocelyn turned me down. She *eschewed* marriage. She actually used that word. So twentieth-century, she insisted. I was crushed.

Still, our relationship was great.

Until Devesh.

I always figured I'd meet Devesh sooner or later, since Jocelyn was his project manager, and he was always calling her cell. I have a cell—a flip-phone. I mourn the loss of rotary phones, although I never used one.

As to any goings on, I had no clue. I was curious, though, why Devesh and Jocelyn didn't have enough time to do business at the office. Occasionally, she worked from the apartment or a coffee place, but usually she took the first express bus to the office. I'd still be in bed. I rise promptly at eight. I open the shop at nine-thirty and close at six. At six-twenty, I take the first sip of my martini. Dr. Rosenblum allows—*condones*—one a day. Then I cook. Jocelyn bought a microwave oven, but I refused to use it. I dine at seven-thirty. All the while I play—used to play—Big Band records on a '50s Grundig Majestic console stereo. It has a dual acousticon speaker worthy of my collection of 78s. Jocelyn inherited the Grundig from her Mexican grandmother.

Jocelyn often returned home after I finished dinner. "In the oven," I'd say. "Couldn't you get home earlier?"

She'd stroke her long brown hair. Dyed. "It's not just a job," she'd say. "I have a career."

A degree in English can take you anywhere.

One day, Jocelyn opened the door and there was Devesh holding a pink box from a Chinese bakery. He looked like India's version of a geek Pillsbury doughboy. Black jeans—the skinny version for portly fellows. Gray jacket covered with pockets and zippers. Gold sweater. I got the impression he was trying to appear taller than me given the abnormally thick soles of his checked sneakers. Thick like the lenses in his glasses. Black frames.

He offered the box. "Barbecued pork buns."

"No thanks," I said. "For Asian food, I prefer Vietnamese."

"You mean *East* Asian food," he said. His eyes locked on Jocelyn's. She nodded.

"In San Francisco," he said, "passing on pork buns is like, a sacrilege."

"And you're from where?" I asked.

He smiled. "Just another Hindu from Houston. Stayed home and went to Rice. Escaped to Austin for grad school. Got a job there. Been here for like, eighteen months. I still love Indian food and barbecue and Tex-Mex, but when in Rome—"

Jocelyn reached for a pork bun.

Devesh grinned.

Devesh showed up every few weeks, always with food. His sweaters failed to conceal the stomach flopping over his belt. For a guy in his mid-thirties like us, that seemed wrong.

Not, however, to Jocelyn.

"Devesh is such a fun person," she said in his presence marked by Greek yogurt cake with orange syrup.

I took one small bite as a courtesy. Dr. Rosenblum frowns on sugar.

"You're a fun person yourself, Joc," Devesh said.

Another time, Jocelyn said, "I'm thinking about taking off a few pounds. What do *you* think, Dev?"

Devesh spread butter on half a warm raspberry muffin. "Nothing wrong with a few extra pounds, not that *you* need to worry." He looked at me. "What do *you* think, Adam?"

I thought Jocelyn might be onto something but shrugged.

She frowned.

"Joc is thinking of going blonde," Devesh said.

I scratched my head. My finger used to get lost in my Jewfro, but I had it clipped back when I took a job selling baby furniture on Sacramento Street. "First I've heard."

Once, Devesh brought Italian wedding cookies from a bakery in North Beach. He and Jocelyn finished every last one over a Monterey County Pinot noir and coffee.

"What else besides eating does Devesh do for fun?" I asked one night.

"He's totally engaged with code, but he also loves video games, German rock bands, food trucks and polka dancing."

"Likes a good time," I said.

She studied herself in the mirror. "Don't we all?"

One night, Devesh brought pupusas—thick Salvadoran corn tortillas stuffed with pork or cheese. I'd gone to dinner and a movie with Scott, a furniture refinisher who refers clients now and then. We saw Humphrey Bogart as the private eye Sam Spade in *The Maltese Falcon*. Probably for the tenth time.

When I walked into the living room just before midnight, my attention went straight to the coffee table. It was littered with dirty plates, crumpled napkins, wine glasses, a half-eaten pupusa and an empty bottle of Napa Valley Sauvignon Blanc.

A note peeked out from under the bottle. I assumed it came from Jocelyn's printer. The font looked like handwriting so the reader would take the message personally.

I did.

The next morning, I went to Wells Fargo. School was out, and two young girls were selling candy bars. I bought three and dropped them into a pocket of my trench coat. Then I emptied our joint checking and savings accounts. Jocelyn questioned the idea of joint accounts. We weren't married. I countered that we weren't much of a couple without some kind of partnership. Some degree of trust. The accounts held a token few hundred dollars each, which represented a commitment. Jocelyn maintained her own bank accounts elsewhere. I kept mine across the street at Bank of America.

When I came out, I saw pigeons flocking around an old lady—the short, dumpy babushka-type in a kerchief and a baggy gray overcoat that might have been stylish in the USSR when Brezhnev was in power. Thick ankles rose out of blocky black shoes. As she emptied a paper bag of yellow-gold feed, the pigeons beat their wings and shoved each other out of the way on the shit-covered sidewalk. There was enough food. They were probably stuffed. But what do you expect from pigeons? In some respects, they're no different from people.

As the pigeons finished pecking and gobbling, the old lady muttered in Russian to someone who wasn't there.

I shook my head. Why was I watching pigeons stuff themselves like miniature Jocelyns and Deveshes when it was time to open the shop? Still, I stood and stared.

The old lady ignored me. Maybe she was mocking me. Maybe she intuited that Jocelyn had taken off, and no woman would leave a *real* man. Or maybe, as Dr. Rosenblum would say, I was projecting my anger onto her.

She slipped the bag into her coat pocket. The pigeons flew up to a long ledge above the sidewalk. Even before I turned, a gob of wet splattered on my right shoulder. Shit rained down like a winter storm from Alaska. The winged rats left the old lady untouched.

At loose ends, I made simple mistakes in the shop. Sleep all but eluded me. Worse, whenever I left the apartment, I heard footsteps. But who would trail *me*? And why? I kept the same unwashed sheets and pillowcases on the bed so Jocelyn's scent would comfort me. They didn't.

"I can write you a prescription," Dr. Rosenblum said.

I said, "No thanks. I have to handle this myself."

After that, before I went out, I slipped the .38 into the pocket of my trench coat.

Two weeks after Jocelyn deserted me, I went to the BofA on Geary to get cash. Jocelyn used her phone to pay for everything, even soy lattes and ice-cream cones. I have credit and debit cards, but cash keeps spending digital money from getting out of hand. My gaze drifted across the street. I shoved my glasses against the bridge of my nose to make sure I wasn't seeing things. My breath caught. Jocelyn was standing outside Wells Fargo. Her hair was blonde, but she wore the same green Day-Glo raincoat. Maybe she'd come back to complain about my withdrawing our money.

My hand wandered to the .38 in my pocket. The gunsel in *The Maltese Falcon* came to mind. How many people can tell you he was played by Elisha Cook, Jr.? How many of them know he was born in San Francisco?

I started to cross the street—three lanes in each direction—but the light marooned me at the traffic island. A Mercedes stopped. Jocelyn got in. I was sure the driver wasn't Devesh.

I feared hyperventilating. Was this guy someone Jocelyn worked with? Or had she left Devesh? I was not a happy camper. I'd wanted to take out the .38 and give Jocelyn the scare of her life. I'd wanted to do it because I felt dirty—not like pigeon shit, but the kind of dirt you can't wash off.

* * *

The night I saw Jocelyn again was the night I thought I saw her and didn't then did.

My pre-dinner martini offered minimal comfort, and I didn't feel like cooking, so I took out a vintage Pyrex bowl and mixed tuna with mayonnaise and relish. What appetite I had slunk away. I went to the bedroom and opened the door to Jocelyn's closet. All her stuff hung there except her precious DayGlo raincoat. She probably planned to buy a whole new wardrobe. Get Devesh to pay. Or the guy driving the Mercedes. New man, new clothes, new life and me opening cans of tuna.

I ran my hand over one of her dresses, the material smooth and cool. Touch stirs memories. So does smell. Touch and smell are what you do when you make love.

My appetite returned. I didn't feel like tuna, so I decided to go to the nearby Mexican place Jocelyn and I enjoyed. I thought I'd find comfort in old memories.

Across the street from Wells Fargo, I saw the old Russian lady feeding the pigeons. I caught a green light, strode across Geary and slipped into a doorway. The filthy birds gorged themselves, as if they weren't fat enough. Can't old ladies see the mess they help make? Don't they know they could slip and break a hip and die? No question, the old lady wasn't all there upstairs. Dr. Rosenblum says few people are.

Then a woman with long blond hair wearing a DayGlo green raincoat popped up. I'd broken the case. Jocelyn was tailing me, so she could find a time and place at her advantage to confront me about our money. Chances were, Devesh was skulking around. Or the guy who drove the Mercedes.

I slipped my hand into my pocket and stepped out of the doorway but kept silent. Let Jocelyn speak first. Try to weasel out of what *she'd* done to *me*.

She ignored me.

I took a deep breath. Dr. Rosenblum's advice.

As the old lady folded up her empty bag, Jocelyn took her arm and said something in Russian.

Jocelyn didn't speak Russian. Also, the shape of her eyes suggested a genetic heritage from Central Asia, which isn't China and Mexico.

"I'm sorry?" she said. Not the sorry I wanted from Jocelyn but a statement that *you* should be sorry for intruding.

I beat it back across the street and kept going until I reached the

Mexican joint. Inside, I made a beeline for the far end of the counter. A familiar waitress flashed a half-smile asking, *Where have you been, and why are you alone?* They don't serve martinis, so I asked for a margarita. Then I ordered the combination plate *numero dos*. Extra guacamole. I ate it all.

Approaching the register, I spotted the actual Jocelyn cuddled up in a corner booth with a guy who looked like the guy who drove the Mercedes. If it weren't for the staff and the customers, I might have emptied the .38. Anyone would have understood. As it was, I should have walked up to Jocelyn and told her off. Not having Dr. Rosenblum to support me, I pulled my collar up and headed out the door.

The next day, Jocelyn's clothes were gone—all but a purple scarf huddled in a corner of her closet. No note.

It had to be Jocelyn because there was no sign of forced entry, and all my stuff was there. She left the TV and the juicer. The Grundig hi-fi, too. And my records. It dawned on me that I never had the locks changed. I'd hoped she'd let herself in one night, crawl into bed, apologize and cry herself silly.

I took a martini into the bedroom and turned on the TV. The last thing I remember was an audience laughing at some talk-show host's lame joke. The real joke was on me.

The day after, Devesh called me at the shop. "I really feel bad about all this," he said. "I had no intention of hurting you. That would only hurt *me*. Karma and all that. It's just that Joc is—was—*is* such a special person. Things kind of got out of hand. Like a super-virus."

"You've got balls," I said.

"I hear your pain. What I hope is, you can find it in your heart to forgive me. Show compassion like Vishnu."

I knew next to nothing about Hindu gods, and frankly, I didn't give a damn. Calling up my best imitation of Bogart, I suggested that instead of lighting incense or something like that, he perform a feat anatomically impossible.

"I deserved that," he said. "I feel better."

I didn't.

* * *

You hang around a bank on a Sunday afternoon, people get suspicious. So I settled in at a donut shop by Wells Fargo. I hate that spelling—d-o-n-u-t. Mocks the language to save three whole letters in the name of efficiency.

What was I doing there? I couldn't help myself. Two cups of coffee and two crumb *doughnuts* later—Dr. Rosenblum would be displeased—bingo! The old lady showed up. Was I stalking her? That was obvious. But why? Did she represent Jocelyn's dark side to be put in her place? Had I fallen under the spell of *my* dark side?

As always, the old lady emptied her paper bag. As always, the pigeons beat their wings, indulged in their gluttony and spread their filth.

Mission accomplished, the old lady headed down the street. She rocked back and forth like a World War Two-sailor on a bender the night before shipping out from San Francisco.

I followed the old lady to a Russian deli and waited outside, my cell phone at my ear to divert anyone's suspicions. When she came out, I tailed her to a one-story cottage with a stucco exterior painted a nondescript cream. She went in.

I went home.

The phone in the living room rang late that night. It's a landline. I keep it because an earthquake can take cell towers down.

"My grandmother's stereo," Jocelyn said. "I told Steve about it. He's the guy I'm living with now. He says I should have it."

"You don't listen to records," I said. "You can have the TV."

"Steve has a TV. His is bigger than yours."

"So *that's* what this is all about?"

"His *TV*, Adam. The stereo, as you well know, was my grandmother's. Maybe I sort of gave it to you as a birthday present but not officially. We were high that night. Anyway, the Grundig might be community property if we were married, which we're not, so it's mine. That's what Steve says. He went to Stanford Law. He does IP."

"Which is what?"

"Intellectual property. Patents. But all lawyers know about community property."

"I assume he knows we lived together for almost three years."

"Now *you're* a lawyer?"

"And you *did* give me the Grundig for my birthday. I kept the card that came with it."

"Men don't keep birthday cards."

I followed Dr. Rosenblum's advice and took a deep breath, then a second. "I tell you what. I'll give you your half."

"Adam, what are you talking about? You think this is like the baby King Solomon was going to cut in half because two women claimed to be its mother?"

"It worked."

"You don't want to bluff a lawyer," she said. "Besides, Steve says this is about protecting a woman's rights."

"But *you* walked out on *me*. For *Devesh*."

"My point. Women aren't property. Steve's going to rent a van, and Devesh is going to help. He's a good friend of Steve's. That's how we met. Steve and me."

"They're *still* friends?"

"You keep living in the past," she said. "That might have been charming. Once."

I eased into a chair, closed my eyes and sucked in another deep breath. "This is ridiculous," I said.

"Steve says that if you need to, you can think about if for a week."

I thought about it. I also thought there might be a way out. Jocelyn's lawyer was her boyfriend. Wasn't that a conflict of interest? Also, he was committing adultery with my wife—or the woman who would have been my wife if we'd gotten married. But these things get complicated. For the money it would cost me to hire a lawyer, I could find a dozen or more old Grundigs. If that many still existed.

Over the following days, I closed the shop early and took a long, circuitous route home. I drank my martini followed, with all due respect to Dr. Rosenblum, by a second. I barely ate. A good wind off the Pacific could have blown me halfway downtown. I didn't listen to music. I didn't read. When the walls closed in on me, I walked the streets.

One night, I walked right up to the edge and staked out the old lady's house. A woman rang the bell. The house lit up then the door opened. The long-haired, Central-Asian-eyed blonde stepped out. The two women walked down the street arm in arm. I figured they were going to dinner or a movie. They didn't strike me as the types to go clubbing. Not that you ever know. What had I known about Jocelyn?

I leaned against a tree and tried to sort things out. Then my eyes drifted down to the sidewalk in front of the house. It was spotless.

I should have gone home, but I couldn't see letting the old lady off the hook. People do ugly, thoughtless things in other people's figurative backyards, and no one calls them on it. I decided to send her a message.

I pulled Jocelyn's scarf—the one she left behind—from my coat pocket and covered my face. Then I rang the bell. After maybe thirty seconds, the old lady appeared behind the beveled glass panel that made up most of the door.

I stuck the muzzle of the .38 against the glass—right between her eyes. Then I pulled the trigger.

She never flinched. Didn't offer an expression of shock or fear. Not even of gratitude, since I hadn't loaded the gun.

The week Jocelyn said Steve gave me was ending. I called her. "The Grundig. Steve and Devesh or whoever can pick it up tonight. Nine o'clock. I'll leave it in the lobby. You still have a key to the front door of our building."

"You can't carry something that big down the stairs," she said.

I didn't appreciate the putdown, but I refused to let Jocelyn get to me. "Nine o'clock. The lobby."

The rest of the day returned to normal. Before closing, I locked the .38 away in the shop. In the apartment, I went to work. At eight-fifteen, I made the first of several trips down two flights of stairs down carrying the disassembled pieces of the Grundig. I laid them out on the lobby floor with a note asking my neighbors to bear with me. All Steve would need was a few tools and the doggedness of Philip Marlowe or Sam Spade to identify the small electronic part wrapped in Jocelyn's purple scarf nestled in back of my top dresser drawer.

White on White

WHAT DOES A nine-year-old Black girl know about art? Give me a break. Not that I don't love the kid for what she did. I know artists who'd pay a fortune to get my kind of exposure. Actually, they do that. Pay a fortune. What do they get? *Bupkes*.

Fact: People come to see an exhibit by Garrett White because Garrett White defines art. I told that to *Vanity Fair*. I told that to *Slate*. I told that to Terry Gross although you can't see my work on the radio. And *The Times* still trying to make some kind of point that I was born Gary Weisbrod in Queens? What? Frank Gehry wasn't Frank Goldberg? It's all part of the mystique. Garrett White reinvented himself so he could reinvent art. Michelangelo, Rubens, Degas, Picasso, Henry Moore. That was then. Ditto for Warhol and everyone who followed right up to the millennium and past. Garrett White is *now*. That's what I told *American Art Collector*.

As to the girl, if I was writing a screenplay, I couldn't come up with a better story. She and her parents walk into my exhibit, *White on White*. The father's a doctor like Bill Cosby on the old TV show. The mother teaches Comparative Lit at Columbia. I forget their names. The kid's name I can't remember, either. But that's not the point.

The point is, the story's simple. Like art should be simple. Too many artists make things complicated. Garrett White doesn't do complicated.

He does simple. *White on White?* A room. A cube, actually. Twenty by twenty by twenty. Walls? White. When the entry and exit doors close, you can't see them. Floor? White. Ceiling? White. Very white because it's the light source. It gives each surface the same value of brightness. More or less. Not *exactly* the same. Garrett White does simple. Making everything exactly the same? That's complicated.

Visitors walk into the room ten at a time. Ten's the max. They get two minutes to take it all in. Then they leave as the next group enters. Before the kid came, some groups had only five or six people. Maybe as few as three. But ten, that was the max. More than ten screws up the experience. The curator's notes say that on a placard outside the entry. It's a quote from me, actually. "More than ten screws up the experience." I don't say why. Why say why? An artist doesn't explain himself. Other people do the explaining. The artist does art.

So *The Times* reports that someone in a particular group—a full ten by the way—starts talking as soon as she enters the room. It's the girl. They describe a pink blouse, purple jeans and pink sneakers. Her hair's braided with all these beads—pink, yellow, turquoise. A real work of art, *The Times* says. So anyway, the girl blurts out, "There's nothing in here." Her parents try to shush her. At nine, the kid's a critic? The kid won't pipe down. "There's nothing in here," she says. "Isn't there supposed to be something in here?"

The rest of the group remains silent. These are New Yorkers—or visitors who know the local customs. Their silence cuts deep. What, these people paid a special admission fee to see nothing? They're stupid? These are doctors and lawyers and professors and business people and students and other artists. Or their spouses or partners or friends or whatever. They may not know what they like, but they know art.

That's a joke.

What goes down is no joke. The next Sunday, *The Times* runs an article in *Arts & Leisure*. Might they be a little tardy? Hell, yes. Waiting ten days after the opening before reviewing Garrett White? That's like televising the State of the Union Address in February.

The headline reads, "There's nothing in here." This, no question, would lead the reader to believe that *White on White* has just been chucked down a hole and Garrett White's reputation with it. Which, no offense, would make the reader wrong.

The thing is, the writer is ambivalent. Is *White on White* great art? Or is Garrett White putting something over on us? She can't say. Am I disappointed? Hell, no. You can't pay for that kind of ink—or digital composition. Now, everyone who gives a shit about art has to see *White on White* in order to weigh in. *White on White* is topic one on the East Side, the West Side, in Chelsea, in the Village. The hipsters down on the Lower East Side, they're all over it. Aside: Can you believe my immigrant grandparents once lived there? The same goes in DUMBO, in Williamsburg, out in the Hamptons. If you don't have an opinion on *White on White*, why did someone invite you to that that cocktail party or dinner?

Some people suggest hard feelings towards the kid on my part. No way. I'd take her to the zoo or out for gelato if I liked kids. It's simple. She called it as she saw it. Just like an artist. But what does a nine-year-old know about art? *Bupkes.*

Here's what she *should* know when she gets ready to make her way in the world. The media takes a comment and runs with it. Maybe the comment's not positive. Maybe it's negative. Could be what they say is even true. Doesn't matter. It's all about the buzz. Some kid speaks. People start talking. A museum gets into crowd control. Galleries raise their prices on every Garrett White piece they have. Still, they sell out. They call my rep for more. *Demand* more. We, as they say, take it to the bank.

So what's to know? It's simple. Creating something from nothing—*that's* art.

"White on White" appeared online in The Summerset Review (2013).

Max

ASK ME ABOUT something that happened last week, and I'll have to think hard and probably screw up the details. That's if I remember at all. Nineteen fifty-four? What happened to Max and what happened after I can tell you like it was yesterday.

That summer, I turned ten. The Yankees, who I loved, won 103 games—they only played 154 then—but the Cleveland Indians won 111 and the American League pennant. Bobby Avila, the Indians' second baseman, led the American League in hitting at .341. Al Rosen, the Tribe's (no pun intended, but we were all proud) Jewish third baseman, hit .300 with 24 homers and 102 runs batted in. Still, the Giants, not long for New York, swept the Indians in a World Series featuring Willie Mays' incredible catch off Vic Wertz and Dusty Rhodes' four homers.

The mind's an attic that requires periodic sorting and cleaning. I find the task problematic.

Max scorned the Yankees. Technically, he was Uncle Max, my father's older brother by a year, but he insisted I call him Max. At home, I'd slip up now and then. My father would say, "*Uncle* Max. Show respect."

He was a Dodger fan, since he lived most of his adult life in Brooklyn. At best, I was indifferent to the Dodgers, but I loved Max. I thought everybody in New York did. Whenever I went anywhere with him, people laughed at his jokes, and gave him food and liquor and cigars. I felt almost like a grown-up.

Things started changing the last Saturday morning of July '54. My father was at the pharmacy he and his partner Larry had just bought on Queens Boulevard in walking distance to our apartment in Rego Park. He worked Shabbos because while we were Jews, we were hardly observant.

I was up on the roof of our building. My mother thought I was in the street with the other kids, which I had been. If she knew I was on the roof, she'd have taken TV away for a month. Maybe a year. The risk was worth it. My friends and I liked to throw a tennis ball or one of those old pink Spaldeens from down in the street up onto the roof above the sixth floor. We took turns up there retrieving the throws that succeeded. Sure, you could lean over the parapet to catch a ball with not quite enough steam on it and topple over, but the last thing a ten-year-old thinks about is mortality. When my mother called me from our living room window, my friend Marty shouted up, "Danny went to the candy store. He's coming back in a minute." Hearing that exchange, I counted to two hundred then walked down the stairs to the fourth floor.

"Uncle Max called," my mother said. "He has tickets to the Yankees this afternoon. He wants to pick you up early."

This was no ordinary game. The Yanks were playing the Indians, who they trailed by maybe a game in the standings. Before my mother could remind me to be a good boy, I shot out the door and leaped down the stairs. I didn't want to make Max wait. The year before, he'd moved to a similar six-story building only two blocks away. *To be close to the mishpachah.* We had two bedrooms. I shared that second bedroom with my older sister Karen until she married Stan. Max had one. He was a lifelong bachelor. *Women!* he'd say then lick his lips the way Mel Allen did when he delivered commercials for Ballantine beer on the old black-and-white Yankees TV broadcasts. *But marriage?*

Max pulled up in his '53 Cadillac Coupe de Ville with its ice-blue body and white top. Two bullet-shaped pieces of chrome extended from the rear bumper suggesting the rocket ships in the old Flash Gordon serials on TV—the ones with Buster Crabbe. Max intended to keep the Caddy till the '55s came out. *It ain't broken in yet.* My father drove a '49 Hudson Commodore, gray inside and out.

On the way to Yankee Stadium, Max detoured. We stopped at candy stores in Elmhurst, Corona and Jackson Heights. Each time, he had me wait in the car. He'd return empty-handed and tap me on the arm. *Business before pleasure, kid.* What that business was eluded me. Max, I knew, was treasurer of a union local involved with delicatessens, not candy stores.

I was all for our extended drive to the Bronx because it offered more time to talk about baseball and life. The former centered on our Yankee-Dodger rivalry and my boasts about the Yankees beating the Dodgers in the '52 and '53 World Series. The latter concerned sports in general, money, women and the usual caution for me to look out for myself. The world was a tough place. *Your father—Without me, he wouldn't have made it through high school, forget college and pharmacy school.*

As Max told it, the Irish and Italian kids in Manhattan always looked to beat up the Jews. Once, they went after my father. Big mistake. At fifteen, Max already was six feet and a muscular two-ten. Max and my father were walking home from school, Max trailing behind, talking to a girl. *Goddam kike!* some guys yelled as they rushed my father. *There were four of those fucking goyim*, Max told me more than once. *I beat the shit out of them. After that, your father was off limits.* Not long after, Max dropped out. *I left word about your father. Anyway, I got an education in the real world, not crap from books.*

As always at the Stadium, I was awed coming out of the tunnel beneath the grandstand and seeing that huge expanse of green. We settled into our box seats ten rows behind the Yankees dugout along the first-base line to watch infield practice—a tradition long gone. Max bought us hotdogs, a Coke for me and a beer for him while Mickey Mantle loosened up throwing knuckleballs to Yogi Berra. Max's smile was as big as mine.

The Indians scored a run in the first inning off Allie Reynolds. In the bottom of the inning, the Yankees wasted a two-out triple by Mantle. After the Indians scored again in the third to lead 2-1, Max left our seats to make a phone call. Cell phones? Two-way radios like Dick Tracy's were still a fantasy. Max brought back ice cream.

In the middle of the fifth with the Yanks down 3-1, Max excused himself again. "Gotta make another call, kid." He brought back peanuts then signaled the vendors for another Coke and another beer.

In the bottom of the seventh, the Yanks tied the score. Max left to make yet another call. When he came back, he said, "Gotta go, kid." His eyes decreed that the matter wasn't up for discussion.

We caught the end of the game in the car. The Indians scored two runs in the top of the tenth. In the bottom of the inning, the Yanks came up short with only one.

"Tough luck, kid," Max said when we pulled up in front of my building. "Anyway, I can't come upstairs. Got a fire to put out."

"A fire?" I asked.

He made a fist and lightly tapped my shoulder. "Everything you get in life? It comes with a price."

The next night I was in bed under my sheet—we didn't yet have air-conditioning. I'd watched *The Ed Sullivan Show* with my parents. Now I was supposed to be asleep to get up early for day camp at our synagogue. Instead, I was reading a Tarzan comic book with a flashlight. Karen, a CIT—counselor in training—at the same day camp, was sleeping over at a friend's across the street. The telephone rang in the foyer, which shared a wall with my bedroom. I heard my mother say, "Sid's in the shower." Then silence. Then, "Of course, come over now."

Five minutes later, the doorbell rang.

"The dinette," I heard my father say.

Preoccupied, my parents forgot I could hear everything in the dinette, which shared another wall with my bedroom. Also, the dinette windows, opened to catch a breeze, were only a few feet away. I spun to the foot of the bed and stuck my right ear against the screen.

Chairs scraped the floor. Plates and silverware clattered on the table's marble top. That afternoon my mother had baked chocolate babka.

"What?" my father asked.

"These people," Max answered.

"These people," my father repeated.

"They aren't happy," said Max.

Silence.

"You can make it up to them, I'm sure," my mother said.

"Depends," said Max.

Another silence.

Perhaps wary, they switched to Yiddish, which they often spoke with my grandparents. Maybe they struggled to make themselves understood, because they returned to English.

"High school, already you were a bookie and what?" my father said. "They threw you out." What startled me wasn't the revelation that Max was a bookie as well as a union official but the anger in my father's voice. "And to gamble yet? How do you lose twenty thousand dollars? Twenty thousand! And to pay back, borrow from the union?"

My mother whimpered.

"These people," my father went on, his voice rising. "*They* rob the union, not *you*. These people are gangsters!"

"I *know* these people," said Max. Suddenly, he sounded as calm as my father was upset. "I can reason with them."

"Reason?" my father asked.

"I told them I'd have the money by Friday. I just need a loan, is what I need."

"Twenty thousand?" my mother moaned. "Everything Sid and I have is tied up in the store."

"Ten," Max said like a neighbor asking to borrow the proverbial cup of sugar.

More silence.

"Five, that would help. You got five?"

"Max," said my father. His voice blended disappointment with fear.

"Even two or three. Anything to show I'm acting in good faith."

"Two or three would help?" my father said.

"These people," said Max.

One more silence.

"It was a mistake, okay?" Max said. "That's what you want to hear, right? Okay. But don't worry. These people, they don't care about me. They only care about the money."

By Tuesday, I'd forgotten the matter. When you're ten, the world of adults is as complex as a cobweb and just as weightless. I figured one of my parents had gone to the bank and withdrawn enough cash for Max to satisfy "these people" for a while. Max would find a way to get the rest. And that was that.

Friday, day camp let out mid-afternoon for Shabbos. Karen and I stopped at a deli for knishes. When we got to the apartment, my father stood in the foyer swinging his arms as if he was swatting away ghosts. My mother sat in a high-backed chair next to the radio-bar they bought before I was born. Her eyes were red. She seemed to be cannibalizing her lips.

My father's arms fell. "Sit," he said.

We sat.

"Uncle Max—"

"What about Uncle Max?" I asked.

Karen, who got my father's drift, shot an elbow into my ribs.

"Uncle Max," my father repeated. "An accident."

I figured Max had twisted an ankle on the curb or cut his hand slicing a bagel.

Karen burst into tears.

My mother released her lips. "This morning. Early. They found him outside his building. On the sidewalk."

My father took out a handkerchief and brushed his nose. "The police didn't call me until lunchtime when I was out of the store. When I got back, there was this note to call them. Someone—"

"Sid!" my mother cut him off.

"Ma, I'm ten years old," I protested.

Karen went silent.

My father sighed. Although he was smaller than Max, I'd never thought of him as weak and vulnerable. "Last night, they said. Someone. Probably two people. Pushed him off the roof."

Three weeks later on a Sunday morning, we sat in a small, dark-paneled funeral chapel. Jewish custom says you bury the dead the next day, or two or three days after if family is coming from out of town. But the State of New York required an autopsy and whatever else before releasing the body.

We'd arrived early so my father could look into the casket. *Sometimes they bury the wrong people.* I fingered the slit black mourner's ribbon pinned to the lapel of my sport coat as if I could summon a genie who would bring Max back or at least explain the unexplainable.

Max and my father were my grandparents' only surviving children, so there was only a sprinkling of mourners. One was a cousin of my father's—a heavy, gray-haired woman I'd never met—and her husband. Several adult relatives from my mother's side offered support along with a smattering of friends and neighbors. Larry had to stay at the store. A few men I didn't know occupied the back row. Sobs and whispers most notable for their lack of accompaniment periodically interrupted the silence while I stared at Max's closed coffin wondering what it felt like to be dead. Also, since I was the center of the universe, why this had happened to *me*.

Rabbi Goldfarb—Max wasn't a member of our synagogue but my parents asked for a favor—approached the small lectern in front of the casket. Just as he cleared his throat, the doors at the back of the chapel opened. Heads swiveled. Two workers appeared with a huge arrangement of white carnations.

An almost-choral gasp rose from the mourners. Ours was a Conservative synagogue. Flowers—a symbol of life—had no place at a Jewish funeral where death was seen not as a new beginning but as the end.

Rabbi Goldfarb held up his hand like Moses parting the waters.

The workers retreated.

"My God," my mother whispered. "Who?"

We observed a sort-of Shiva, the seven-day mourning period. My parents ignored traditions like covering our mirrors or sitting on hard boxes. *We're Americans!* Wednesday, my father went back to the store until dinner. Stuck at home, Karen and I chafed at my parents' hypocrisy. They wouldn't allow us to watch TV. They also limited what we could read in the usual four or five newspapers to the comics and sports pages. But we knew as they did that by now, Max's story was old news.

We spent our confinement playing Monopoly and seven-card gin rummy. I read Chip Hilton sports novels, Karen teen romances. We could go out twice a day but only to walk around the block. "You do not cross the street," my mother instructed. "If I find out you went to the candy store—"

After dinner, visitors brought rugelach and cookies in pink or white bakery boxes fastened with string. We were allowed our treats then banished from the living room so the adults could talk.

We heard enough through our bedroom door. The police were still working on who killed Max, but the bigger topic of discussion was the shanda of the flowers. Unknown to my folks until the funeral, Max once had been married. The scandal? The woman wasn't Jewish! She hadn't shown at the funeral, so, where was she? No one knew or cared. What we knew now was that Max had two daughters in their early twenties. They didn't feel comfortable coming to the funeral, so they sent the flowers with a signed card. *The life insurance,* everyone confided knowingly. But Max's daughters never contacted my parents. Besides, Max had no coverage.

A few years back, Karen took another run through our parents' papers and found Max's death notice from the *Daily News*. Probably sent by the funeral home.

A hundred words, the notice painted Max as a loving brother, brother-in-law and uncle. It left out his sins—and my long-lost cousins—as if truth constituted an offense so great that the dead must be disguised and thus disfigured. This suggested that if the dead were rendered as imperfect—read that human—we would no longer love them.

Disgusted, I balled up the yellowed clipping and tossed it in the trash. Since then, I boycott obituaries.

Closure

MINUTES AFTER GORDON emerged from his post-op fog—Carole smiling at his bedside while dabbing at tears—his survivor's elation gave way to guilt. Yes, he'd just been given a new heart. And yes, while he'd be on a regimen of nasty medications to fight rejection, he and Carole had reason to believe—not just hope but have faith—that their life together would extend beyond the middle of middle age. This while his ever-prudent doctors cautioned that life expectancy after a transplant remained up in the air despite the accumulation of plentiful and, for the most part, encouraging data. An actuary at an insurance firm, Gordon understood that he represented only a single data point among thousands whereas Carole, inherently optimistic, saw the glass half full. More than half. However-many their remaining days, she insisted, each would be a joy given the alternative. *My heart tells me that. The heart knows.*

As Carole spoke words of comfort and encouragement, Gordon silently asserted that his guilt demanded its due. During seven months of suspended animation on the waiting list, receiving someone else's heart seemed abstract—surgical procedures, medications, side effects and the like. Something other people experienced. Now, reality jolted him. Another human being had died for him. Well, not *for* him. The dead man was an organ donor. Not that Gordon had asked the man—or anyone—to give up his life so a medical team could harvest his heart along with any other salvageable organs. When Carole informed him that his donor died a hero, the kind of person they made movies about, Gordon made a weak fist as a gesture of homage.

The guilt grew.

Not long after he achieved a reasonable measure of clarity, guilt transitioned to unrest. Gordon didn't fear his body rejecting someone else's tissue or the risks posed by cyclosporine—at least as much as he might. He understood that statistically, the odds were in his favor. Rather, he found himself unnerved because the beating heart within his chest posed unanticipated questions. Did another man's heart make him— Gordon—any less Gordon? Might he, without his consent, become more like his donor? Know what his donor knew? Feel what his donor felt? He summoned enough presence of mind to dismiss those questions as fit only for tales by Edgar Allan Poe or Stephen King.

Another equally vexing set of questions supplanted them. Did the new heart place him under some obligation to the donor? More relevant, to the donor's family? Did it require him to be a hero, too?

An ICU nurse looked in. "Gordon, how are you feeling?"

Gordon grunted. Damned if he knew.

The Mayor attended Eddie Byrne's wake. A Yale-educated African American—some thought him the next Obama—the Mayor commiserated with Eddie's family and the chief of police and Eddie's captain and Eddie's lieutenant and all the uniform guys—and women. He was too smart to call them gals. When a beat cop from Eddie's precinct sang "Danny Boy," the Mayor bawled with them. When it came his turn to raise a glass, he couldn't praise Eddie enough. Eddie was a cop's cop who laid it on the line to defend the people of the city from crime, chaos, cataclysm. A hero who chased down an ex-con wanted for armed robbery and shooting an elderly woman. Lord Jesus, what got into people? After he spoke, and everyone resumed drinking, the Mayor offered a shoulder to Kathleen, Eddie's wife and the mother of their two-year-old twins. Beautiful Irish girls. The Mayor often reminded voters in certain precincts that he had an Irish great-grandmother. And damn right, he'd be just as proud if he discovered Italian blood flowing through his veins. God bless the ethnic vote. God bless America!

The Mayor spoke at the funeral. The story had to be told and retold. Eddie and Quinton Clark—his partner and an African American the record should note—corner the suspect. The suspect points a gun. Eddie inches forward. He tries to talk to the gunman, find common ground, calm him, avoid a tragedy. The suspect, determined never to return to prison, grows more agitated, charges, fires. Eddie takes a bullet. Quinton empties his weapon. The suspect goes down. Blue suicide.

Murmurs rose among the thousand or so mourners at St. Brendan's. *Good for Quinton, but too bad it wasn't Eddie who killed the motherfucker. Thank Christ, Quinton got him, but if only Eddie—"*

The media was all over the funeral as they'd been all over the story the past week interviewing cops, friends and neighbors. The family, withdrawn and understandably so, offered only a few innocuous comments through one of Eddie's uncles. Who could blame them for keeping their own counsel? This wasn't, he said, their first tragedy. But Eddie knew his duty. A cop with a new family—a second chance—risked everything to bring some scumbag to justice. Only the media never aired the word *scumbag*. They heard it a lot, but they had to be careful about what they broadcast even if their viewers shouted the same words and worse at their TVs and radios. They even aired a parishioner's statement about Father Felipe at St. Brendan's. *No disrespect, but how is it the diocese can't find an Irish priest?* Still, people said, Father Felipe would get the ball rolling on Eddie's canonization. Father Felipe had not expressed such an intention, but the media wanted to demonstrate how beloved Eddie was. The mourners— those who knew Eddie Byrne personally and those who didn't but felt like they did, and those drawn to tragic events seeking catharsis—would never forget him. A husband. A father. A hero. A goddam saint. One thing everyone knew: Eddie Byrne was in heaven right now sitting at Jesus' right hand.

Oh, and didn't somebody get Eddie's heart?

Dr. Scheinwold glanced at the reddish scar running down Gordon's chest. "Very nice for two months out. I should do this for a living."

Gordon let the surgeon's humor pass. "But what about my blood pressure?"

Dr. Scheinwold smiled. "A little high but not unexpected. You're doing fine. By the way, have you met the family?"

"The family?"

"The donor's family. The widow and the children. Twins, if I remember."

Gordon, to whom the matter of the donor leaving twins still proved unnerving, shook his head.

"Maybe it's a little too soon," Dr. Scheinwold said. "For you and them, too."

"I guess."

"Well, you're doing fine. You've got a good heart."

At three months, Gordon felt almost normal. He was back at work Monday, Tuesday and Thursday. He came in late and left early, but he got a lot done, and his co-workers gave him their full support. Maybe better, he and Carole were talking about resuming sex. *If you feel ready*, Dr. Scheinwold advised, *you probably are. Or you will be soon.* That sunny prognosis seemed achievable because the data supported it. That and his newfound confidence. Each night, after he kissed Carole goodnight and turned out the light and rested his head on his pillow, Gordon truly believed he would wake up the next morning. More, he would feel even stronger. As his self-assurance grew, his guilt dissipated. Life was good.

Then the dream popped up, unbidden and disturbing. It retreated for several days, reappeared, took a week's hiatus then again imposed itself. Gordon, lacking a biblical Joseph to interpret it, had no idea what it signified. What he *did* know was that the dream, particularly because of its repetition, always left him awake and panting, his pajamas sweat-soaked. One night, he summoned the will to unburden himself.

"The same girl each time?" Carole asked.

"The same."

"You're sure?"

"It's *my* dream."

"A child?"

"Seven. Maybe eight. Like Sheryl at that age."

"She looks like Sheryl?"

"Sort of.

"*Is* it Sheryl?"

Gordon took a deep breath. "No."

"A child you know?"

"No, I don't know her."

"And you see—"

"Always the same thing. Her face and the top of her shoulders. She's pretty the way Sheryl was. The way all little girls are pretty. Light brown hair. Long. Like how little girls—their mothers, I guess—let it grow." He went quiet.

Carole took this as a signal he had more to reveal. "And?"

"It's her eyes." Pressure filled Gordon's chest. He clutched his blanket. Was the new heart expanding? Would it blow up to the size of a beachball then explode? On the plus side, he was breathing. He was agitated, but he could breathe. He decided that what he really felt was a heaviness, as if Dr. Scheinwold had stuffed his chest with a rock.

Carole placed her hand on his forehead as she did with the twins when she suspected they might be coming down with something. Sheryl and Marty were off at college now, each at a different school to explore their separate identities. The costs would give anyone nightmares. She withdrew her hand. "Does she say anything?"

"She just stares. It's the eyes."

Dr. Scheinwold swiveled in his chair. "That adjustment in your cyclosporine— Just what the doctor ordered."

Gordon shifted his weight on the examining table.

"As far as your dreams go, I doubt it's the medication."

"Then what? It's all in my mind?"

Dr. Scheinwold wrote something on his tablet. "Where else would dreams be? But seriously, that's someone else's area of expertise."

"A shrink? You think I should see a shrink?"

Dr. Scheinwold looked up. "What do *you* think?"

"Isn't that what shrinks always ask?"

"Gordon, for me transplant surgery is routine. Always challenging, sure, but you know what I mean. On the other hand, how many new hearts have you received? It's hardly uncommon for a patient to experience donor guilt."

Gordon buttoned his shirt. "Okay, but the girl. What does she have to do with anything? And as far as my donor goes, sure, I still feel bad he died. Was killed. But it's not like I *wanted* him to get killed."

"Of course not."

"I had nothing to do with it."

"Exactly." Dr. Scheinwold put the tablet down. "So it's five months. You still haven't met the family?"

Gordon shook his head.

"Ever seen them? A photo, I mean. TV."

"TV, sure. The funeral. It was on the news. I kind of got a glimpse of the wife and the twins, but I had to turn it off."

Dr. Scheinwold stood. "Gordon, I'm a heart guy not a head guy, but maybe your dream is telling you something. A cop loses his life which, with a little assistance from yours truly, gives you the rest of yours. He leaves a wife and two little children. Of course, the children are too young to understand what it means that some man has their daddy's heart inside his chest. Still, maybe you need to meet them. Maybe you need to say thanks. Get closure."

Conflicting emotions battered Gordon. It sounded reasonable that the Byrne family—the widow and, in whatever way, the children—might also seek to shut some kind of door on their grief. But how was that supposed to work? The widow would still slip into bed each night alone and wake up each morning staring at a smooth pillow. The twins would grow up with only photos and videos and newspaper clippings of their father. And his badge, probably. These would be keepsakes, not memories.

Still, he was curious as to what the Byrnes were like. What would Mrs. Byrne tell him about the husband and father they had loved and lost? And given that Eddie Byrne's heart beat inside him, what comfort could he give them? Surely, he owed them something. *Something?*

The dream took a break then reappeared, playing in his head each night like a movie with an extended theatrical run. The girl remained in close-up, wide-eyed. This time she spoke but, as in a silent film, produced no sound. Gordon read her lips. *No. No, please. Please. Not again.* She repeated those words as if the film was looped. In place of an orchestra— or at least someone on the piano—Gordon heard the sledgehammer pounding of his heart.

In a small room adjacent to the Mayor's ceremonial office, the Mayor's chief of staff, a young African American woman with close-cropped hair and lime-green designer eyeglass frames, praised Gordon for seeking closure. "Mrs. Byrne is looking forward to meeting you."

The chief of staff had selected that Tuesday morning as a perfect time to get breaking radio coverage plus airtime on the noon TV news not to mention the early and late evening news broadcasts. "Social media exposure, of course." At first, her remark took Gordon back, but he wasn't naïve. Everything was grist for the media mill, and if the Mayor earned a few political points, fine. Eddie Byrne's memory deserved the honor, and Gordon had no right to take that away from Kathleen. He thought of Eddie's widow by her first name now. Kathleen's family also would be there, as would Eddie's.

"If you'll excuse me," said the chief of staff. "My executive assistant will be here in a moment." She left them to await their cue.

Carole adjusted Gordon's tie. "Nervous?"

"I can hear our heart beating," he said.

"You sure you're okay?"

He patted her hand.

She smiled. "When Mrs. Byrne and her family meet you, they'll feel a lot better."

"You think?"

"I know."

Precisely at ten, the chief of staff escorted Kathleen Byrne, wearing a gray pants suit, and the twins, dressed in pink, through an opposite door connecting to the oak-paneled ceremonial office. The remaining Byrnes followed along with Kathleen's family, the O'Connells.

The chief of staff's young executive assistant winked at Gordon and Carole. "We'll let the Mayor have a minute with Mrs. Byrne," he said. "Make her and the family comfortable."

Gordon and Carole nodded in unison.

"He's a great people person, the Mayor," said the executive assistant. "Reelection next year will be a snap." He grinned. "I know we can count on your support."

The door opened. The executive assistant nudged Gordon forward.

Gordon clutched Carole's hand.

TV cameras and reporters filled the room. Gordon had never been the center of this kind of attention—of any kind of attention. Following the transplant, the media focused on the Byrnes while he insisted on anonymity. Now, he'd be all over the news. Hardly a celebrity, though, which was the last thing he wanted. This was about the Byrnes. And the O'Connells. And upholding Eddie's memory.

The Mayor stood with Kathleen as Gordon and Carole approached. Kathleen's cheeks struck Gordon as a bit hollow. Her eyes glistened.

The Mayor gently squeezed Kathleen's forearm. A supportive squeeze. A brotherly squeeze.

She smiled at Gordon.

Gordon smiled back. He owed Kathleen so much. She and the extended families on both sides. But he felt a special responsibility to the twins. They would never experience the simple joys his twins had shared with him—movies, vacations in the country or at the beach, pizza after Little League or volleyball, bedtime stories. Gordon gave the twins the biggest smile he could muster. He had to be there for them in whatever way he could, to honor Eddie's memory so *they* would honor it.

Kathleen extended her arms.

Gordon staggered back half a step then rocked forward and hugged her. He had to demonstrate that he understood what she'd gone through. Well no, he couldn't really understand, but he felt her pain on a very deep level. They shared a new normal.

After the hugs and tears and awkward but comforting words, the Mayor assured the media, and through them the families and the city, that Eddie Byrne indeed had been a hero, in death had given someone in need a new life. Everyone could find a big measure of comfort in that. For that matter, Kathleen and her—their—beautiful little twins, enduring the unimaginable, also were heroes. Not to forget Gordon. Gordon was the worthy recipient of a noble heart.

Then the Mayor excused himself, and the chief of staff thanked the media for coming and guided Gordon, Carole and the families to a nearby room for coffee and a little private time. Kathleen and her mother excused themselves and took the twins to the bathroom. The remaining Byrnes and O'Connells filled the room in subdued clusters.

A broad-shouldered blonde introduced herself as Rosemary McDermott, Eddie's sister. "This hasn't been easy for any of us, but I think knowing you're the kind of person you are makes Kathleen and the rest of us feel so much better."

His throat constricted, Gordon nodded.

"So anyway, you've probably noticed that my family might seem a little stand-offish," she said. "They're not angry. It's just, you being alive thanks to Eddie— They're good people. We're good people. But we've had more than our share of tragedy what with me losing my husband five years ago and two months after that losing Marie and Robyn."

Carole took her hand.

"Marie, she was Eddie's first wife." Rosemary raised her free hand to her mouth. "You didn't know?"

Gordon shook his head. Neither the chief of staff nor her assistant had said anything about a dead wife and child, and he'd avoided researching the family on his own.

"Well, I guess not," Rosemary said. "After the operation, that would have been too much, I guess. But now you know. His wife. Their daughter. Hit and run."

Gordon's shoulders heaved.

"I'm so sorry," Carole said. "*We're* so sorry."

"I hope you don't mind my telling you," Rosemary said, "but I feel like I have to. Is that wrong?"

"No," Gordon managed to say.

Rosemary nodded. "So, Eddie married Kathleen eighteen months later. He was eleven years older, but they were perfect together. We love Kathleen like we loved Marie, even though Marie was a wop." She shook her head. "Why do people make bad jokes at times like these?"

Although not a touchy-feely kind of guy, Gordon patted her shoulder much as the Mayor might have.

"Eddie and Marie and Robyn," Rosemary said. "A beautiful family. Oh God, Robyn— You never saw such a pretty girl." She cleared her throat, reached into her purse, opened a caramel-colored leather wallet and held up a photo. "School portrait. Second grade. Robyn was what? Seven? Seven-and-a-half actually. I have no kids, and I was a very proud aunt. Crazy proud. I used to call her my little dream girl."

Gordon raised his right hand to his heart.

Carole grasped his arm.

In the moment it took Gordon's lungs to expand and his hand to fall, he conceded that the Byrnes had suffered more than he knew—more than anyone knew. It was only right that he help them bear their burden, hold high the flame of Eddie's memory all the days of his life, which also would be the days of Eddie's life. That settled, he made no effort to hold back his tears as he gazed at the face of the seven-year-old—seven-and-a-half actually—the familiar face framed by long, light-brown hair and marked by eyes that concealed the torment transplanted to him. A dream girl.

Facing Down the White Bull

THE SECOND TIME I screwed over Burt Weinstock involved a woman forty-five years younger, and I never laid a finger on her. It began innocently enough with an invitation to our latest alumni gathering touting a cash bar, which would keep me from drinking more than I should, and nibbles, which would cover dinner.

A little after six-thirty on the designated date, I rode up the elevator of a hip hotel in the East Twenties with alumni three and four decades younger. All wore suits. That included the women. I took them for investment bankers, attorneys, CEOs, surgeons. People who wrote—or at least *could* write—big checks with no little frequency. Wearing gray slacks and a twenty-year-old navy blazer with a frayed lining, I stood behind them in silence as they mumbled amiably to each other while staring at their cell phones. My cell remained nestled in the left-front pocket of my slacks. I suspected they had no clue I was going to the same event.

Speakers in the Celestial Room blared some or other female pop star singing some or other catchy tune. Two-dozen alums chatted amiably, drinks in hand. Beyond them, floor-to-ceiling windows gazed down onto Park Avenue. It being winter, lights glowed like stars in a wilderness sky published by *National Geographic*. This being Manhattan, the stars above failed to make an impression.

A volunteer asked me to fill out a name tag. I told her I had a thing about name tags. She was cheerfully insistent. I glumly complied and made a beeline to the bathroom. At seventy, you've learned to pre-empty your bladder which can pre-empt discomfort for maybe an hour. No point in interrupting a conversation or missing out on the arrival of more hors d'oeuvres.

At the cash bar, I ordered Scotch on the rocks. I'm not a cocktail drinker, although a quick survey of the room revealed alumni downing cocktails in a variety of neon colors. By the time I stepped away, the crowd numbered over fifty. A dozen more alumni were checking in. The din rose. I turned my hearing aids down.

I spotted Burt with the aforesaid young woman. The ages of women under fifty—under sixty—elude me, but I didn't think myself too far off guessing twenty-five. Her dark brown hair, thick and wavy, streamed damn near down to her waist. There's something about all that hair. Lovely face. Slim figure. Nice breasts. Is it old-fashioned to call them perky? Or sexist? I've given up worrying about that, although I consider myself "woke," whatever that means. At any rate, I give myself credit. I still notice.

Burt and I shook hands. "This is Valentine," he said.

"Valentina," she corrected.

"Valentina," Burt repeated. "Class of—"

"I'm in grad school at NYU," she said. "Part-time. Working on my MFA."

"Given that you're chatting with Burt," I said, "creative writing. Working on a novel. Figuring you'll teach until you can give up your day job."

She smiled.

"Well, Burt's your man," I said.

Burt raised his free hand to his cheek as if he'd been slapped.

I wondered if he'd taken my compliment as some sort of sly put-down. It wasn't. Unless it was. We had a history.

We were in the same class at our prestigious university, both English majors and so acquainted, although we traveled in different circles. After graduation, Burt landed a junior editing job at a major publishing house and quickly ascended the ranks. I taught English at a Catholic high school in the Bronx—the faculty's lone Jew—and devoted nights and weekends to writing. I had a few short stories accepted by respected publications before working up the courage to embark on my novel. Several years later, the novel and my marriage both finished, I summoned the courage to approach Burt—this after a number of agents rejected the manuscript. Burt bought it, proving that agents know a lot less than they'd have you believe. We developed a business relationship and, over time, something of a friendship. Then everything went south.

As the room continued filling with alumni, Burt looked at Valentina then held a hand out towards me. "Oh, God. I haven't introduced Mike. This is the author I mentioned was coming. One of my favorites, and believe me, authors can be difficult."

I assumed Burt was demonstrating that bygones were bygones, unless he was dissing me. We both knew what was what. Or what had been what.

I wish I could say I had a wildly successful career as an author and made Burt's company a ton of money, burnishing his reputation in the process, but my "promising" debut novel was followed by a "disappointing" second novel. After my third hit the remainder tables with a thud, Burt offered his regrets. There'd be no advance for my next novel. Art was art, but tell that to the marketplace and the accountants who were taking editorial matters out of his hands. I told him I got it, which represented a half-truth. I had a hunch other factors came into play.

One factor.

Fortunately, before Burt severed ties with me I took a day job as a copywriter at an ad agency working on a major beer account. Scott Fitzgerald, Dorothy Sayers, Joseph Heller and Don DeLillo—also Salman Rushdie—worked as copywriters, but *before* their literary careers took off. The only thing I knew about advertising was the stuff I saw in the papers and on TV, but the creative director I interviewed said he admired me. All copywriters want to be novelists or playwrights or screenwriters, and all art directors see themselves as painters, sculptors or filmmakers.

After several years praising beer then wristwatches, I went freelance to give myself sufficient time to write a novel that would re-launch my literary career and mark my entrance into the pantheon. I did okay but got sick of advertising, so I turned to teaching creative writing and committed myself to living on less. The new venture represented a middle-class version of Bohemian life holed up in a garret on the Left Bank, except I had a small apartment in the Village where I still live. Building a clientele proved more of a strain than I imagined, but I got by.

The manuscript—typewritten—sits unfinished in a desk drawer.

The years passed. What happened to them? Life, I suppose. In this observation, I reveal the limits of my prose. Anyway, I reduced Burt to a disappointing memory. More accurately, a guilty one.

Then two years ago, one of my students, an octogenarian fellow alumnus, asked me to accompany him to a similar alumni gathering. A retired investment banker, he had no past writing fiction and no future in literature, but he churned stuff out with admirable enthusiasm and paid my admittedly inflated fees without hesitation.

As now, the crowd was basically under fifty. Probably under forty. Only a few of us older types dared to show. That included Burt.

I almost didn't recognize him. When I did, I considered ducking out, but my student and I had only just arrived. Also, Burt spotted me. We maneuvered around the room at a distance like modern dancers, who wander the stage but never approach each other let alone touch. Aging being what it is, we ended up in the restroom one urinal apart.

"Burt," I said.

"Michael," he said.

We each would have been satisfied with that, but in came my student.

Men don't prattle in men's rooms. My student didn't give a shit. He introduced himself to Burt. "All those children out there," he said. "So nice to see another mature alum. Do you know Michael? Let me buy you both a drink. Whoever came up with the concept of the cash bar, anyway?"

Burt and I surprised ourselves by chatting with a measure of geniality.

My client was fascinated that Burt had been an editor and years later—post-me—a successful agent. He described the novel he was working on, looking at me every ten or fifteen seconds for support.

I met each glance with a smile.

My client bought another round then popped the question: Would Burt come out of retirement to represent him?

Burt advised my client to seek representation elsewhere.

My client went home.

Prodded by momentum and fresh drinks, Burt and I exchanged reminiscences of small delights balanced by inevitable regrets. We discovered we were both free agents. Neither of us had remarried. Neither of us had kids. We also acknowledged that eating solo offers merits but excludes the joys of conversation. We agreed to get together every now and then for coffee, drinks or a meal. Sometimes, I went uptown. Others, he came downtown. We often ended up splitting the difference and met in midtown. I found myself tentative at first, but Burt never laid a guilt trip on me. He had the right.

The social aspect aside, reconnecting with Burt inspired me. I developed an idea for another novel to put me back on the map—although I'd barely established a Pluto-like position in the literary world and hadn't written fiction for what seemed like forever.

One Sunday at brunch on West 81st, I tossed him a "what if." He encouraged me to explore the idea. I wrote a detailed outline and noodled character studies. With no little trepidation, I started a first draft.

Four chapters in, I pitched Burt that given the time he had on his hands, representing me would constitute a healthy diversion. Obviously, it would mean a great deal to me. The novel had renewed the sense of purpose I no longer found in teaching. Also, I fantasized about boosting my finances. My relationship with money always had been one-sided and never in my favor.

I survived the old days because Gayle, my ex, never hit me up for alimony. At twenty-one, she came into a trust fund but hoarded it even after our wedding, anticipating the day when the blue skies of our marriage would go gray then blacken and drown us under a series of cloudbursts. Her lawyer told her she was insane not to take me for every nickel—they were few—but she insisted on demonstrating that she was the bigger person. No protest from me.

Burt responded to my proposal by chewing on his bagel.

I followed up that representing me offered him a measure of rejuvenation. Everyone needs a reason to get up in the morning beyond going to the bathroom.

Burt put the bagel down, signaled the waitress for more coffee then said he'd give the matter some thought. Meanwhile, another alumni get-together was coming up. It would be a lark. We might even run into an old friend, although the odds were dwindling.

I wasn't all that enthused but agreed to go. My life was in Burt's hands, since he said he might have an answer by then.

A week later, he called to say he hadn't decided yet, but he'd see me at the alumni event.

Now, here we stood, feet starting to ache, with Valentina.

I extended my hand.

Valentina's brow furrowed—as much as a child-woman can furrow her brow. "Did I once read one of your stories in a survey course?" she asked.

Had she paid me a compliment or thrown an old dog a bone. "Possibly," I said. I could have said "probably" but knew better.

"Are you working on something now?"

I glanced at Burt.

His mouth hinted at a grin. His eyes betrayed rejection.

Valentina displayed a reaction more upbeat. "I'd love to hear all about it," she said, having no idea what stood behind the furtive communication in which Burt and I had engaged. "I'm fascinated with the writing process."

"I told Valentina earlier," said Burt, "there's no one way to write a novel. Successful authors just go to it. The rest find redemption in codifying the rules."

I fought against frowning.

He gave me his glass. "Just be a moment," he said and walked off towards the restrooms.

"I think writers have to learn their craft," Valentina said.

The noise level near deafening, I leaned in.

"And starting a new novel at your age. That's so exciting."

"More like scary," I said.

Her eyes widened. "Didn't Hemingway say something about a blank sheet of paper being a bull or something?"

I nodded. "The writer has to face down the white bull—that blank sheet of paper in the typewriter. In ancient days. A laptop screen can be just as terrifying. Maybe more, since you're always tempted to wander off on the internet. Anyway, I wrote my senior thesis on Hemingway. I didn't think they taught him anymore."

She cupped her hand behind her right ear.

"Hemingway," I half-shouted. "Listen, maybe we should go down to the lobby bar where it's quiet."

She looked towards the restrooms.

"If he wants, Burt'll find us."

Her eyes wandered around the room.

I assumed she sought out better prospects—hardly a difficult task.

She looked back at me, her eyes sparkling. "Sure."

In spite of my delight, I hesitated. This wouldn't be the first time I took a woman away from Burt.

Forty years earlier, I got involved with Burt's wife Fran. I plead extenuating circumstances. I was divorced, so it wasn't like I was cheating on Gayle, who'd suffered a miscarriage a few years back. Some couples bond after that kind of thing. Others chew on each other. Also, Burt and Fran's marriage occupied that particularly bitter space just before the lawyers come in and try to separate the combatants. So technically, sure, I was aiding and abetting adultery. Postscript: Making that case calls on the letter of the law but not its spirit.

Our fling was prosaic and short-lived. Later, pangs of guilt crept up on me. Adultery—I cop to it now with the afore-mentioned caveats—is a sin. Everyone knows that. Of course, almost everyone gives it a shot. What vexed me was that Burt and I were engaged in an artistic/business relationship. I betrayed the trust that's supposed to entail.

In the elevator going down, I considered that deserting Burt represented another betrayal, one that would overcome him with disappointment. It wouldn't concern a lost opportunity for sex. I for one didn't anticipate a roll in the hay. What I was taking from him was a moment of chaste romance like the courtly love Chaucer wrote about. Valentina wouldn't understand, but people Burt's and my age? Absolutely.

You ease out of bed one morning and your joints creak. After a shower, you lift your razor and stare into the mirror. Your stubble's turned gray or white, intersected by lines and creases in once-smooth flesh. When you dress—no pressing business at hand—your fingers fumble with your shirt buttons. You reject all this as an aberration, because part of you thinks you're fifteen and always will be. Meanwhile, what hair you have continues to thin while your belly thickens, and as much as you try to clamp down on the brakes, you keep heading downhill.

Eventually, you concede that you're old. Worse, society wants little to do with you. You had your shot, old-timer. Leave us be and go play out the string. You take your place in the ranks of ancient historians lamenting the loss of a glorious past, a relic occasionally considered by the young to be amusing but most often archaic.

Then you meet a woman who's young and pretty and full of life. Her smile makes you tingle. She laughs at your jokes, and if she's more deferential than wholehearted about that, fine. Looking at her is like looking into a magic mirror. You see the dim reflection of the man you once were, and it doesn't take much of a flight of fancy to believe that you can be that man again.

Crossing the lobby, it occurred to me that Hemingway got it wrong. The blank page a white bull? More a calf. Growing old, you confront something much more terrifying than setting down the right words in the right order. I suspect that's why, three weeks before he turned sixty-two, Hemingway raised the barrel of a shotgun and slipped the muzzle into his mouth.

I concluded that delusion has its merits. The days dwindle down and all that, but I prefer to see the glass as half full. Also to believe that alone in the ring, the sounds of pawing and snorting obscuring the pounding of your heart, you can will yourself to stand up to, and maybe face down, whatever the day's white bull may be.

We sat at the bar.

I ordered drinks.

The bartender looked at Valentina.

She turned to me and smiled.

The bartender grinned.

I winked.

Borrowed Time

FROM THE DECK of my condo, I see four men kicking up bursts of sand as they sprint towards the Pacific. Three are local fishermen who docked earlier in the morning with their catch and returned to the seaside café next door to knock down a cerveza or two. The fourth waits tables there.

The aroma of amberjack on the café's grill mingles life and death.

A small crowd gathers. Americans, Canadians and no few Europeans who prefer getting off Baja's beaten track but not too far. They watch the men charge into the surf and hurl themselves at the breakers. White foam churns around brown shoulders.

I set down my bottle of Negra Modelo and pick up my binoculars. Early winter, gray whales migrate down from Alaska to calve. Late winter, they swim back to feed in cooler waters.

In a few weeks, I'll make my own migration.

The rescue party reaches a man flailing his arms and *thisclose* from going under. Two keep his head above the surface while a dinghy approaches.

I live off the ocean, but I fear it. From a distance, it's smooth and peaceful. Inviting. Seductive. On the water, swells hurl you into the air. You can see for miles. Then you drop into a trough like being cast into a well. The sky shrinks. The beach disappears. You lose your bearings. Below the surface, scary things lurk while unseen currents wait to pull you away then under.

Just like life.

As the dinghy's rower, his oars dangling in the water, helps pull the man over the gunwale, a voice rises from the crowd on the beach. *¡Tiburón!* Two swimmers crawl in after him. The other two hang on to the stern as the dinghy heads back to the beach.

I have a relationship with boats. Actually, ships. I take a cruise—five- and six-star lines only—once or twice a year. Not that I'm wealthy. I work. My work takes me on cruises.

Arriving at the beach, the rescuers wrestle the victim out of the dinghy and carry him towards the shade of a palapa. The man's head rests, face up, against one of the men's pillow-like belly. Blood covers his left thigh.

A slim woman wearing a lime-green cover-up and a straw sunhat fastened with a purple ribbon rushes forward.

A rescuer gets her into something of a bear hug. He thinks it best she doesn't come closer.

Her howl overwhelms the screeching of gulls.

The other rescuers urge the crowd to retreat a few steps. Few onlookers comply.

I train my binoculars on the victim. His left leg below the knee flops to the side at an odd angle. My guess is a Great White. What I *know* is that he lies terribly still.

A siren wails. It almost reassures me. Everyone, from tourism officials in Mexico City to the locals, wants visitors and ex-pats like me to feel safe. It's how you do business.

I know how to do business. Three basic principles guide me: Be personable. Listen attentively. Never get greedy. The last remains open to interpretation.

I started my business in my mid-thirties after the risk-reward ratio of a previous undertaking proved unfavorable. After more than a decade with more ups than downs, I know what works: Stay in shape. Drink moderately. Dance like a professional.

I check my laptop. I admit to a small fetish: I continually monitor my investments, although the markets remain out of anyone's control, so I rarely trade.

What I *can* control is my spiel. I always let my fellow passengers get things started, prod them with questions. When I see they're comfortable,

I let drop my earlier cruise experiences, some of which I shared with my late wife. Until her fatal illness.

Before launching my new enterprise, I found the right disease and studied it in depth. Commiserated in chat rooms with others who'd lost loved ones to determine how best to compose my own response to unexpected death. Honed my story to achieve accuracy and consistency. I can't chance running into someone I've met on a previous cruise but fail to recognize calling me on this detail or that. I deliver a performance, and it's always restrained. Never maudlin. It's important to meet every sympathetic word, glance or touch with grace and propriety.

I return my attention to the beach. The body lies on what I assume to be a stretcher beneath a glistening white plastic sheet.

Someone hands the woman in the lime-green cover-up and straw hat a large yellow bag as she accompanies the stretcher to the ambulance. I assume she gets in. It's parked out of sight.

On a future cruise, I may meet that woman. Widows and divorcees of means try to escape their loneliness. In doing so, they often provide access to what men like me want. The right prospect will be too preoccupied—or confused—or willing to deceive herself—to review her portfolio. Long before she suspects something's not kosher, I take my leave.

No worries. The good time a woman had provides a counterweight to her monetary loss. Her sense of victimhood. She keeps her accountant and her lawyer in the dark. Embarrassed but wiser, she moves on.

I look out towards the horizon. I wonder what plans the victim and his wife—or girlfriend—made for that evening. What they had in mind for the rest of their stay. The weeks following. The balance of the year. Life.

A gray whale breaches, spins and lands on its side. Whitewater explodes.

My breath catches. I thrill at the creature's sheer joy, its ability to live in the moment.

I recall an old saying: Man plans, God laughs. My own horizon takes me only to the next cruise. I'm a realist. Somewhere out there is a woman I'll misjudge. Things will go sideways.

Like the whales, I take it day by day.

We all live on borrowed time.

Taj Mahal

As THE AIR-CONDITIONED car returned to the hotel in Gurgaon, Delhi's new technology hub, Liz and Mel found themselves drenched with sweat. The driver, pounding his horn, zig-zagged through the plodding late-afternoon traffic. Unlike in California, no markers defined the two lanes in their direction, which the swarm of vehicles turned into three and four.

Janash, their guide sitting to the driver's left, waved his hand. "In Delhi, it is always rush hour. But in the end, we are all going to the same place." He turned. "Of course, I mean home."

Liz turned her attention to a small motorcycle carrying a young family stoic in the congestion and heat. The father drove. The mother sat behind him, two small children on her lap. A third child—Liz speculated she might be ten—perched behind her mother.

A rib-flanked cow sauntered in front of the motorcycle.

The father braked.

Liz's heart leaped up towards her mouth then dropped to her stomach.

The car halted within inches of the oldest child's dangling legs.

"Oh, my," Liz whispered.

None of the family seemed bothered.

Liz uttered a silent prayer combining supplication with thanks.

The young father nudged the motorcycle forward.

The car followed, the driver leaving no room for what Liz considered the barest margin of safety. She wondered if Delhi offered anything remotely resembling safe spaces.

Traffic oozed on. Taxis, cars, buses, trucks and swarms of orange-and-green motorized rickshaws lurched left and right to speed their trips by a second here, a second there. Their progress paled as measured against streams of pedestrians. Men dressed in long-sleeved shirts despite the heat and carrying briefcases, and women in midriff-baring saris of brilliant reds, blues, yellows and greens maneuvered with and against the traffic. Unlike the homeless cows left unmolested as objects of Hindu veneration, they strode with visible purpose towards their bus and metro stops.

Liz turned her attention to the side of the road where women squatted over charcoal braziers and chatted while children played or slept. She bit her lips.

Mel shook his head. He'd been briefed on Indian street life before the trip but still found it alarming.

As if he had eyes in the back of his head—or had managed a glance in the rear-view mirror—Janash said, "One must understand that India is a very complex country just as every individual human being is a complex organism."

Mel reproached himself. Who was he to pass judgment on a culture so old? Moreover, only he and Liz seemed out of sorts. "In a way, this reminds me of the Brits," he said, trying to make light of the situation. "How you drive on the other side of the road."

Janash turned again and arched his eyebrows. "With all due respect, sir, hardly the *other* side. Far more people live in India than in the U.S. A billion-three, I believe it is now." A smile lit his tea-colored face. "I myself have only two children. Boys. Have you children?"

Liz took a breath. "A son."

"*Had*," Mel corrected. An accountant, he insisted that any inventory of his life arrive at an accurate sum rather than one distorted by fantasy or regret.

"I am so sorry," Janash said. He swiveled back to face the road.

Liz imagined Janash searching for additional words to supplement his brief condolence. As to Mel, she could not understand his compulsion to mention Paul's death to every stranger he encountered. Granted, after ten years, fond memories remained. But despite weekly therapy sessions, so did torments and recriminations. Deflecting the possibility of further inquiry, she asked Janash, "Have you been to America?"

"Sadly, no," Janash replied. "One day, I hope. But I *have* been to Argentina. I worked as a translator. I speak Spanish. Here in Delhi, I have many Spanish-speaking clients."

The driver found a miniscule opening, sped up, swerved then halted abruptly. Nonplussed, he resumed inching forward.

Mel gripped his daypack, a boundary marker of sorts squatting on the seat between Liz and him. He had no regrets about coming to India. Uncharacteristically for a man who valued routine and the familiar, he'd suggested the trip to break out of the rut common to any marriage of thirty-two years. Liz, opposed to the petty tyrannies inherent in tour groups, consented when Mel, again contradicting his nature, promised they would go it alone. Of course, a travel-agent friend would plan their itinerary, book their flights and hotels, and secure trustworthy English-speaking guides.

Now, Mel wondered if they'd overextended themselves. Perhaps, following the sixteen-hour flight from San Francisco to Abu Dhabi and the four-hour hop to Delhi, they should have rested this day, their first in-country. Not that he had a complaint beyond the traffic and the vehicle exhaust that obliterated the anticipated aromas of exotic flowers and spices. Since dawn, they'd added one sight after another to their joint memory the way a lepidopterist collects butterflies: the Qutb Minar, a 237-foot sandstone tower built at the end of the twelfth century, Humayun's Tomb, a pedicab jaunt through the ancient Chandni Chowk market, and a ride past New Delhi's presidential palace and British-designed parliament building. They'd even managed a brief, sweaty stroll along the Rajpath to the India Gate memorializing Indian soldiers killed during and after World War One.

Meanwhile, it made sense to enjoy the symbols of gaiety anticipating Diwali. Streams of lights suggesting waterfalls dangled over the sides of buildings. Buses and trucks displayed vivid colors complementing the women's saris. Certainly, their spirits would rise when they arrived at their sleek, luxurious hotel—a welcome bridge between cultures.

"I was thinking," Mel said. "We should shower, have dinner and get to bed early. See if those pills kick in. Big day tomorrow, the train to Agra and all."

Liz offered her own perspective in a voice barely audible. "Everything is so different." She made no effort to continue. The time change having kept them awake most of the previous night, they'd eaten breakfast in silence and barely spoken since. Let Janash carry the conversation.

Yielding chatter to Janash, however, went beyond fatigue. While Mel and Liz presented a cordial front following Paul's death, silence quickly became their new normal. This, as opposed to their early years when Liz's liveliness overcame Mel's introversion so that they shared experiences and dreams with torrents of words and formed a couple rarely seen apart. Pre-Brangelina, friends called them Melizabeth. Post-Paul, the remains of their social circle viewed their silences with regret and discomfort.

"Just ahead," said Janash.

The car approached a gray wall, slowed then stopped at a ten-foot-high gate constructed of metal plates painted black. Three men in gray uniforms, assault rifles slung over their shoulders, stepped forward. Another poked a long-handled device with mirror on one end beneath the car.

"For explosives," said Janash.

Liz gasped.

"I think guards made the same search last night when we got in from the airport," said Mel. "I'm sure it's just routine."

"It's not routine in America," Liz said.

"We're not *in* America," said Mel.

"How can you be so calm?" she asked, the pitch of her voice rising. "So calm and resigned to everything?"

"Everything?"

"You know damn well what I mean."

The guard withdrew the mirror.

Liz released a weary sigh.

Two other guards opened the gate. A third saluted.

As the car rolled into the courtyard, Liz's right hand fell over her heart. "Oh, my," she murmured.

Two police vehicles stood to the left of the hotel's covered entry.

A young, light-complexioned man in a blue blazer accompanied by an older, heavy-set woman in a blue-and-green sari greeted them, palms pressed together, fingers pointing skyward. The man opened the left-side passenger door.

Mel stepped out and offered Liz his hand.

She ignored it.

Roses, zinnias, marigolds and wave petunias produced fragrances almost dizzying. The heat seemed even more intense.

Janash wandered off.

Looking at the young man, Liz observed that some Indians weren't nearly as dark as Janash or the woman while others were even darker.

"Welcome back. I hope your day was a pleasant one," the young man said in barely accented English suggesting college, perhaps even high school, in the States.

Liz bit her lip. The young man reminded her of Paul.

The woman, identified by her name tag as the hotel manager, stepped forward. She appeared to be the only member of the staff not in her twenties. Again, she placed her hands in front of her chest. "*Namaste*," she said.

Mel and Liz returned the traditional Hindu greeting.

The woman acknowledged the puzzlement on their faces. "We've had a little fuss," she said. "Not to worry."

"Fuss?" Liz asked.

"At any rate, I am so glad you have returned at this hour," she continued, attempting to deflect Liz's anxiety. "We are offering free cocktails in the bar. Our Manhattans are the finest in India. And of course, should there be anything you require—" She presented a business card with two hands.

Mel thought only the Japanese did that, but what did he know? They'd never been to Japan.

The woman stepped away to greet more guests.

Janash reappeared. "Please. Let us go inside."

In the lobby, Liz embraced the cool air then froze.

An armed guard stood near the front desk.

Mel took her arm.

Believing she had every right to be alarmed and not patronized, she shook it off.

A young woman offered bottles of water.

"This so-called fuss," Liz said to Janash. "Obviously, the manager didn't want to tell us anything. But police cars? And those men?"

"Security guards," said Janash. "Standard at five-star hotels. There were guards last night when you arrived."

"India," said Mel, "doesn't strike me as a country where a lot of bad stuff goes on."

Janash took a water bottle from his daypack. "I do not say there is crime in India, but I do not say there is none. Really, you should not be concerned."

"But I *am* concerned," said Liz.

Janash studied the white marble tiles beneath his feet. "I spoke with one of the police," he said in a near-whisper. "It seems there was an incident. A woman. A guest. It appears she— It appears she left her door open while she was changing shoes or something like that, and someone—"

"We should go to another hotel," Liz said. "You can find us one. Or the manager can."

Mel placed a hand on her shoulder.

Liz shook it off.

"What are the odds," Mel countered, "something like this happens again tonight? I mean, with all these security people and police? And tomorrow morning, we're taking the train to Agra."

"Early," said Janash. "We should leave the hotel at six. Traffic."

Reconciling herself to the probability that she'd sleep no better at another hotel and too drained to argue, Liz nodded.

"So then," said Janash, "I will meet you here in the lobby tomorrow morning. The hotel puts out a continental breakfast for early risers beginning at five-thirty. And as you are traveling first-class, you will enjoy a full breakfast on the train."

"And you?" Liz asked.

"I will be in second class. My wife will prepare a meal for me. Most important, tomorrow will be a wonderful day. We will visit the Red Fort and then, when the afternoon light makes it sparkle, the Taj Mahal."

"And *this* afternoon, free cocktails," Mel said, having applied to the situation a brief cost-benefit analysis.

Janash raised his hands. "*Namaste.* Sleep well."

"*Namaste*," Mel and Liz returned.

As Janash stepped outside, Liz turned to Mel. "If that were me and not that poor woman in her room, you would have protected me, wouldn't you?"

"Oh, my god," Liz shrieked the next afternoon even before the bellman finished showing them their hotel room. She ran to the large window. "We have a view of the Taj Mahal."

"That's what we paid for," said Mel.

Liz again considered the possibility that the Taj Mahal, a symbol of enduring love, might rekindle the flame in their marriage.

Mel calculated the more mundane prospect of bringing their emotional accounts into more of a balance.

Both accepted that the visit would be bittersweet. As a child, Paul once decided that he wanted to be an architect and design beautiful buildings. He constructed a model of the Taj Mahal out of sugar cubes and cardboard. It was graceless, but being good and loving parents, they praised him. He'd made the effort. Not long after, that ambition, like so many others, melted away amid countless temper tantrums and schoolyard fights, three arrests, four therapists and two stays at rehab.

Liz focused her attention on the marvel they'd come so far to see. Even from a distance, its white marble façade glistened.

The bellman, young, gracious and fluent in American English, asked, "May I be of further assistance, sir?"

Mel shook his head and slipped two 200-rupee notes into the bellman's hand. After the door closed, he opened his daypack, withdrew binoculars and joined Liz at the window. "Well, look at that," he said.

"At what?" she said without turning.

"Scaffolding. There's scaffolding or something covering one of the towers."

"Minarets. They're called minarets."

"I knew they were doing some work, but I thought they'd have it down by now. The scaffolding."

"It's still beautiful," she said.

Mel handed the binoculars to Liz. "I hoped everything would be perfect."

Thirty minutes later and slathered in sunscreen, Liz and Mel met Janash in the lobby. A slender young woman in an orange sari—all the staff were trim, good looking and unfailingly attentive—presented bottles of water. Before going out into the courtyard, baking in the afternoon heat, they put on wide-brimmed hats. Janash led them to a motorized cart. The driver's beard was as white as his turban.

"Following a brief ride, we will enter the gardens," Janash said. "They are most impressive. As we walk, I will tell you about Shah Jahan and his love for his second wife, Mumtaz Mahal. She died at the age of thirty-eight giving birth to their fourteenth child. Fourteen. Can you imagine? The building you will see is actually her mausoleum."

Inside the marble-and-red-limestone southern gateway, one hundred feet high, a walkway led across a broad lawn. To their right shimmered a long pool of blue water. In all directions, visitors strolled, chatted, took photos. Most were Indians—families of two and three generations, couples and school groups enjoying the Diwali holiday.

Liz walked forward, her gaze fixed. She remembered a friend's remark that no matter how the Taj Mahal appeared in photographs or videos, it was even more beautiful in person. Now she understood.

Mel experienced mild disappointment.

Liz stopped and took photos of two Indian grandparents holding the hands of their granddaughter—perhaps three—wearing a pink dress with neck, sleeves and hem edged in silver.

A young Indian couple held up an iPhone. In perfect English, the woman asked if Liz and Mel would pose with them.

Following post-selfie smiles and handshakes, Janash led them to a marble bench where a dozen people stood in line. "Perhaps you would like me to take your photo here?"

"This is a very nice spot for a picture," Liz said.

"Oh, yes," said Janash, his face radiating pride. "This bench is quite famous."

"Famous?"

"Princess Diana sat here on her visit in 1992. Thus, it is known as Diana's Bench."

When they sat, Liz handed Janash her phone.

Janash motioned them to move closer together.

They inched towards each other.

"Just a little more," he said.

They held their positions.

Janash took several pictures. "You will treasure this forever," he said.

Mel and Liz joined him to study the results. "Beautiful," she said.

Mel nodded his assent, although he noticed that their smiles seemed forced.

Janash motioned them away from the bench and extended an arm towards the Taj Mahal. "From here, you can explore by yourselves and, of course, go inside. The tombs for Mumtaz Mahal and Shah Jahan, who died thirty-five years after his wife, are very beautiful. But things are not always as they seem. The tombs are symbolic. Following Muslim law, the Shah and his wife are buried beneath the main chamber in a plain crypt. After, you can walk around the building and look out over the river. It is called the Yamuna. It rises in the foothills of the Himalayas and flows into the Ganges. The Hindu goddess of the river, Yami, is the sister of the god of death."

Liz gasped. "Is it clean?" She raised a hand to her mouth. "Is it rude of me to ask?"

"No, it is not rude. And no, the Yamuna is not. But it is even worse in Delhi and downriver from there. I am ashamed—"

"So let's drop it," Mel said.

Janash managed a pained grin. "At any rate," he said, "you must now leave your water with me, and I will meet you back at the entry. Shall we say, one hour?"

At the foot of the steps, Liz and Mel slipped plastic coverings over their shoes, ascended the steps and went inside. Conjoined with the steady flow of visitors, they admired the main chamber. The ceremonial tombs stood on raised platforms and displayed inlays of semi-precious stones depicting life-affirming vines, fruits and flowers. Keeping pace with the crowd, they exited the rear of the building and emerged onto the marble terrace overlooking the river.

"I've never thought about the back side of the Taj Mahal," Liz said. "Very nice but not as striking." She stared out at the river. "I never even knew this river was here. What did Janash call it?"

"The Yamuna, I think. You don't see it in photos. They only show you the front."

"What people want to see, I suppose."

Mel grimaced. Shah Jahan had built a timeless symbol of love, yet now that they'd seen the empty tombs and walked out back, the Taj Mahal struck him as an illusion. Like marriage. When two people committed to a life together, they envisioned building their own emotional Taj Mahal. But all the glittering possibilities amounted to nothing more than a façade. Time, dispassionate and relentless, thrust them into the bowels of the life they constructed—dark, soul-chilling rooms hollowed out each day from disappointments unforeseen and inevitable.

A young Indian man wearing a lime-green shirt buttoned at the wrists approached. "Excuse me," he said He gestured towards a young woman in a purple and gold sari, and two small children—a boy and a girl—then raised a selfie stick. "Would you mind having your picture taken with us? And that is your wife? Would she mind?"

Mel smiled. He enjoyed being considered exotic.

Liz joined them. "Your children are beautiful," she said. "Your son, he's six?"

"Seven," said the boy, proud of his proficiency in English.

"And your daughter? I'd say four."

The girl nodded then stared at her pink sandals. They revealed toenails painted a brilliant vermilion.

"You must have children of your own," the woman said.

Liz swallowed. It was that perfectly innocent comment that, after the first year, pushed her towards solitary pursuits like gardening, reading and long walks on the beach.

"We had a son," Mel answered, risking Liz's displeasure. Still, he preferred a moment of pain now followed by the predictable reproach to constantly denying a past that clung to them like their skin.

Liz sighed in resignation.

The father's face radiated awkwardness.

"He was twenty," Mel said.

The couple looked down at their son. "I am so terribly sorry," the man said. Then, in the manner of people who live in more crowded and intimate circumstances than most Americans—or perhaps because Mel might offer a measure of wisdom that might serve to protect his own children—he asked, "Did he take ill?"

"No, an accident," Mel answered. Fearing he'd gone too far, he said, "Thank you," as if he'd just concluded a small business transaction and had an appointment to keep. He regretted lacking the courage to say, *Take ill? I wish. No, Paul had over twice the legal limit of alcohol in his blood and all these drugs when he took this curve on a two-lane road up in the wine country at ninety miles an hour—that's something like a hundred thirty-five kilometers—and the police called at four in the morning.*

The Indian couple's eyes expressed the puzzled sadness of parents who, while acknowledging another's loss, could not comprehend its soul-crushing nature. Taking their children by the hand, they uttered hushed goodbyes and walked off towards the nearby mosque.

Like polished ballroom dancers, Mel and Liz spun in unison and stared out at the Yamuna. Each pictured the collapsed remains of a sugar cube-and-cardboard Taj Mahal abandoned to a shelf in their garage.

Big Truth

WHAT ARE THE odds four alter kakers sunning themselves at a baseball game get into a fistfight?

The ruckus began with Jeffrey, who wore his frail heart on the sleeve of the blue Cubs jersey he flaunted at Dodger Stadium on the third day of a road-trip reunion. Jeffrey, Gary, Arnie and I hadn't been a foursome since maybe our sophomore year in college fifty years earlier. Given Jeffrey's condition, he was the last one you'd expect to drag us to the brink. Unless you knew his contempt for restraint. Which we did.

Agitated when the Dodgers' leadoff hitter approached home plate after the Cubs stranded two runners in the top of the first, Jeffrey croaked, "Fuck you! Fuck the Dodgers! Fuck L.A.!"

Arnie, on Jeffrey's right, shouted "Jesus!" I, stuck on Jeffrey's left, choked on my Dodger dog. Arnie and I, residents of the Bay Area where the Giants-Dodgers rivalry is palpable, had warned Jeffrey it would be judicious to keep a damper on his enthusiasm.

Gary, the only one of us who'd stayed in New York, sat on my left. As in San Diego and Anaheim, he'd commandeered the aisle seat and maintained his distance from Arnie. Grimacing with an air of theatricality, he raised his hand to his chest as if Jeffrey had pushed his recurring heartburn over the top. At each game, Jeffrey bought the first round of beer and insisted it be accompanied by hotdogs. Dropping his hand, Gary looked up. "The color of that sky," he said, only partly to me. "Diebenkorn. Hockney. They knew. The sky in California? Money."

The Dodger hitter halted outside the batter's box, stretched his neck, readjusted his batting gloves and dropped a hand to his crotch.

Jeffrey picked up his theme. "Fuck L.A.! Fuck L.A.! Fuck L.A.!"

His level of antagonism overcame the frailty of his voice, leaving me as much puzzled as disturbed. Displays of undisciplined passion may be common in youth, but that train left the station long ago. Over drinks, maybe at our first dinner, possibly in the car, Gary, Arnie and I acknowledged our diminished interest in baseball, although the four of us made up the starting infield on one of Queens' best high school teams.

Unsure as to how far Jeffrey's rant carried, I found a measure of comfort in sitting among several dozen Cubs fans wearing matching blue or white jerseys. Men, women and kids who also disdained the Dodgers but acquiesced to the rules of decorum and hopefully offered us some measure of protection.

The hitter lined a fastball over the leaping Cubs shortstop—Jeffrey's position. Rounding first base, where I played, the hitter pointed both index fingers skyward then retreated to the bag. I wondered if God kept me from hitting .300 our senior year.

As the cheers died down, a couple of Dodger fans several rows behind us expressed their delight by taking umbrage at Jeffrey's remarks. "Fuck *you*! Fuck the *Cubs*. Fuck *Chicago*!" Their voices suggested each had at least forty years on us accompanied by sufficient muscle tone to make Jeffrey think better of responding.

As Jeffrey smoldered, Arnie shrank in his seat. Gary stared at the sky.

I lowered my eyes and examined the remains of my Dodger dog as if I was poring over yesterday's box score. I gave thought to turning around to see who might pose a threat to four guys approaching geezerhood—though more likely we'd arrived. I concluded that my curiosity might be misinterpreted as incitement.

Jeffrey slowly unfolded from his seat until he stood stooped like a wilted flower. His left hand—papery skin, protruding veins, liver spots and a wedding band in need of downsizing—trembled as he clutched the armrest between us.

I reached up and rested my hand lightly on his shoulder. Any pressure might have broken something.

"Fuck you!" a Dodger fan bellowed several rows behind us. I imagined a bearded, beer-bellied 250-pounder with biceps the size of bowling balls.

Jeffrey shot him a bony finger.

The antagonist, although slow on the uptake, evidently discerned Jeffrey's situation and refrained from further comment.

Jeffrey collapsed into his seat.

The Dodgers' number-two hitter stepped in. The Cubs' pitcher shook off his catcher, checked the runner, shook off his catcher again and stepped off the rubber. The hitter stepped out of the box. Baseball shuns any restriction imposed by time, which taunts every other aspect of our lives.

"Sorry," I called out without turning around. I hoped the fans around us, whichever team they rooted for, would grant Jeffrey forgiveness.

Arnie made his own attempt at reconciliation by whispering something to the woman next to him, a Cubs fan with rosy cheeks and a generous Midwestern girth. I couldn't make out her answer, but Arnie nodded then stared out towards the hills beyond the centerfield bleachers to signify their understanding.

Gary nudged my arm to draw my attention then ambled up the aisle. He handed a dollar bill to a broad-shouldered man wearing a white Dodgers tee-shirt and blue Dodgers cap, worn backwards in a display of eternal adolescence. No beard. Beer belly? Hard to say. I imagined he was the Dodger fan at odds with Jeffrey's sentiments.

"That's a fuckin' hundred, dude!" he said.

Gary smiled, held up his phone and bounded up the steps to the concourse. Business was business. More accurately, art was business.

Believing a confrontation had been avoided, I turned to Jeffrey. "What the hell was that about?"

He winked. "Who doesn't hate the Dodgers?"

I swept my left hand across the filled stadium.

"Anyway, you don't know how much I suffered until the Cubs finally won it all. Now, I can die in peace."

His nonchalance got the better of me. "You could have died right here, asshole," I said. As kids, we hurled that and other epithets at each other with great frequency, usually with no offense taken, occasionally countered with an "Up yours!" or, if the wound went deep enough, a shove or even a punch. I regretted saying it, but the word had flown from my mouth like an arrow discharged from a bow, beyond recall.

In a gesture of noblesse oblige, Jeffrey lifted his beer to his lips. His doctor prohibited alcohol.

I patted his knee. Despite our serious differences some years back, I gave Jeffrey credit. He still had balls. For starters, he was here. When the four of us met at our hotel in San Diego, he laughed at the shock our faces expressed when we saw how thin and pallid he was. He assured us he'd live to a hundred. I'd spoken with his wife before the trip. She said three to six months.

Why Jeffrey chose this trip for his last hurrah, I have no idea. As he told it, his life had been the stuff of novels and movies. He could have taken his wife someplace far-removed and exotic, and while his doctor would have protested, Jeffrey wouldn't have cared. For that matter, his doctor wasn't thrilled about his leaving Chicago. But Jeffrey wanted to spend several days in July touring ballparks in California with Gary, Arnie and me. He planned the itinerary. And since he loved trains, the next morning we'd take the Coast Starlight up to San Jose then Caltrain to San Francisco.

I inclined towards Thomas Wolfe's admonition that you can't go home again, but what could I do? Jeffrey had little time left. In a way, so did I.

Years earlier, after retiring from banking—the marketing side, not financial stuff—I went back to writing short stories. When my wife Evelyn's cancer upshifted to rapid decline, writing morphed into therapy. It may sound selfish—or more likely the way writers are—but her suffering created an opportunity to take my fiction to a deeper level. I wouldn't emerge as a new Malamud, Doctorow, Heller or Roth, but I'd do a better job of appraising the life I'd experienced.

I amassed rejections the way philatelists collect stamps. Mule-stubborn, I embarked on a novel. Before long, I felt like an engineer shuttling a train from one track to another, knowing his destination but baffled as to how to get there. I concluded that telling a story that throws some weight involves more than stringing words together. You have to reveal some Big Truth that explains why we're born, why we die and why we fuck up in between. The problem is, Big Truth teases you like one of those old-time burlesque strippers who removes her bra only to reveal nipples covered with pasties. Then, while your hunger peaks for a glimpse of that last tantalizing bit of flesh, she retreats behind the curtain.

Jeffrey? I empathized. But I really came along hoping that the trip would give my creative juices a kick in the ass.

The next morning, we slumped in Goliath-size leather armchairs filling Union Station's Spanish Colonial/Art Deco waiting room—painted beamed ceilings, soaring arched windows, floors of marble and tile. Our ten a.m. departure was listed as delayed. Exhausted by dissecting careers, wives, kids, travels and, yes, baseball—truth and lies mixed like assorted nuts in a holiday gift pack—we turned inward like mourners at a funeral. Our collective silence sent a mental text: *We've been getting too close.*

Jeffrey interrupted what doubtless passed to the few other waiting passengers as tranquil reflection. "Eleven-oh-eight."

Arnie looked up. "Meaning what?"

"That's when we'll leave."

Gary and I turned to Jeffrey.

"I didn't hear any announcement," Arnie said.

Jeffrey revealed a Cheshire-cat smile.

Gary shook his head. "We should have flown," he said, refusing to take the bait involving Jeffrey's supposed sixth sense. "A whole day from L.A. to Frisco? My assistant in New York can charter us a plane."

She could. According to *Forbes*, Garrett White, the iconic painter and sculptor, boasted assets pushing $200 million. The figure seemed even more impressive considering he'd gone through four divorces. The last time I saw him, he was struggling to pay college tuition as Gary Weisbrod.

"What's the rush?" Jeffrey asked. "Where do you think we're going?"

"How about San Francisco?" Arnie said.

"And after that?" Jeffrey replied.

We retreated into our disparate thoughts.

Half an hour later, a disembodied voice summoned us to our train. We rose stiffly like pensioners rocking on the buckling porch of a dilapidated Borscht Belt hotel answering the call to dinner. Our faces betrayed further proof of decline.

Gary's revealed attempts to duplicate the timelessness Michelangelo chiseled into David. "Marty Cohen," he boasted our first night together. "Best plastic surgeon in Manhattan." His hair, as full as in high school, gleamed Photoshopped-silver. "Alan Goldfarb," he informed us.

Arnie and I had been content to go with nature's flow. Still, when we met at SFO, we startled. In addition to broader waists, we sported creases in our foreheads, folds in our cheeks and turkey wattles staking out territorial claims beneath our jaws. Our thinning hair had gone gray. But more than our appearance unnerved us. Half a lifetime had passed since we reconnected in San Francisco, me settling in the city, he across the Golden Gate Bridge in Sausalito. Things hadn't gone as I'd hoped, which I admit translated into a measure of justice. Although in allied professions, we avoided each other.

Jeffrey stunned us. Splotches of gray stubble erupted in no discernable pattern from a speckled scalp the texture of wrinkled parchment. His sunken cheeks and skeletal body made Mick Jagger look like the old body builder Charles Atlas.

"I'll take your suitcase," Arnie offered.

Jeffrey shook his head.

Arnie frowned.

Gary shrugged.

Resigned to Jeffrey's determination to pull his weight, I led a slow procession to our train.

Onboard, we stowed our bags in the overhead racks. That task beyond Jeffrey, he accepted Arnie's assistance.

Gary's bag wouldn't fit.

A conductor advised he'd find space downstairs by the bathrooms.

"This is Louis Vuitton, special edition," Gary protested. He turned to us and stage whispered, "Not that I can't buy them by the dozen."

The conductor cocked his head.

Gary took the bag downstairs.

We gave Jeffrey the window seat on the left side so he could admire the Pacific on the trip north.

Gary, who claimed the seat next to him, returned and adjusted Jeffrey's footrest. Then he studied the newest photo of Garrett White in *Vanity*

Fair. Pleased with the image he'd shown us every day, he glanced around at the car's dozen or so fellow passengers. "Jesus, it's like being shut up with those Okies from *The Grapes of Wrath*."

I feared Dodger Stadium all over again, only maybe more dangerous without a Praetorian guard of Cubs fans.

The train lurched forward without incident.

I checked my watch. "Eleven-oh-eight."

Jeffrey smiled.

Arnie, in the window seat to my right, grimaced. "Naturally we're leaving late. This is Amtrak."

"It's not about leaving late," Jeffrey said. "It's the time we're leaving. Down to the minute like I said in the waiting room."

In junior high, Jeffrey positioned himself as the outlier among us, always boasting of psychic powers and being in tune with alternate realities. We laughed. In high school, we attributed his claims to pot and whatever other drugs he was doing that we weren't. But on that first night in San Diego, he pinky swore that after Harvard Law, he went to San Francisco to work for a major law firm handling Silicon Valley clients. A few years later, he underwent an out-of-body experience, divorced and decamped for an ashram in India. Spiritually purified, he went to Chicago to help a law-school buddy build his estate-planning practice, found a new wife then launched a successful practice of his own. That last accomplishment brought us together again. Unfortunately.

The train slithered past factories and warehouses noted only for featureless gray walls—a Southern California scene movies and TV show only when they involve drug dealing or murder. The conductor approached to check our seat cards.

Jeffrey rummaged through the pockets in his slacks. "I know I have it," he said. His head dropped like a puppet with its strings cut.

My breath caught.

He raised his chin, reached into his shirt pocket and extracted the card. It's weight seemed to resist his effort.

The conductor moved towards the back of the car.

Gary held up *Vanity Fair*. "Philistines!" he blurted out. "I gave the fucking writer two hours of my valuable time—*two*—and they print this shit?"

"You mean you never read the story until now?" Arnie asked.

Gary ignored him. "Not that Garrett White's prices won't shoot up anyway. Only one thing counts in the art world. Exposure."

I glanced at Arnie for corroboration. He'd chucked a major career in advertising to paint, but his status came nowhere near Gary's—as Gary remarked more than once.

Arnie's grunt put a full stop to what passed as our conversation.

At one-thirty, we went to the dining car and settled into a booth with red plastic seats and a white tablecloth of similar chemical composition. The waiter took our drink orders then offered his sympathies. Lunch was down to roast chicken or hamburgers, either with potato chips. We could, however, start with salad, and he'd bring rolls. Only a few pieces remained of chocolate lava cake—they hadn't been provided enough—so he could take that order now.

Every other subject exhausted, we bitched about breakfast. Jeffrey insisted we get to Union Station early to eat at its restaurant. We found it closed. An Amtrak employee mentioned a place not far in an underground mall across from City Hall. Gary called a car. The menu consisted of breakfast burritos. Just breakfast burritos. They weren't especially tasty. How do you screw up a breakfast burrito?

The waiter returned with our drinks. Gary ordered chicken, the rest of us burgers.

Jeffrey fumbled with a can of Diet Coke.

I lifted his hand—it felt like bone wrapped in paper—and popped the top.

Jeffrey tried to pour. Soda spilled over the side of the plastic cup.

Arnie finished the job.

Gary twirled his Chardonnay and eyed Jeffrey. "All those chemicals can't be good for someone in your condition."

Jeffrey grinned. "*Nothing's* good for someone in my condition."

Nervous chuckles nudged the tension towards the window-end of the table to share space with the salt, pepper, sugar, ketchup, mustard and paper napkins.

Gary smirked.

"What?" Jeffrey asked.

"Remember Diane Rubin?"

We all smirked. Diane Rubin represented the wet dream of every boy at Forest Hills High. After Christmas vacation our junior year, Gary announced he'd screwed her. The news left me thrilled but also crestfallen. We saw ourselves as brothers, but sex left every man for himself. Gary had scored. I was still struggling.

"Diane's been collecting me for years," Gary said. They hooked up after she divorced the CEO of a restaurant chain then buried some Park Avenue surgeon. "Her favorite piece is in her bedroom."

Jeffrey smiled. "Diane was outside the principal's office that afternoon Officer Taylor—"

"Tyler," I cut in. "The school cop was Tyler." If we were going to bring up old memories, I thought we should strive for a reasonable level of accuracy.

Jeffrey nodded. "Tyler takes us to Dr. Brennan's office because someone snitched that we smoked pot at the baseball field after we beat Van Buren."

"Bayside," I said.

"Not Newtown?" Arnie asked.

"Unless it was Jamaica," I said.

Jeffrey attempted to shrug. "Anyway, there's Diane—"

"No, I remember now," Gary said. "Emily Horowitz. Long brown hair. Big zits but big tits."

Arnie shook his head. "Linda McMullen."

The waiter brought our salads—iceberg lettuce brown at the edges, a bit of radish and a slice of tomato the color and texture of a sun-faded plastic toy.

Gary's eyes shot open. "Jesus, they wouldn't serve this at McDonald's."

Arnie stared at Gary. "How do *you* know what they serve at McDonald's?"

Gary sighed. "Don't be so fucking literal."

I held a packet of vinaigrette dressing up to Jeffrey.

"Not gonna hurt *me*," he said.

I poured half onto Jeffrey's salad, the rest onto mine.

Arnie started laughing. "Brennan was pissed, especially at Gary."

Although it seemed a physical impossibility, a furrow gouged itself across Gary's forehead. "Fuck you!" he said.

Gary bought pot before the game, although scoring weed was Jeffrey's job. A kid named Chuck Berkowitz, who wanted to be part of our tight-knit group and who we rejected simply because we could, snitched. Dr. Brennan summoned our parents. Drinkers and smokers, they objected to any drug with which they lacked familiarity. Word came down from on high. Every morning before school for the rest of the semester, we cleared the sidewalk on 110th Street of old newspapers, candy bar wrappers, cigarette butts and Trojan wrappers. Occasionally, used Trojans. Lunch periods, we collected dirty trays, plates and utensils. Still, we played baseball. Rumor had it Dr. Brennan made a hefty wager with half-a-dozen principals on who would win the Queens championship. We lost in the finals and left the field crestfallen but not totally.

We were never sure if that was why Brennan also barred Gary from graduation.

"Not that I gave a shit about wearing a cap and gown in the Queens College gym," Gary said.

"You didn't miss anything," said Arnie.

Gary raised his fork and impaled his tomato like a small boy sticking a pin in a spider. "I didn't miss anything? Fucking Brennan knew someone at Pratt and had my scholarship pulled. I had to go part-time and work at an art-supply store. My dad took a night job driving a cab. Around midnight one night, he's coming home from the garage and some fucking drunk T-bones him."

Remembering that Mr. Weisbrod had been killed but not knowing he was driving a cab—and why—we stared into our salads.

After an awkward minute, I asked, "Did you blame yourself? I mean, for telling that schmuck Berkowitz about the pot?"

Gary raised a fist.

Jeffrey's hand floated onto my arm like a fallen leaf. "I always thought *you* told Berkowitz, Steve."

I took a deep breath and exhaled slowly. I hit critical mass anyway. "Where the fuck did you come up with *that*, asshole?"

Jeffrey rocked back in his seat.

I couldn't believe what I'd said to a dying man—again—although an outburst Jeffrey's way was long overdue.

Gary fondled his wine. "So, I didn't tell Berkowitz and Steve didn't. Then who?"

Arnie glared at Gary. "Really? Not *you*? The guy always bragging about breaking the rules and screwing the Man? The Man who buys that crap you call art?"

Gary thrust a finger towards Arnie's nose. "You should have settled for winning awards selling pizza and tampons. You're not the only failed artist who wishes he was Garrett White."

Arnie's cheeks turned an orange-red suggesting our untouched tomatoes. "Failed? That beats stealing."

I envisioned myself having lit a match near a powder keg—as clichéd an image as there is and maybe one of the reasons my writing had gone nowhere. Then I perked up. Somewhere in all this mess, I sensed Big Truth.

"Stealing?" Gary asked. He rolled his eyes.

"Painting my mountain outside Tucson?" Arnie said.

Gary puffed up like a blowfish bluffing a predator. "And Constable shouldn't have painted the English countryside because Turner did?"

"Painting it *pink*?"

The story shot out of Arnie like metal shards from one of those improvised explosive devices they targeted our troops with in Afghanistan and Iraq. A few years back, Arnie showed Gary studies of this mountain in Arizona, all in shades of pink. Gary laughed. No major gallery would accept paintings in which pink was the dominant color.

"Then you fuck me over," Arnie said in a stage whisper. "You do a whole show of *my* mountain in every shade of pink imaginable."

Gary's face took on a yoga-like calm. "For ninety-nine-point-nine percent of artists? Pink won't fly. Garrett White creates a market because he's Garrett White."

Arnie's jaw dropped like that of a boxer buckled by a hard right, his only defense against a knockout punch to wrap up his opponent's arms. Then his eyes gleamed. "Did you guys know Steve was engaged to Joyce?"

I took a long, slow sip from my beer—my own version of clinching an opponent.

Gary scratched his head. "Joyce your *sister?*"

Arnie nodded.

Jeffrey stared.

"Joyce who went into fucking therapy," Arnie said.

That Joyce had taken things *that* badly was news to me since I took off for San Francisco less than a week after breaking our engagement. There'd been someone else, but I'd broken off with her, too. And why would a woman want to marry a man who didn't love her? The revelation embarrassed me but left me hopeful. Big Truth hovered.

Jeffrey paled, if that was possible, and took three quick, shallow breaths.

"You okay?" Gary asked.

Jeffrey nodded.

I waited for Arnie to say I was as big an asshole as Gary.

He turned towards the window.

What passed for Jeffrey's color returned. "Really, Steve, I always thought more of you than that," he said.

It hit me that the four of us carried way more baggage than what we'd lugged aboard. I preferred keeping mine locked, but Arnie had pried it open. "So how about what you did to Evelyn?" I asked Jeffrey.

Jeffrey stared as if I was a child who'd confused a mundane parental quarrel for a sign of imminent divorce.

The waiter interrupted us with four lava cakes and coffee.

I figured our attention would shift to dessert. No such luck.

After picking at his cake, not quite thawed, Arnie dropped his fork and looked at me. "So this thing with Jeffrey and Evelyn?"

I cursed myself for having been foolish enough to give away something I didn't want to deal with. Not here, anyway. Not now. I shook my head.

Jeffrey, rejecting our offers to open a packet of creamer, said, "Just routine legal stuff."

I flashed on a possible Big Truth: The gravitational force of self-righteousness rivals the Sun's. "It started with Norman, Evelyn's brother," I said.

Jeffrey waved me off. "Sam would have understood."

Sam, my father-in-law, had been a macher in Chicago real estate. When he wanted to update his estate plan, a business associate suggested Jeffrey. Jeffrey found out I was Sam's son-in-law and mentioned our childhood connection but never called me. Not that after Sam told me about the coincidence, I called Jeffrey. Maybe I'd latched onto another Big Truth: People who create new identities go to great lengths to protect them.

Jeffrey set up several complicated trusts. The assets were supposed to go to Norman and Evelyn fifty-fifty, but being old school, Sam named Norman sole executor, even though he'd long labeled Norman a fuck-up. After their folks died, Norman tried to control the assets and dole out money to Evelyn like she was his daughter receiving an allowance. We hired a lawyer in San Francisco, but Evelyn feared confrontation, and given different state laws, we failed to get an agreement. Our lawyer suggested an attorney she knew in Chicago—a shark. He convinced Evelyn that blood can be thinner than water. She should threaten to take Norman to court and have him removed as executor. They settled.

Jeffrey rested his hand on mine. It felt cucumber cool while my cheeks burned jalapeño hot.

I tried visualizing a mountain stream, trees swaying in the breeze, birds flitting from branch to branch. The water dried up, the trees toppled, the birds flew off.

The waiter returned with more coffee.

Jeffrey made a writing motion.

Arnie yanked the bill from Jeffrey's hand. "I don't want to leave anything on the table except this lava cake." He turned to Gary. "I told Chuck Berkowitz because I was pissed about you screwing Diane Rubin."

Gary attempted to raise an eyebrow. "Putz!"

Back in our car, *Lord of the Flies* sat on my lap as I stared out the window.

North of San Luis Obispo, the tracks bent right near ninety degrees. I had complete views of both the locomotive up front and the car at the rear where the old-time caboose used to go. The train brought to mind the arc of a life. The cars in the rear contained vast stores of memories—some happy, some painful, many time-clouded. The cars up front held shrouded clues to each individual's future. They'd reveal themselves in due course but remained subject to change. Free will and all that. No question, Jeffrey would be the first of us to find out what life meant—his at least—after leaving it. If death opened up some window on life. And if life meant anything. My spirits picked up. I had a grip on Big Truth: Every life's journey rolls along what appears to be a common route, but each is singular. The kicker is, we all wind up at the same destination.

The track straightened. I shook my head. Can a man at seventy be that sophomoric? Still, I conceded that Big Truth exists. And it's not as complicated as we think. The problem is, it hides in plain sight. Like when you look for something in the dark, if you stare straight at it, you'll never see it.

We chose the late seating for dinner. Mistake. The kitchen ran out of chicken, so we gritted our way through more burgers.

Back in our car, we gave the past a rest and chitchatted about the next day's Giants game followed by dinner at a seafood place on the Embarcadero with floor-to-ceiling views of the Bay Bridge arcing its way towards Oakland.

Gary insisted he'd pick up the tab.

Jeffrey seemed particularly upbeat.

An hour from San Jose we dozed. Thirty minutes later the conductor awakened us. All bags should be taken off the train.

We found Jeffrey's seat empty.

Ten minutes later, still no Jeffrey.

As daylight faded, Arnie walked towards the back of the train to see if Jeffrey had gone to the lounge car. Gary headed to the front to cover all the bases. I stayed put. "In case Jeffrey mystically appears from a visit to another dimension."

Five minutes later, Arnie returned with Jeffrey.

"I just wanted to enjoy a drink at sunset," Jeffrey said. "How many more of those am I going to have?" He glanced around. "Where's Gary?"

"He went to look for you," said Arnie, "but he's probably downstairs guarding his precious Louis Vuitton bag."

I told Arnie to wait with Jeffrey and went downstairs. I saw the bag. No Gary. Not knowing what else to do, I peered into the unoccupied bathrooms. No Gary there, either. Two bathrooms displayed red OCCUPIED signs. I knocked on one. A woman complained, "Hold your horses for Chrissakes." The other offered no response.

I went for the conductor.

Police and EMTs met us in San Jose. They had questions. The police didn't seem to suspect foul play.

Had it been Jeffrey, I could see the logic to his deciding to end things on his own terms, the next day's game a ruse. It also made sense poetically. For many people—myself included—California represents the end of the rainbow.

But Gary?

An EMT approached me. "I can't give you an official cause of death," he whispered, "but if you find out it was his heart, don't be surprised."

A police officer said they'd contact the NYPD to locate Gary's assistant in New York. I asked if we should stay with the body. "The coroner's gonna look into this," she said. "Nothing you can do, unless you're family."

I wanted to tell her we *were* family, but I didn't think she'd understand. For that matter, I wasn't sure I did.

Arnie summoned an Uber. No way would we ride the commuter line to San Francisco.

Waiting in front of the station, something clawed at my gut. Gary's death was hitting me harder than Evelyn's. I lived with Evelyn almost forty years, fathered her children, always found a way home when the tracks laying out the route of our marriage diverged. The Bible talks about clinging to each other and becoming one flesh, but you both know you're two people.

Gary was another matter. At first, I thought it was the suddenness. Evelyn took a long time dying, and we were both relieved. It was something else. Jeffrey, Arnie, Gary and I went back to the beginning or as close to it as we could remember. We shared the kinds of experiences you seldom do with siblings because they're older or younger, and your parents imposed them on you. Friends you choose. Over time, your victories together, your defeats and the vast majority of days consumed with small talk, inane laughter and trivial irritations make a major impact on who you become. Or don't.

When Jeffrey's time came, I'd feel the same way.

I wasn't sure I'd arrived at Big Truth, but I sensed I was close.

A black SUV arrived. I helped Jeffrey get in back between Arnie and me and buckled his seat belt. Then I collapsed into the leather seat and closed my eyes. As we started off, I attempted to put things in perspective.

Arnie screwed Gary, although he never anticipated the consequences. Later, Gary screwed Arnie, consequences be damned. Having dumped Joyce, I guess I screwed Arnie, too. In San Francisco, after I'd succeeded then failed and needed a job, Arnie revenge-screwed me, although things worked out. Jeffrey played a major role in trying to screw Evelyn, therefore me. But who screwed Jeffrey? Who abandoned him to endure day-in, day-out pain that would grant relief only in death?

Process of elimination left God or a random universe. Neither offered consolation.

A song drifting through the car's speakers interrupted my musing. I found myself nodding along with a standard the Mills Brothers made big way back in the 'forties and now covered by a lone male vocalist. He seemed familiar, but I couldn't figure who. As I wrestled with the singer's identity, an inner voice—maybe like one Jeffrey claimed to have heard—enlightened me. I'd led myself down a blind alley. Big Truth is a fantasy. We seek it when we're in pain, which is most of the time, expecting some platitude will empower us to sweep away life's messy complications and vaporize the memories that torment us like emotional chicken pox.

Then it came to me that the singer was Ringo Starr. Really. Ringo.

A eureka moment followed. What enables us to maintain our balance when we totter on the edge of yet another abyss? To see the sun rise after every dark night of the soul? Little truths. The trick isn't to pursue them but be ready when—if—they appear to us.

With that, I embraced a newfound little truth and sang softly with Ringo: "You always hurt the one you love."

CPSIA information can be obtained
at www.ICGtesting.com
Printed in the USA
BVHW031000140419
545372BV00031B/74/P

9 781532 071454